THE BROTHERS O'BRIEN
SHADOW OF
THE HANGMAN

THE BROTHERS O'BRIEN
SHADOW OF THE HANGMAN

WILLIAM W. JOHNSTONE

with J. A. Johnstone

PINNACLE BOOKS
Kensington Publishing Corp.
www.kensingtonbooks.com

PINNACLE BOOKS are published by

Kensington Publishing Corp.
119 West 40th Street
New York, NY 10018

Copyright © 2012 William W. Johnstone

All Kensington titles, imprints, and distributed lines are available at special quantity discounts for bulk purchases for sales promotions, premiums, fund-raising, educational, or institutional use. Special book excerpts or customized printings can also be created to fit specific needs. For details, write or phone the office of the Kensington special sales manager: Kensington Publishing Corp., 119 West 40th Street, New York, NY 10018, attn: Special Sales Department; phone 1-800-221-2647.

PINNACLE BOOKS, the Pinnacle logo, and the WWJ steer head logo are Reg. U.S. Pat & TM Off.

ISBN-13: 978-0-7860-3302-7
ISBN-10: 0-7860-3302-9

First printing: April 2012

13 12 11 10 9 8 7 6 5

Printed in the United States of America

First electronic edition: November 2014

ISBN-13: 978-0-7860-3624-0
ISBN-10: 0-7860-3624-9

Chapter One

"You'll hang, Patrick," Sheriff John Moore said. "There ain't nobody can save you, and that's a natural fact."

"I didn't kill her, John," Patrick O'Brien said. "Molly Holmes and I were good friends."

"I know you didn't kill her," Moore said. "But three people saw you leaving the barn, and they say otherwise." The sheriff, a middle-aged man with tired eyes, moved his checkers piece. "Crown that."

Patrick sat back in his chair and smiled. "I give up, John. I can't beat you at this game."

"How many is that? Eighteen in a row?" Moore asked.

"Twenty-three to be exact," Patrick said.

"Maybe you'll win next time."

"I doubt it. You know what move I'm going to make before I make it."

"That's the secret to being a good checkers player, Pat."

The office door opened and Moore rose to his feet. His hand dropped to his holstered Colt, the ingrained habit of twenty-five years of law enforcement. But when he saw who stepped inside, he smiled and stuck out his hand. "Sam, good to see you again."

Samuel O'Brien took the proffered hand and said, "Howdy, John. I brought Patrick some books." He laid a stack of volumes on the sheriff's desk. Then to his brother he said, "How are you holding up?"

"All right, I guess," Patrick said, examining the book spines. "Except that John keeps beating me at checkers."

"John beats everybody at checkers," Samuel said.

"Ah," Patrick said, his face brightening, "a brand-new volume of Keats."

"Lorena's idea. She said he's your favorite poet."

"Poetry should be great and unobtrusive," Patrick said, "a thing which enters one's soul, and does not startle it or amaze it with itself, but with its subject."

"Hell, Pat," Moore said, "did you just set there and make up them highfalutin words?"

"No, the poet John Keats made them up sixty years ago."

"Oh," Moore said. "It would take me a spell to work all that out in my mind." He looked thoughtful. "I wonder if that Keats feller played checkers." He got no answer to his question and put his hand on Patrick's shoulder. "Sorry, Pat, but I've got to lock you up again." The sheriff's face was apologetic. "It's for appearances' sake, like."

Patrick rose to his feet, his leg shackles clanking. "I understand, John. You've got a job to do."

"Do you really need to keep my brother chained up like an animal?" Samuel said, his anger flaring.

"Sorry, Sam, but it's the law."

"Whose law?"

"The Vigilance Committee of Georgetown, fairest city in the New Mexico Territory."

"Who says it's the fairest?" Samuel said.

"The Vigilance—"

"I get it, John," Samuel said.

Patrick shuffled toward his cell, partitioned from the rest of the office by a limestone wall and steel-reinforced door. Before the door slammed shut behind him, Patrick turned and said, "How's the colonel taking this, Sam?"

"As you might expect," Samuel said. "He says if there's any move to hang you, he'll burn down this town and shoot every man who had a hand in declaring you guilty."

Suddenly John Moore was worried. "Samuel, any more talk like that from your pa and I'll bring in the army to keep order. Patrick was tried and convicted of rape and murder by a jury of his peers, sentenced by a judge, and there's an end to it."

"Do you think my brother is guilty, John?" Samuel said.

"No, I don't."

"Then who is?"

"I don't know that, either."

"John, Dromore won't stand aside and see one of its own hang for a crime he didn't commit."

"Pat was found guilty in a court of law, not a court of justice," Moore said. His eyes hardened, became dangerous, and the warning signs of the former gunfighter glowed in their blue depths. "I'll enforce the law, Sam, any way I have to."

Samuel nodded. "Our quarrel is not with you. Somebody raped and murdered Molly Holmes and pinned the blame on Patrick. Whoever and wherever he is, I'll find him."

Moore turned his head and looked at Patrick. "Remember to turn the key in the lock when you get inside, huh?"

After the iron-bound door closed behind Patrick, Moore said, "Sam, I'll help you any way I can, but you've only got seven more days and your brother hangs. I don't know if it was a poet who said it, but time flies."

Samuel stepped to the window and stared outside. The hard work of running a cattle ranch in an unforgiving land had drawn him fine. He was tall, slim, dressed in a worn blue shirt crossed by wide canvas suspenders. Shotgun chaps, boots, and a brown, wide-brimmed hat completed his attire, but for the Colt he wore, horseman-style, high on his right hip. His dragoon mustache and hair were both neatly trimmed, a little dictate of his wife.

Samuel's eyes roamed over the single dusty street that made up the fair city of Georgetown. Clapboard, false-fronted buildings elbowed each other for room, and two saloons, both of adobe, stood near the railroad spur and cattle pens.

Only the town's more respectable element braved the midday heat, businessmen sweating in broadcloth, women in cotton dresses, carrying parasols, and a few booted and bearded miners just in from the hills. The rough crowd, a few of them leftovers from the recent Estancia Valley range war, would not show up until lamps were lit in the saloons and the girls from the line shacks came out to play.

Georgetown was a mean, miserable burg, held together with baling wire and spit, and Samuel O'Brien figured it had not earned the right to hang a man.

He turned away from the window and said, "John, I've got to be going. If Patrick—"

"Needs anything, I'll see he gets it," the sheriff said.

Samuel smiled. "You read minds, John."

"Yeah, I do, and that's why I keep beating your brother at checkers."

The office door burst open with a bang, the calling card of a man determined to make a grandstand entrance.

Elijah Holmes strode into the room, his boots thudding on the rough pine floor. He held a Bible in one hand, a coiled bullwhip in the other.

"I want to see him, Sheriff," he said. "I will read to that papist son of iniquity from the book, then whip the fear of the one true God into him."

Moore blocked Holmes's path. "I told you already, Elijah, you can't see the prisoner."

The farmer was a tall skinny man wearing stained overalls. He had a shock of gray hair, and a beard of the same color spread over his narrow chest. His eyes blazed the wild look of a mentally unbalanced fanatic.

Samuel thought Molly Holmes's husband looked like a deranged Old Testament prophet, and he placed himself between the farmer and the door to the cells.

"Sheriff, he raped my wife, then crushed her skull with a blacksmith's hammer," Holmes said. "It is my right."

"You'll attend Patrick O'Brien's hanging," Moore said. "That's the only right you have."

"Damn him to everlasting fire," Holmes screamed. "Did you see my wife's body?"

Moore nodded, remembering. "I saw it."

"Naked, bitten, torn, ravaged, a red-hot poker thrust into her sinful womanhood." He shoved his face into Moore's, saliva dripping from his lips. "Did you see it?"

The sheriff nodded, but said nothing.

"She was a whore!" Holmes shrieked. "Patrick O'Brien seduced her with his books and his smooth ways, reading poetry to her and filthy novels. There is only one book that should be read." He raised the Bible high. "The one I hold in my hand."

Suddenly Holmes looked crafty. "Do you see this?" He shook the bullwhip. "How many times did

I use this on her, trying to make her change her ways and return to the sweet bosom of the Lord?"

"I don't know," Moore said, his face stiff.

"A score! Two score! Yet she continued with her vile fornications under my very roof." Holmes stopped for breath, then said in a quieter tone, "Then, 'twas the last time I whipped her, she vowed to change her shameful ways. But what happened? Along came Patrick O'Brien with his books and silken tongue, and she refused to give him what he wanted." Holmes let his thin shoulders sag. "Enraged, he forcibly satisfied his wicked lusts, then killed her, finally despoiling that which she had refused to uncover to him willingly."

His gorge rising, Samuel said, "Mister, your wife had a name."

"I know she did, O'Brien, and be damned to ye for being kin to evil's spawn."

"What was it? What was her name?"

"I won't sully my tongue with the name of a whore," Holmes said. He glared at Moore. "Let me pass, Sheriff."

"You're not going in there," Moore said. "This is a jail, not a carnival sideshow."

"I won't give him the whip, since it troubles you so much, Sheriff. But I'll read to him from Scripture and reveal to him the error of his ways."

"Mister," Samuel said, his hand close to his holstered Colt, "this is a friendly warning—one step toward the door to the cells and I'll drop you right where you stand."

Holmes's eyes widened in shock. "Sheriff Moore, did you hear that?" he gasped. "This man threatened me."

"I didn't hear a thing," the big lawman said. "Now get the hell out of here, Holmes, before I arrest you for disturbing the peace."

"So that's it," Holmes said, "you're in cahoots with the high-and-mighty O'Briens and their millionaire pa."

"Holmes," Moore said, his face tight with anger, "scat!"

The farmer nodded. "I'll scat, all right, but I tell you one thing"—he directed his gaze at Samuel—"the day your brother hangs, O'Brien, I'll dance on the gallows and piss on his grave."

The farmer turned and flung through the door, but he stopped, turned, and stabbed a finger at Samuel. "O'Brien, from now on, your life ain't worth spit."

"Right nice feller, isn't he?" Samuel said after Holmes was gone.

"He's a mean one," Moore said. "I think he gave Molly a miserable life." He sat at his desk. "Then Patrick got her interested in books and she found a way to escape, at least for a while." The sheriff opened a drawer and produced a bottle of Old Crow. "Too early?" he said.

"I could use a drink," Samuel said. He took the

glass from Moore's hand, then said, "You think Holmes could have killed her?"

The sheriff took a sip of his bourbon before he spoke. "He could have," he said. "That red-hot poker thing sounds like something he'd do."

"Was Holmes ever a suspect?" Samuel said.

"No. He was seen as the grieving husband. If he murdered Molly, he sure acted the part of an innocent man."

"Why didn't you suggest that Holmes could be the killer, John?"

"Sam, I can't accuse a man without proof," Moore said. "Holmes and two of his hired men saw Patrick leave the barn at a gallop. When they went to investigate, they found Molly's naked and very dead body. The proof of Patrick's guilt was hard to refute. Just ask lawyer Dunkley."

"Lucas Dunkley did his best for Patrick," Samuel said. "He was up against a stacked deck from the git-go."

Moore held up the bottle. "Another splash?"

"No, I'm fine," Samuel said.

Moore poured himself another drink, then said, "At the trial you said Patrick rode to Dromore and reported the murder. I never could understand why didn't he come to me?"

"He was in shock, John. He'd just found a woman he liked raped and murdered, and he came to Dromore for help. About a dozen of us went to the Holmes farm, but we found nothing."

"But you did, Sam. You found that the only tracks

to and from the barn were made by Patrick's horse."

Samuel nodded. "Yeah. That was pretty damning, huh?"

"At least that's how the jury figured it."

Samuel laid his glass on the desk. "Thanks for the drink, John. I've got to get back to Dromore." As though he'd just remembered, he added, "The colonel sent for my brother Jacob."

At first Moore seemed to take that last in stride, but then he shook his head and made a small groaning sound. "That's the worst news I'll hear today," he said. "Or any other damned day."

Chapter Two

Samuel O'Brien was about to swing into the saddle when a voice from the opposite boardwalk froze him in place, his left boot in the stirrup.

"Sam, a word with you, if you please."

Lucas Dunkley stood outside his office, a rare smile on his face.

"Be right with you," Samuel said. He led his horse across the street, looped it to a hitching rail, and stepped onto the walk. "What can I do for you, Lucas?"

"Let's go inside," the lawyer said. "The heat is intolerable."

Samuel agreed with that observation.

The sun, burning like a white-hot coin, had climbed higher in the sky and mercilessly hammered the land. Only the El Barro Peaks to the north, purple in the distance, looked cool. Georgetown smelled of hot tarpaper, pine resin, horse dung, and the sharp odor of the cattle pens down by the railroad spur. A faint breeze lifted skeins of dust from the street and fanned the perspiring cheeks of the respectable matrons on the boardwalks.

Lucas Dunkley's office was small, dark, and dingy. The ledgers and law books on the shelves were dusty, as was the black mahogany furniture and the lawyer himself. Despite the heat, Dunkley wore dusky broadcloth, much frayed at the sleeves, and a high, celluloid collar. A small pair of pince-nez spectacles perched on the tip of his pen-sharp nose, attached to his lapel by a black ribbon.

After bidding Samuel to take a seat, Dunkley said, "I'll be brief."

The little man seemed to expect an answer, and Samuel said, "Yes, of course."

"And to the point, you understand?"

"Yes."

"Very well then, we can proceed. Your brother, the condemned Patrick O'Brien, is not guilty of the rape and murder of the late Molly Holmes."

"I know," Samuel said. "I wish you could've convinced the jury of that."

"I did not have all the facts then," Dunkley said. "I do now."

Samuel leaned forward in his chair. "What? I mean—"

The lawyer held up a white, blue-veined hand. "Be circumspect, Mr. O'Brien. Be judicious. Be wary. Facts are indeed facts, but in a court of law they must be proved to be facts and not fancies. Do you understand?"

Samuel said he did, but in truth, he didn't.

"Your brother is a pawn, Mr. O'Brien. He will be sacrificed so that a most singular evil may prosper and fulfill its ends." Dunkley looked over his steepled fingers. "The evil was spawned here, in this territory, and it's a cancer I intend to root out and expose to the world."

"What sort of evil?" Samuel said. "Damn it, Lucas, give me something."

"I can't, not yet. Allow me a couple of days and I'll reveal all."

"We don't have much time," Samuel said. "Patrick hangs in seven days."

"I am aware of that," Dunkley said. "And I know that my own life is in terrible danger." The lawyer smiled his wintry smile. "Yet I will proceed, perhaps more carefully. I must be cautious, prudent, circumspect, as you must be, Mr. O'Brien. This town has eyes and ears. You will be suspect because there are those who will think that you now know what I know. Do you understand?"

Samuel nodded. "Suppose I send a couple of my vaqueros as bodyguards, men good with the iron? You'd be safe then."

The lawyer shook his head. "No, that would hamper my freedom of movement and hinder my investigation. I will carry a small revolver on my travels, and that will be sufficient."

"Travels? Where?"

Dunkley smiled. "Not far, just out of town a ways." He rose to his feet. "Mr. O'Brien, at the moment

I am all that stands between your brother and the gallows. I will not fail him." He picked up a pile of papers from his desk and riffled through them. "Now, business matters press, so if I could beg your indulgence?"

Samuel rose to his feet. "Yes, of course."

"Come back and see me two days hence at this same time," the lawyer said. "I believe I shall have news of the greatest import then."

"Take care of yourself, Lucas," Samuel said.

As he left, the office wall clock chimed noon, as solemn and foreboding as a tolling church bell.

Samuel O'Brien rode west toward Dromore, the great plantation house his father had built at the base of Glorieta Mesa. He wanted to be there when Jacob showed up, if only to head off the usual friction between his brother and the colonel.

Pa insisted that Jacob's place was at Dromore, running the ranch with his brothers, not forever roaming restlessly from place to place, earning a living by the speed of his gun.

It was a case of an irresistible force meeting an immovable object, and both parties were too hard-headed to realize there could be no compromise and no winner.

Samuel smiled and shook his head, remembering past clashes between the colonel and Jacob. He'd no confidence that this time would be different, though the fact that Patrick's life hung in the balance could change things.

Samuel crossed Apache Canyon and was a mile west of the Pecos when he spotted dust on his back trail. At first he thought it a trick of the shimmering heat, but when he looked again he saw a veil of yellow lift above a ridge just a couple of hundred yards behind him.

A man on a horse makes a fine rifle target, and Dunkley's warning had made Samuel wary. He swung out of the saddle and led his buckskin to a stream that ran clear and cold off the mountains. He let his mount drink, his eyes on the ridge. The dust was gone.

Samuel got down on one knee and with his left hand cupped cold water into his mouth. His eyes moved constantly in the shadow of his hat brim. The hilly, treed land around him was still, silent, waiting . . . but for what?

The answer came when an exclamation point of water spurted from the stream, followed by the roar of a rifle. Samuel dived to his right, rolled, and fetched up against a barkless tree trunk, its white branches rising above his head like skeletal arms. He drew his Colt, wishful for the Winchester on his saddle, and raised his head above the trunk.

Samuel saw nothing, but a second bullet chipped splinters from the dead tree. Whoever the bushwhacker was, he had him pinned.

A drift of white gun smoke rose from a stand of juniper and piñon about fifty yards to Samuel's right. He thumbed off a shot in that direction, a forlorn hope with a short-barreled Colt's gun. He'd no idea where his bullet went.

A couple of minutes ticked past. Samuel had no shade, and the relentless sun hammered him, drawing sweat from his armpits and the middle of his back. The land undulated in the heat as though hiding behind a row of transparent snakes. Nearby, insects made their small sound in the grass, and a bashful breeze stirred the pines.

The crack of the rifle and the burn of the bullet came at the same time.

Samuel felt a sting on the outside of his right knee. He glanced down and saw that his pants were torn and already bloodstained.

He cussed a blue streak. The bushwhacker had moved, and the bullet had come from behind him to his right. He should be dead, but wasn't. That could only mean the would-be killer was not a fair hand with a rifle, and Samuel wasn't about to make it easy for him.

He rolled on his back and pinpointed the smoke drift, a gray smear forty yards away among a stand of juniper and scrubby wild oak.

They say that fortune favors the brave, and Samuel was about to try to prove it.

He swallowed hard and rubbed sweat from his gun hand. Then he fisted the Colt again, jumped to his feet—and charged.

His wounded knee felt a little gimpy as Samuel ran for the trees, but it was holding up well. A bullet kicked up dirt at his feet, and a second one split the air close to his head. He shot at the smoke, shot again—wild, inaccurate fire—hoping it might keep the gunman's head down.

As it turned out, he'd played hob.

The rifleman stepped out of the trees, a Winchester to his shoulder. The man seemed unhurt, but Samuel figured his bullets must have come close enough because the bushwhacker was looking to end it.

The distance was twenty yards, and for a moment the eyes of the two men met and held, and Samuel read the signs. He moved to his right just as the rifle roared. A clean miss. Samuel dived for the ground, rolled to the shelter of a mesquite bush, and then scrambled to his feet. He raised his Colt to eye level with both hands, sighted for an instant, and fired.

The bushwhacker took the bullet high in his chest. Blood staining his mouth, he tossed the Winchester away, signaling that he was out of it. The man was a back-shooter who lacked sand and bottom, and now, hurt bad, he wanted no part of Samuel O'Brien.

The would-be killer hunkered down, and when Samuel came close enough, he said, "I'm done, mister. I'm done for good. Hell, I'm leaving . . ."

"Who paid you to dry-gulch me?" Samuel said. "Damn you, tell me."

But he realized he was looking into the stiff face and distant eyes of a dead man.

Samuel studied the dry gulcher. He was small, thin, with the haggard look of someone who'd gone hungry as a child. His entire outfit, a ragged high-button suit a size too big for him, black bowler hat, and scuffed, elastic-sided boots, was worth maybe a dollar, if that. But the Winchester was almost new, a model of 1886 in .45–.70 caliber. The rifle cost around twenty-one dollars, or an ounce of gold, more than this bushwhacker could ever have afforded.

Samuel O'Brien reloaded his revolver, but his mind was elsewhere.

Somebody had hired this man to kill him, and that somebody had supplied the murder weapon.

But who? And why?

He had questions without answers.

He didn't know whom, but he was certain that Patrick and lawyer Dunkley were a major part of the why.

Samuel had a choice, and he contemplated his options: ride on to Dromore or return to Georgetown and report the bushwhacking to Sheriff Moore. He settled on the latter. If someone in town had hired the man, the sight of his would-be assassin's bloody body draped over a horse might flush him out. Then again, it might not. But until he heard from Dunkley again, all Samuel could do was roll the dice.

Chapter Three

"Sure I know who he is," Sheriff John Moore said. He let go of the dead man's hair and let the head drop. "Name's Arch Harris, and he didn't come to much. Did odd jobs around town for whiskey money and stole a chicken now and then. He lived with his wife and two kids in a tarpaper shack just outside of town when he was to home, which wasn't often." He looked at Samuel. "Arch had a real liking for whores, when he could afford them. He was involved in a cutting over a six-foot-tall whore who went by the name of High Timber, but that was a few years back."

"Is the mustang his?"

"Yeah, I guess. I seen him ride it before."

"What about the Winchester, John?"

"He never owned a rifle like that in his life. He either stole it or somebody gave it to him."

"To murder me?"

"Seems like, Sam. Unless he had a beef with you, personal."

Samuel shook his head. "I never saw this man before in my life."

"Well, he doesn't have any money on him, but that don't mean nothing," Moore said. "Probably it was to keep him sober until the job was done."

"Who hired him, John?"

"Hell if I know," the lawman said. He glanced at a washed-out blue sky streaked with purple strings of cloud, like an upturned porcelain bowl that had spent too long in the kiln. Moore's eyes were tired; he was a hard-nosed lawman who'd done too much thinking of late. "I'd say whoever murdered Molly Holmes hired Arch to kill you, Sam. That's what I'd say. But the hell of it is, I've got no way of proving it."

An excited crowd had gathered around the dead man hanging belly-down over his horse, and Samuel O'Brien looked past them to Lucas Dunkley's office across the street.

Moore read Samuel's eyes. "Lucas ain't there, Sam," he said. "He rode out of town about half an hour after you did."

"Say where he was going?"

"I didn't speak to him."

The meaner the town, the more prosperous the undertaker.

Jasper Light, in broadcloth and a silk top hat, pushed through the onlookers, tiptoed to the sheriff's side, and said, "And who is the deceased?"

Moore looked at the undertaker with all the enthusiasm of a man regarding a fly in his soup. "I swear you can smell 'em, Jasper," he said.

Light wrung the undertaker's hands, his narrow shoulders hunched like a carrion-eater. "Mine is a competitive profession, Sheriff Moore," he said. "The early bird gets the worm, you know."

"He's got no money on him, Jasper," Moore said. "The normal burial rate set by the Vigilance Committee applies."

Disappointment clouded Light's eyes. "Oh, dear, yet another pauper."

"I'm afraid so," Moore said. "Plant him in a pine box, then send your bill to the committee. Three copies, mind. You didn't do that the last time."

"The horse, saddle, and bridle?" Light said, hope rising in his voice.

"Go to his widow," Samuel said. Like Moore, he had no liking for the man. He reached into his pocket, then peeled off a ten-dollar bill. "Take this," Samuel said, "and treat him decent."

Light reached out and grabbed the money like a striking rattlesnake. "He'll go first class all the way," he said.

"He'd better," Samuel said. "I'm bringing his wife and kids to the funeral, so make sure he's boxed and ready to go in an hour."

Light smiled. "It will be as you say, Mr. O'Brien." He gave a little bow. "And how is your dear father, the colonel? In good health, I trust?"

"He's not ready for you yet, Light, so don't get your hopes up."

"Ah, a little joke," the man said, his thin face empty. "Those in my profession do appreciate them so."

"Get him ready," Samuel said. "I'll swing by your place and pick up the horse."

The undertaker gave another little bow and led away the mustang with its swaying burden.

After Light was gone, Moore said, "Sam, you really going to talk to the widder woman?"

"Yeah, I reckon."

"She won't thank you for it, you being the one who did the killing an' all."

"Maybe so, but I can't kill a man, then walk away from it like he never existed."

"A lot of men don't think that way, Sam."

"Then their way isn't my way."

The sheriff hesitated, about to say something that didn't set easy with him. Finally he said, "I have to make a report on the death of Arch Harris, Sam. It's a formality, you understand, but the Vigilance Committee will probably want to talk with you."

Samuel smiled. "They going to lock me up, John?"

"Hell, no," Moore said. "Two O'Brien brothers in the same jail are more than this town can handle."

A wind had picked up, blowing fair off the Santa Fe Mountains, and across the way the batwings of the Sideboard Saloon rattled like a snare drum. Somewhere a screen door banged open and shut, and a dog barked, then fell silent.

Moore looked at Samuel for a long time, studying the younger man. He looked as though he wanted to say something but first had to get the words straight in his mind. Finally he said, "See this hand I'm holding up?"

Samuel smiled. "Yeah, it's your gun hand; looks like a bear paw."

"See the palm right here?" Moore scraped his fingernails back and forth across the hard skin. "It's been itching like hell since Molly Holmes was murdered. Know what that means, Sam?"

"You're going to shoot somebody, maybe?"

"No, it means hard times are comin' down, Sam. Killin' times."

"I already worked that out for my own self, John."

"You be careful, Sam," Moore said. "Somebody wants you dead real bad, and next time they won't send an amateur."

The Harris shack, a sagging frame-and-tarpaper structure no bigger than a hatbox, lay on the bank of a dry wash a mile to the east of Apache Canyon. A few cottonwoods and piñon grew close to the cabin, suggesting the wash had an underground stream, and stands of cholla dotted the dusty landscape. Farther east, rugged mountain peaks stood like silent sentinels against the sky.

It was a pleasant enough spot, Samuel O'Brien decided, but the shack itself was a mean, miserable place, sadly neglected, its only sign of prosperity the few scrawny chickens that scratched in the dirt around the front door.

As good manners dictated, Samuel sat his horse and called out, "Hello, the cabin."

The door opened almost immediately, and a thin, careworn woman stepped outside. Her eyes went to Samuel, then to the mustang he led. Before her visitor could speak, the woman said, "He's dead, isn't he?"

"Yes, ma'am, he is," Samuel said.

The woman showed no surprise, no grief, only a numb acceptance of a day she'd known would inevitably come. "How did it happen?" she said.

Samuel shifted his weight in the saddle, dry-mouthed and uneasy.

The woman saw his discomfort and said, "I see."

Samuel finally found his tongue. "I believe someone hired your husband to kill me," he said. "He bushwhacked me south of Georgetown and—" He stopped, hunting for the right words.

"And you defended yourself," the woman said.

Samuel nodded. "That's how it stacks up, ma'am. He left me with no choice." He held up the mustang's reins. "I brought back your husband's horse."

"Thank you," the woman said. "Thank you kindly."

Mrs. Harris was not pretty and had never been pretty. She was thin, slack-breasted, and barefoot. Dust had settled between her toes, and the bottom of her threadbare calico dress was much stained and frayed. Two silent children, a boy and a girl, joined her at the door. The girl, dark circles under her huge brown eyes, looked to be about ten, the boy a year or two younger and frail.

"Is there anything I can do for you, ma'am?" Samuel said.

The woman shook her head. "No, there's nothing you can do for me."

"May I escort you to your husband's funeral?"

"No, I don't want to see Arch go under the ground," Mrs. Harris said. "What words could I add to the ones that have already been said between him and me and those I've said to our God?"

"Did he abuse you, ma'am?" Samuel said.

"No, he was a good enough husband when he stayed away from whiskey and fancy women." She met Samuel's eyes. "He brought home a whore's disease that will kill me sooner or later. But before I die, I want to see my children settled."

The afternoon was hot, oppressive, and Samuel O'Brien felt penned up, as though the day was crowding him close, refusing to let him move. Sweat trickled down his back and seeped from under his hat brim and stung his eyes.

Now he tried hard to do the right thing.

"Mrs. Harris," he said, "you and your children would be welcome at my ranch. There's always plenty of work to be done around Dromore, and you'd have a steady wage and a place to live."

"You're one of them O'Brien boys, aren't you?" the woman said. She had faded gray eyes, the color of wood smoke.

Samuel touched his hat and smiled. "Yes indeed, ma'am. My name's Samuel, or Sam if you like."

The woman nodded. "That's a very kind offer, Mr. O'Brien, but we can fend for ourselves."

"But how will you live?"

"We'll get by."

Samuel felt a twinge of desperation. "You'd be happy at Dromore, Mrs. Harris, and we can bring in a doctor to treat your"—he searched for a kinder word than disease—"misery."

The woman was silent for long moments, then she said, "The day is hot, Mr. O'Brien. I must get the children inside."

Defeat weighing on him, Samuel said, "Mrs. Harris, about your husband . . . I'm sorry."

"One way or another, we're all sorry, Mr. O'Brien. Some of us are even sorry that we were ever born." She turned and pushed the kids inside, and the door closed behind her.

Samuel sat his horse, feeling drained and lethargic in the heat. Finally, he swung away from the shack and headed west toward Dromore. He felt he'd lost something, a part of himself that he'd never regain. But as to what it was, he had no idea.

Chapter Four

Samuel O'Brien rode up to the big house at Dromore under a flaming sky that roofed the timbered high country with bands of scarlet and jade. The heat of the day was over and the dust had settled, leaving clean air that smelled of pine resin and the wildflowers night-blooming among pinnacles of mountain rock.

When Samuel swung out of the saddle, a Mexican boy ran to take his horse. "Is Señor Jacob here?" he said to the kid.

The boy shook his head. "No, patron. He did not come, I think."

Disappointed, Samuel nodded and stepped inside. The butler met him in the foyer and told him that his wife and son were in the study with the colonel.

"Jacob didn't arrive?" Samuel said, hoping that the boy could've been mistaken.

"No, sir," the butler said. "Dromore has had no visitors today."

When Samuel walked into the study his wife ran to meet him. She threw her arms around his neck, kissed him, and then stepped back, studying his face. "You look tired, Samuel," she said.

Samuel gave her a weak smile. "It's been a long day, Lorena." He looked over her shoulder. "Pa, are you spoiling my son again?"

Shamus O'Brien sat in his wheelchair, the white bundle that was his grandson in his arms. "Young Shamus is too young to know I spoil him," the colonel said.

Lorena smiled. "He'll know soon enough, and then watch out. First the pony, then the twenty-two rifle, and then—"

"And then whatever he wants," Shamus said. He lifted his eyes to Samuel. "Son, you've been through it."

"I reckon."

"Maybe you better tell us about it."

Lorena's pretty face was suddenly concerned. "Samuel, it's not about Patrick, is it?"

Samuel nodded. "Patrick's just fine, but yes, in a way it's about Patrick, about all of us."

He poured himself a drink, sat by the fire, and accepted a cigar from his father.

"Tell us what happened, Samuel," the colonel said. "From the beginning."

Using as few words as possible, Samuel recounted his visit with Patrick and then his conversation with

Lucas Dunkley. By the time he'd ended his account of the bushwhacking and his meeting with Mrs. Harris, his cigar was half smoked and his whiskey glass was drained.

In the silence that followed, Lorena noticed her husband's knee. "Samuel," she said, "you've been wounded."

"It's nothing," Samuel said. "I got burned by a bullet, is all."

But Lorena wouldn't let it go. She fussed her way out of the study and returned with a basin of warm water, washcloths and bandages, and some brown stuff in a bottle that Samuel knew from bitter experience stung like hell.

Shawn, looking worried, followed Lorena into the room. "Damn it, Sam, how did you get shot?" he said.

"Hardly shot," Samuel said. "I got burned."

Shawn grabbed a chair and sat beside his brother. "How did it happen?" He glanced at the knee that Lorena now exposed when she rolled up Samuel's pants leg. "That looks ugly," Shawn said. "Some ranny beat you on the draw-and-shoot?"

"I'll tell this story one more time, then I'm done," Samuel said, wincing as Lorena liberally applied the stinging stuff.

He gave Shawn the same account as he had his father, dwelling longer on Dunkley and his suspicions. Then he said, "And that's all I've got to say."

The study door swung open and Luther Ironside, Dromore's segundo, thudded into the room, his spurs chiming. "Sam," he said, "tell me how the hell did you get yourself all shot to pieces?"

"What do you reckon, Luther?" Shamus O'Brien said.

Taking his time, Ironside lifted the baby off Shamus's knee, kissed the little one on the cheek, and handed him back to Lorena.

"Colonel, I say we do as Sam said and get a couple of men into Georgetown to look out fer that lawyer feller," he said finally.

"Shawn?"

"Makes sense to me, Colonel. Whoever wanted Samuel dead is sure as hell targeting Lucas Dunkley."

"Lucas says he's taken to carrying a revolver," Samuel said. "He knows he's a target."

Shamus lit a cigar and studied Ironside through a blue haze of smoke.

Luther had served under him in the late war as a top sergeant and later had helped found Dromore. He'd fought Apaches, rustlers, and bandits up from the Mexico border, and had been wounded in the Estancia Valley War. He was long past the first bloom of middle age, but there was steel in him and his bottom. He was fast on the draw-and-shoot and he'd killed men, but he'd never sought a gunman's reputation. Still, he was the kind of man that named gunfighters called "Sir" and allowed the road. Luther was a brave man, there was no doubt about that, but he was also reckless, impetuous, insubordinate, quick-tempered at times, and a mite too fond of bonded bourbon and painted women.

In other words, he was just the kind of heller the colonel needed in Georgetown. Him and Shawn. And Jacob. If he ever arrived.

"Luther," Shamus said, "I want you and Shawn to head out at first light tomorrow for Georgetown. Keep an eye on lawyer Dunkley and make sure nobody guns him."

When he saw Ironside and his son nod, Shamus added, "And I want Patrick safe. I don't trust John Moore and never did. He's got a long Yankee face on him, and I don't cotton to that."

"I catch your drift, Colonel," Ironside said.

"John Moore's all right, Pa," Samuel said. "He knows Patrick didn't murder Molly Holmes and said it out straight at the trial."

"He still plans to hang him though, doesn't he?" Shamus said.

Samuel could only stay silent and nod his agreement.

"No son of mine will ever hang," Shamus said, his face reddening. "Jesus, Mary, and Joseph, and all the saints in heaven bear witness that I'll destroy that damned town and everyone in it before I'll let them murder my blood." He glared at Samuel. "Yes, it's about the blood, Samuel. The same blood that runs in my veins runs in Patrick's, and I'll never turn my back on my own blood. Remember that well, because blood and honor are the very foundations of Dromore and all it stands for."

"And Ma's hearthstone," Samuel said, smiling.

For a moment Shamus was taken aback. Then he smiled. "Yes, Shawn, you're right. Saraid's hearthstone is the bedrock for all the rest, for what has been and for what is still to come."

"Colonel," Samuel said, "I understand what you say about the blood. I won't watch Patrick hang."

"I know you won't," Shamus said. "But a lesson once given is worth repeating."

"Colonel," Ironside said, "why don't me and Shawn just ride into town, spring Patrick from jail, then hide out in the mountains for a spell?"

"It's a thought," Shamus said.

"I'll put a bullet in Moore, if you like," Ironside said, beaming, as though he'd just clinched the deal.

The colonel was lost in thought for a while, but he looked up and said, "No, for the time being we'll do it legally. Let's wait and hear what Dunkley has to say."

"But it's an option, though, huh?" Ironside said.

"Yes," Shamus said. He pushed his wheelchair to the window and stared out at the fading day. "It's an option."

Chapter Five

The bedroom was dark, lit only by the thin blade of moonlight that angled through the drawn curtains. A rising wind whispered slyly around the eaves of the house, and in the distance coyotes lifted their noses and questioned the night.

"He done it again, Cap'n," the man who stood at the bottom of the bed said. "He came home covered in blood that wasn't his'n."

The bed creaked, but the man who sat bolt upright was invisible in shadow. "You were supposed to keep him confined to his room."

"We did, Cap'n, but he slung a chair and broke clean through the window."

"Who was it this time?"

"Woman who lives in a shack over to Apache Canyon and her two kids."

The man in the bed groaned, like someone in pain. "Damn him, damn him to hell," he said.

"I'm real sorry, Cap'n."

"Did you see her? And the kids?"

"Bill Anders rode over there, came back an hour ago. He hasn't talked since, just sits on his bunk holding his head and sobbing, like."

"Bring Anders to me. Now!"

The man called Anders stepped into the room, hollow-eyed, his hat in his hands.

"Tell me," the man in the bed said.

"It's bad, boss."

"Damn you, tell me."

"Near as I can put it together . . ." the man stopped, his words balling in his throat.

"Tell me." A hoarse whisper from the darkness.

"Near as I can tell . . . he stripped the woman naked, then done her good. After he was finished, he killed her and the two kids." The man called Anders hesitated, then said, "That's as near as I can tell."

"Did he . . . did he use a poker like he did the last time?"

"Running iron."

"Oh, my God . . ."

"You have to kill him, Cap'n," Anders said. "Shade is an evil thing that ain't fit to live."

"He's my son."

"He'll ruin all our plans for the ranch, Cap'n."

"No, he won't. By God, I'll keep him chained for the rest of his life if I have to."

"He's tied up already, Cap'n. Me and Clem got

him roped hand and foot in the barn." A sudden edge to his voice betrayed Anders's agitation. "Cap'n, when the Georgetown vigilantes discover what happened, they'll figger out pretty damned quick that they're fixin' to hang the wrong man."

"They won't discover it, at least not the way you found it."

The unsteady breathing of the man in the bed was loud in the quiet. Then he said, "Go back to the shack and set it on fire. I want those bodies burned unrecognizable. As far as the vigilantes are concerned, the woman set the place ablaze by accident and she and her kids burned to death."

Anders pleaded. "This don't set right with me, Cap'n, I mean Pat O'Brien gettin' hung for something he didn't do. Let me kill Shade for you, real easy like."

"No! Damn you, no! He's my son. Now go and do what I told you."

"Like I said, Cap'n, he may be your son, but he ain't fit to live," Anders said.

"I know that," the man in the bed said. "God help me, don't you think I know that?"

After Anders left, the man in the bed spent thirty minutes in tormented thought. Finally, his face stricken, he rose and slipped on a robe. He opened the drawer of the bedside table and removed a short-barreled Colt. He checked the loads, then slid the revolver into his pocket. A tall, graying man with the erect bearing of a former naval officer, Captain Miles Shannon grabbed a pair of crutches that stood by the door and used them to limp into the hallway.

The house was dark, and it took the tall man several slow minutes to hobble his way to the front of the house and step outside.

A haloed moon rode high above Apache Mesa a mile to the north, and around Shannon the wind rustled among cedar and piñon and rippled the blue grama grass. His experienced eye ranged over a couple of yearling steers drinking at the creek, and it pleased him to see that they'd recovered from the hard winter and put on beef.

Ice and blizzards had killed two-thirds of his herd and pushed him to the wall. Only an interest-free loan from Shamus O'Brien had stood between him and ruin. . . .

He supported himself on his crutches and turned his face to the star-strewn sky, sudden tears in his eyes, his conscience twisting inside him like a knife. He would repay Shamus's kindness with betrayal and treachery, and a fine young man would die to save the unspeakable monster he himself had created.

"My son . . ." he whispered, a man in mortal agony . . . "oh, my son . . ."

Shannon's hand slipped into the pocket of his robe and closed on the Colt.

A woman and her two children dead to satisfy Shade's perverted lusts. Anders had been right;

there could be no forgiveness for that. No going back to what might have been. Not now. Not ever.

Shade had to be destroyed, but Shannon would do it himself.

The captain hobbled stiffly toward the barn. He was tormented by grief, but his eyes were determined. It was time to end it and send back to the hell where it had been spawned whatever had possessed his boy's soul.

The barn doors were wide open and moonlight slanted the dark interior. The musky odor of horses mingled with the night smells of cedar, prairie grass, and high-growing pine. A teasing wind slapped Captain Shannon's silk robe against his wooden legs, and strands of iron-gray hair tossed across his face.

Shannon drew the gun from his pocket and walked lamely to the entrance of the barn. Breathing hard, he rested on the crutches and said, "Shade, where are you? Speak up, boy." Moonlight glinted blue on the barrel of the revolver by his side. "Shade?"

Inside, a horse snorted and a hoof thudded on wood. Far off, Shannon heard an owl question the night, and closer by coyotes yipped at a moon as big and round as a silver dollar.

"I know you're in there, boy," he said. "I'm here to cut you loose."

The answering silence mocked Shannon. He stumbled to the lantern that always sat on top of an upturned Arbuckle coffee box to the left of the doorway. A few matches lay next to the lantern, and the captain picked one up . . .

Then screamed as a shocking pain hammered the back of his knees.

Shannon dropped in a heap, and his Colt skittered away from him. He reached for the revolver, then collapsed again as an iron crowbar slammed into his left shoulder and shattered his collarbone.

Through a scarlet haze of agony, he saw the silhouette of a man standing over him, saw the gleam of his teeth in the darkness.

"Hello, Daddy," the man said. "How nice of you to drop by."

Shannon was almost beyond speech, his terrible injuries taking their toll. During the late war both his legs had been amputated below the knees, and now one of his artificial limbs had followed the path of the Colt and lay several yards away.

"I came to kill you, Shade," he said.

"I know you did, Daddy."

"Damn you to hell, you're a monster."

Shade took a knee beside his father and stared into his eyes. "I know that, too. Isn't it fun?"

Captain Shannon made a lunge for his revolver, but the crowbar came down fast and hard and shattered his elbow. He groaned and fell on his back. "Finish it, Shade," he said. "I don't want to live in your world a moment longer."

Shade smiled. "Why, certainly, Daddy." He raised the iron bar and brought it crashing down on his father's head. Only when the older man's skull was smashed into pulp did he stop.

Slowly, Shade got to his feet, his thin chest rising and falling as he struggled to catch his breath. He stood still for a few moments and cursed the asthma that had plagued him since childhood.

He looked at his father's body. *Damn him, not that he cared. Not that anyone ever cared.* Shade kicked the lifeless man again and again, until his building fury was played out.

Gasping again, he stepped from the barn into the mother-of-pearl moonlight, his hands clenched into tight fists, and he stared at the star-splashed night sky, the woman craving ravening at him.

God, he needed a woman real bad.

Chapter Six

"Seems to me," Jacob O'Brien said, "that we can settle this amicably."

"What the hell does that mean?" the older, bearded man standing beside him at the bar said. "Amic . . . ambly . . ."

"It means, my ignorant friend, that we can settle this in a friendly manner, like," Jacob said.

"An' suppose I don't cotton to settling in a friendly manner?" the bearded man said.

"Ah, a good question," Jacob said. "The opposite of amicable is unfriendly, and we don't want that, do we?"

The bartender laid a plate in front of Jacob. "Cheese, hard-boiled eggs, and a stack of tortillas," he said. "That's the best I can do for you, mister."

Jacob smiled. "Hell, I've been living on salt pork for a week. This is a feast and sets with me just fine."

He picked up the plate and stepped toward the

dugout saloon's only table, where a whore from the adjoining hog farm was playing solitaire with a pack of worn, greasy cards. The bearded man's voice stopped him.

"Hey, you, we haven't settled this," he said.

Jacob turned, moved the plate from his left hand to his right, and said, "Yes, we have."

The bearded man was huge, and the bear coat he wore despite the summer heat made him look bigger. His red beard, streaked with gray, spread over his chest, and he wore a couple of revolvers and an enormous pig-sticker in his belt.

"How come we settled it?" he said.

Jacob sighed. "Well, the fact that you didn't know what the word *amicably* means pegs you as an ignoramus. So when you say Grant was a better general than Lee, I realized that you are a simpleton who doesn't know what the hell he's talking about."

The bearded man turned to the bartender. "Hey, Lou, was that an insult?"

The bartender shook his head. "I guess not, Tom. Man is only talking the truth."

The man called Tom slammed his hand onto the bar so hard the whore made a little yelp and jumped in fright. "I know what I know, feller," he said. "And what I know is that Grant"—he removed his hat—"God bless him, was the best general who ever lived, and that includes the Frenchy, what do you call him . . . Nap . . . Napo . . ."

"Napoleon," Jacob supplied.

"Yeah, him." Tom replaced his battered hat and glared at Jacob. "Now it's settled."

"Whatever you say," Jacob said. "Let me buy the man a drink, bartender, seeing as how he won the argument."

Tom grinned. "That's white of you, mister. Bless you, I'll have a glass of rum."

"Be my guest," Jacob said.

The whore watched Jacob eat for a while, then said, "Big spender."

"Spending is better than shooting," Jacob said.

"And you've done your share of shooting, I'd say."

"More than my share," Jacob said. "It wears on a man."

"My name is Amy," the whore said. She looked worn out, and the hog farm was probably her final destination. The only thing lower was to become a soldiers' woman, but she'd know that was the end of the line and fear it.

"Pretty name, Amy," Jacob said.

"So, what's yours?"

"Jacob."

"Hello, Jacob."

"Hello yourself, Amy."

The girl reached out and picked a crumb of tortilla from Jacob's untrimmed mustache, then said, "Where you headed?"

"North."

"Where, north?"

"A ways."

Amy smiled. "You're not a talking man, are you?"

"Sure I am," Jacob said. "When I've got something to say."

He looked at the girl, dark eyes, dark hair, and teeth that were still white and even. She might have been pretty once, but maybe not, it was hard to tell. "What brings you here?" he said.

"Nothing, nothing at all. Somehow I just ended up in this place, at the edge of the world. One day I'll take a walk, fall over the edge, and it will all be over."

Jacob smiled. "There's a lot of world beyond the Manzano Mountains. You wouldn't fall too far."

"A lot of world for you maybe, not for me."

As though she thought she'd stepped over a line, Amy nodded in the bartender's direction. "Lou Rose lets me stay here free of charge, and he feeds me in winter when the miners are holed up in their cabins." Her smile was faint, almost shy. "I guess I shouldn't complain."

"Oh, I don't know," Jacob said. "The world would be a pretty dull place if we'd nothing to complain about."

He pushed his empty plate away, sat back in his chair, and took the makings from his shirt pocket and held them up where Amy could see them. "May I beg your indulgence, ma'am?" he said.

The girl was surprised. "Men never asked me that before."

"Well, they should've," Jacob said. "It's common courtesy when a lady is present."

Amy waited until Jacob lit his cigarette, and then she said, "Jacob, you don't strike me as a man who pays for it, and I'm not a gal who gives it away free." She smiled. "But I'm willing to make an exception in your case."

Jacob laughed. "Hell, Amy, look at me. Do I have the face of a man who sets female hearts aflutter? Of course I pay for it when I get the urge. Now my brother Shawn is different. He's handsome and he has a way with the ladies and—"

The door swung open and a man stepped inside. Jacob stopped talking as alarm bells clamored in his head.

The newcomer was in his midtwenties, tall, thin, with white-blond hair and eyes the color of bleached bone. In a land where men were bronzed brown by weather, the man's skin was fish-belly white, his mustache pale and sparse. He wore dusty range clothes and scuffed boots, but his gun rig of black, tooled leather was of high quality, as was the finely engraved, ivory-handled Colt that rode butt-forward in a holster on his right hip.

It was a professional gunfighter's rig and expensive, but, studying the man, Jacob decided he didn't shape up as a draw fighter, not with that unhandy way of carrying a Colt. A sure-thing killer maybe, but he wasn't a man who made a living with his fancy revolver up close and personal. When the stranger dismissed him with a cold, sidelong slide of his white eyes, Jacob sensed something about the man, something wrong enough to make his skin crawl.

"What can I do you for, stranger?" Lou Rose said.

"I want whiskey and a woman," the man said. His voice was as soft and smooth as velvet drawn across glass, but he wheezed deep in his chest as though he found it hard to breathe in the close dugout.

"The whiskey I can supply," Rose said. "As to the woman, take it up with Amy." The bartender nodded. "Settin' over there with the tall gent."

The stranger's eyes again crawled over Jacob, who felt they'd laid slime tracks all over him, like snails. The man's gaze moved to Amy and lingered.

Finally he said, "I don't want to go dipping into another man's honeypot."

Amy rose from the chair, her professional whore's smile pinned in place. She stepped toward the newcomer, her hips swaying. "I'm available, cowboy. If you've got five dollars."

White eyes looked at the woman over the rim of his whiskey glass, stripping her naked. Then he laughed. "Five dollars for you? You're making a joke, right?"

"Mister, she's the only available woman between here and Santa Fe," Lou Rose said.

"In a pig's eye," the man said. "I can get a dozen Apache women for that much money."

"Then you'd better put it back in your pants and head for the San Carlos," Amy said. Her back was stiff, and a frown gathered between her eyebrows.

"Two dollars," the man said. "Silver money."

"You go to hell," Amy said, turning away from him.

"All right, five dollars," the man said. "And only because I like your sand."

After Amy and the stranger closed the saloon door behind them, the old-timer in the bearskin coat whistled. "Hell, I never paid that much for a woman in all my born days."

"Because you're a real famous cheapskate, Tom," Rose said, grinning.

"Hell, is that right?" Tom Linton said. "So that's how come I'm always left with the ugly, skinny ones."

"You must buy your whores by the pound, huh?" Jacob said.

Linton rubbed his hairy jaw. "I'll tell you something, sonny," he said. "Union whores was a helluva lot prettier than them bag o' bones Reb scarecrows o' your'n."

"Says who?" Jacob said.

"Says me, and when Arkansas Tom Linton says it, you can bet the farm that it's a natural fact."

"Well," Jacob said, "I can't argue with a man who talks natural facts."

"Damn right," Linton said. He looked crafty. "Now, since I won another argument, I guess you should buy me a drink, young feller."

Jacob rose to his feet and walked to the bar. "I guess I should at that. Set 'em up, bartender. I'll have a whiskey."

* * *

The wind picked up and hurled dust against the chattering dugout door and found enough chinks and crevices in the structure to set the oil lamp flames to dancing. The bulk of an entire peak rested on the saloon's stone roof, and the trembling aspen on the slope above tossed and fretted and rustled a frantic warning that the mountain was falling. Howling, the wind tormented the aspen further and tossed down branches that hit the hard-packed earth below with a sound of breaking bones.

Inside, Linton, his eye on another drink, tried to start an argument with Jacob on who had the better cavalry mounts, North or South, but Lou Rose put an end to it.

"We've had enough of your natural facts for one night, Tom," he said. "Leave the gentleman alone." Over the old-timer's protests, he said to Jacob, "It's getting wild out there. You can bed down in the barn tonight if you want."

The barn was another dugout, set at a distance from the saloon and hog farm, and Jacob figured it would be snug enough.

"Thank you kindly," he said. "I'll take you up on that."

"And what about me?" Linton said. "Are you just gonna throw me out into the storm?"

"You know fine well where the barn is, Tom," Rose said. "God knows, you've slept off enough drunks in there."

"Maybe so, and maybe I have, but it's still nice to be invited," Linton said.

Rose smiled. "All right, Tom, you're invited."

"I should think I am," Linton said, somewhat mollified. "A man likes to be asked and—"

The woman's scream drowned out whatever else Linton had to say.

Chapter Seven

Gun in hand, Jacob O'Brien made a dash for the door. The wind pushed against him, and he had to throw his whole weight against the rough timber to force it open.

Behind him he heard Linton yell, "By God, that was Amy!"

Then Jacob was outside in the wind. Ahead of him, a horseman spurred into the torn night, and Jacob thumbed off a couple of fast shots at the fleeing rider. But the distance was too great and the light too dim. He was sure he'd missed the man.

Tom Linton pounded past him, running for the door of Amy's room. Jacob followed at a walk, his eyes on the darkness that had swallowed the rider. He cherished a slender hope that the man with the milky eyes and fancy gun rig would return and shoot it out. But he saw only the gloom of night and the restless rustle of wind-tattered trees.

Jacob directed his attention at Linton. The old-timer slowly backed out of Amy's room, his stiff body betraying his shock. He turned his head and stared at Jacob, a strange, lost look on his weathered face.

Like a broken automaton, Linton opened and closed his mouth, but no sound came out. Jacob rushed past him into the room . . . and entered a charnel house.

Amy had been cut from crotch to breastbone, "gutted like a trout," as Tom Linton would describe it later. She lay spread-eagled on the bed, the sheets she'd fisted in her final agony scarlet with blood. The girl had cried out only once, so it had been quick, Jacob thought. Mighty quick and cruel.

He looked around, but there was no sign of the knife. The killer had taken it with him.

Lou Rose pushed past Jacob, then stopped in his tracks. "Oh, my God," he said. The man swayed and Jacob supported him. "Amy . . . what . . . I mean . . . why . . ."

"She fell off the edge of the earth," Jacob said.

He took a blanket from the bottom of the girl's iron cot and spread it over the body. "I'll come back and help you bury her," he said to Rose.

The man nodded dumbly, but then said, "Where are you going?"

"After the man with the white eyes."

"He did it?"

"Who else?"

"I thought he looked like a strange one," Rose

said. "I told him to talk to Amy. I mean, I'm the one to blame, I should've—"

"You're not to blame, Lou," Jacob said. "The man who murdered Amy is to blame. No one else."

He stepped out the door, only to be stopped by Linton. "Where you headed, young feller?" he said.

"I'm going after him," Jacob said.

"And I'll jine ye," Linton said. He read hesitation in the younger man's eyes and said, "I was an army scout for nigh on thirty years, an' I can track like an Apache." He slapped his guns. "And I don't miss too much with these."

Jacob nodded. "Mount up, Tom."

"Here, what's your name? You never did give it."

"Jacob."

"Mind if I call you Jake?"

"A lot of people do."

The dugout had been blown out of a rock face in one of the Manzano Peak foothills, a mile west of Priest Canyon. It perched on a wide, sandy ledge that sloped gently on its north side into a series of rolling grass meadows cut through by stands of juniper, piñon, and mesquite, miles of rugged country, little traveled. But Tom Linton read the tracks and said the white-eyed man was headed in that direction.

Linton stood by his horse's head in the wind-flung darkness and looked up at Jacob. "And the feller ain't just running," he said. "I reckon he knows right where he's headed."

"How do you figure that?" Jacob said.

"He knows this neck of the woods well enough to cover country pretty fast, and he's keeping low, being mighty careful not to skyline himself." Linton spat. "Damn him, Jake, if he heads into the mountains we could lose him."

"Do you reckon he figures we're after him?" Jacob said.

"I don't know. He might."

"Then mount up. We'll press him close and hope he makes a mistake."

Linton climbed into the saddle, and the two riders headed due north. Ahead of them lay wild country cut through by deep arroyos, high peaks, and the ruins of ancient pueblos laid waste by Apaches. It wasn't a long-riding land in daylight, and darkness slowed Jacob and Linton to a walk as they allowed their horses to pick the trails.

After an hour Jacob's eyes tired from the strain of constantly searching the tunnel of darkness ahead of him. The wind drowned any noise the white-eyed man might make, and to make matters worse, clouds constantly scudded across the face of the moon and turned the night even darker.

Samuel's wire resided uneasily in the pocket of Jacob's shirt, and its brief content, COME QUICK BIG TROUBLE, gave him a world of worry. If the colonel and Samuel needed him at Dromore it meant gun trouble, the kind he was qualified to handle.

He couldn't afford to spend time on a long chase. He'd have to end it quickly.

"Damn it," Linton said, slapping his thigh, "I knew I recognized that ranny with the white eyes."

Jacob lit a cigarette, cupping his hands around the match flame. Through an exhaled cloud of blue smoke, he said, "So who is he?"

"Last time I saw him was a couple of years ago at Fort Union up on the old Santa Fe Trail. He was a second lieutenant in a supply company then, but got himself arrested after he had his wicked way with the wife of a civilian quartermaster."

"You mean he raped her?" Jacob said.

"Yeah, that's what I mean." Linton found his pipe and stuck it in his mouth. "The boy was facing a court-martial, and there were them who said he should be hung, but his pa was a Union war hero with friends in Washington and the lieutenant was allowed to resign. I heard that the boy's pa paid a pile of money to the woman and her husband. A sack of double-eagles helped smooth things over, as they say."

"Can you recollect the lieutenant's name?" Jacob said.

"I'm studying on it, Jake." Linton scowled in thought, then his face brightened. "Shannon! Lieutenant Shade Shannon. I recollect that his pa,

Cap'n Shannon, lost his legs during the war in some sea fight with blockade runners."

"What's Captain Shannon doing now?" Jacob asked.

Linton shook his head. "Now you're asking me conundrums, Jake."

"You mean you don't know?"

"I mean I don't know."

Jacob scanned the wall of darkness ahead of him. "Well, when we find Shade we'll ask him," he said.

As the night shaded into dawn, Shannon's trail faded into the mountains and Jacob's hunt came to an end.

"We've lost him, Jake," Tom Linton said.

"Seems like."

"Well, now what?"

Jacob's gaze wandered over the peaks where morning shadows slanted among the pines and the birds greeted the new-aborning day. "We go back and bury Amy," he said.

"It's a hard thing, letting Shade escape like this," Linton said.

"He hasn't escaped," Jacob said. "One day I'll run into him, and when I do, I'll kill him."

Linton turned and saw the determined set of Jacob's unshaven chin, the blue eyes iced to the color of a gun barrel. "Jake," he said, "something tells me that right about now ol' Shade felt a goose fly over his grave."

* * *

Jacob and Tom Linton helped Lou Rose bury Amy in a rock grave that overlooked a hanging valley where summer wildflowers bloomed.

Linton, who'd stood at the graveside of many soldiers, said the words, and Rose, still racked by guilt, moved his lips in a Jewish prayer for the dead that Jacob reckoned had its origins back in the mists of time.

The sun was directly overhead when Jacob again rode north, this time in the direction of Dromore . . . toward troubles he hoped were less than the ones he conjured up in his imagination.

But he would soon learn that the reality was worse, much worse, than anything he'd envisioned.

Chapter Eight

Shade Shannon rode out of the Manzano Mountains and followed Buffalo Draw west. That night he made cold camp in a mission ruin near Jacinto Mesa and in the morning pushed his tired horse toward the small village of El Cerrito, a cluster of adobe buildings scattered along the south bank of the Pecos River.

El Cerrito was populated solely by Mexicans and the occasional gringo drifter before Joshua De-Clare had moved into an empty casa and made it his temporary headquarters.

Shannon figured that DeClare, that damned, twisted cripple, would help him as he'd helped him once before.

Shannon drew rein on the ridge above the village. He was tired, hungry, and gritty, his white eyes scorched by the morning sun. He reached into his shirt pocket and took a pair of round, dark spectacles from a leather pouch and settled them on the bridge of his nose before he hooked them behind his ears. He could smell the village from where he was, a heady mix of spices, chickens, rooting hogs, and burning mesquite. Women were already bustling around, preparing breakfast. A man stepped out of his house, yawned, stretched, and then threw a disinterested glance at the horseman on the ridge. He went back inside and closed the door behind him.

DeClare and his sister lived at the edge of town, in an adobe with a pole corral, outhouse, and small timber barn at back.

Shannon knew the house well. He'd been there once before, the day DeClare hired him to do that uppity witch of a farmer's wife.

"It's all set up, Shade," DeClare had said. "Just rape the hell out of her and then get out of there without being seen. We'll do the rest."

Shannon remembered that well. DeClare had sat in his wheelchair all pinched and white and sickly, his wasted legs like dry twigs, ready to break in a strong wind.

Shannon's mouth pulled into a tight line. God, he hated cripples. Until he'd done for him, his father had been one, the high and mighty Captain Miles Shannon. Damn him, his mind was as crippled as his body. He never understood that his son needed to hear the dying gasps of a woman like a Chinaman needed opium. Killing a woman after he'd had her nurture him made him feel whole again. Well again.

Cripple or no, Joshua understood that and had recognized a kindred spirit that day in Georgetown when they'd first met. And so did his sister. Dora De-Clare was the most beautiful woman Shannon had seen in his life, even prettier than his own ma, may she rest in peace. He'd do Dora real good one day, but not just yet. Today he needed her. Tomorrow—he smiled—well, so long poor, sweet Dora.

Shannon rode down the rise toward the DeClare cabin. It was time to call in favors of his own.

"Shade, you look terrible," Dora DeClare said. "And you've got blood all over your shirt."

Shannon smiled almost shyly, shuffling his feet like a boy caught stealing apples. "Killed me a whore last night, Dora. Done for my daddy, too."

Dora's expression didn't change as her brother said, "Shade, that was naughty of you."

"They were begging for it, Josh," Shannon said.

"You're a good boy, Shade," Dora DeClare said. "So I'm sure they were."

"Hell, I also killed me a woman and her two kids," Shannon said, a note of pride in his voice.

"When, last night?" Dora said.

"No, the night before that, I think. Father tied me up in the barn afterward, but I escaped, and then I done for him."

Dora said nothing, but her slender throat moved as she swallowed hard, and she didn't look at her brother or Shannon. The last thing she wanted was to meet Shannon's stare, the one that ripped her clothes off and left her naked, or read the madness in his alabaster eyes.

"Dora," Shannon said, grinning, "I guess now you'll spank me for being such a bad boy, like you done before, huh?"

"Yes, Shade, after I wash that bloody shirt of yours and fix you something to eat."

Shannon looked around the cabin. A table lamp that still glowed through the glassy morning light added pinpoints of yellow to his suddenly haunted eyes. "Where is Luke Caldwell?" he said.

"He's out," DeClare said. "Scouting around, I guess."

"I don't like him," Shannon said. "And he doesn't like me."

"Luke doesn't like anybody," DeClare said. "Anyway, I hired him for his gun, not to go around liking folks."

"I will have to kill him one day," Shannon said.

DeClare smiled. "Wait until he guns Jacob O'Brien. Then you can have at him."

"What does he look like, this O'Brien feller?" Shannon said.

"Why do you want to know?" DeClare said.

"After I done the whore at Lou Rose's saloon— you know where that is?"

"I've heard of it."

"Well, a tall, thin feller took a couple of pots at me, then chased me," Shannon said. "It was dark, but I caught a glimpse of moonlight a couple of times and saw him and another man on my back trail."

Suddenly, DeClare leaned forward in his chair, his

pale, thin face alarmed. "You didn't lead O'Brien here, did you?"

"No, I lost him in the hills."

"Are you sure?"

"Of course I'm sure."

"Describe the man you saw," Joshua DeClare said.

"Like I said, a tall, thin man, got a Comanche's face on him except for the blue eyes and big mustache. Wears a puncher's outfit, worn-out and ragged, and totes his gun on his right hip."

DeClare eased back in his wheelchair. "Could be O'Brien, could be a hundred other men."

"If it's him, he doesn't scare me none," Shannon said.

"You ran from him, Shade," Dora said.

"It was the thing to do at the time. Next time I won't run."

"Shade," Dora said, "give me your shirt. Then go outside and wash at the pump. Bacon and eggs all right with you?"

"Anything you cook is all right with me, Dora." Shannon removed his shirt and passed it to the woman. Their fingers touched, and Dora felt her skin crawl.

After Shannon left, Dora watched him from the window as he stood splashing water on his face and chest at the pump. Without turning she said, "Josh, he's a monster."

"We need him, Dora."

"Can you control him?"

"Yes, I can. And if not me, Luke Caldwell will."

DeClare spoke to his sister's stiff back. "Dora, remember that the real monster here is Shamus O'Brien."

"That's something I'm not likely to forget."

DeClare was silent for a while, as though marshaling his thoughts. Then he said, "Dora, fate, destiny, whatever you want to call it, brought Shade Shannon back to us. Now we'll use him again, this time to tear the very heart out of Dromore. When it's done, I'll kill him like the mad dog he is."

Dora turned from the window, blew out the oil lamp on the table that had been competing uselessly against the morning light, and said, "How does a bright young army officer become Shade Shannon?"

DeClare took time to light his pipe. "According to Luke Caldwell, the story goes that he found the bodies of four of his soldiers after they'd been worked over for days by Apache women," he said. "The soldiers had died real slow, a bit at a time, and their intestines—"

"Josh, I understand," Dora said. "You don't have to draw me the picture."

DeClare smiled. "All right, then here's the short version: Something snapped in Second Lieutenant Shannon's mind that day. The way Luke heard it, Shade started screaming, and he didn't stop for three days and two nights. Finally, he went into some kind of deep sleep, and when he woke the man was gone and the monster had taken his place."

"It was then he raped a woman," Dora said.

"Yes. As Shade says, he 'done her good.' He must have done her real good because his father had to call in old favors to get him out of a court-martial and a hanging. He took him back to the Shannon ranch."

"And then we met him," Dora said. She glanced out the window where Shannon was toweling his face and hair. "When do we turn him loose on Lorena O'Brien?" she said.

"When the time is right," DeClare said. "But, never fear, it will be soon." He frowned in thought. "My inclination is to wait until after Patrick O'Brien swings." He looked at his sister, his eyes bright. "The hurt to Shamus will be all the greater then."

"God willing," Dora said.

DeClare's anger flared, and his skeletal hands slapped the arms of his chair. "What has God got to do with it?" he said. "We serve a far more powerful prince, do we not? Do you want him to destroy you, tear you limb from limb?"

Dora's wide, frightened eyes revealed her alarm. "Joshua, please don't talk like that. It . . . it scares me when you say those things about the master."

"You think I'm mad to tell you such things, don't you, Dora?"

"I think Father's death nearly drove you to the brink of insanity." She smiled and laid her hand on her brother's thin shoulder. "But you're better now, Josh, much better."

"And this wasted body of mine, how do you explain it?"

"Josh, you know how it happened."

"Tell me."

"Your horse reared, then fell on top of you."

"Was it God's will?"

"It was an accident, Josh."

"No, it was God's will that I be a cripple." DeClare's eyes burned with black fire, and his mouth tightened into a pale line. "That is why I've turned my back on him."

Dora glanced at her brother's shriveled legs and the unholy light in his stare, and she shivered as though she'd stepped into an icy breeze. "The master wouldn't turn on us, would he?"

"Of course not, I was merely joking. No need to be afraid, Dora," DeClare said. "It is Shamus O'Brien's boast that Dromore has stood against rustlers, Apaches, blizzards, droughts, and floods. We'll see how it stands against me and all the dark powers I can summon."

Dora DeClare felt her stomach spike, from fear or dread or both. Suddenly, she was caught in the terrible twilight shadows that lurk between madness and evil. She glanced outside at Shannon, who stood in the yard beckoning to her, grinning. No, not caught. Dora knew she was no innocent victim. She was part of it, part of the madness, part of the evil, and blood stained her hands. Where and how it would end she had no way of knowing.

She opened the door and stepped outside. Shannon's marble eyes were lost behind dark glasses that glowed red, reflecting the scarlet-rippled sky. Suddenly, she felt sick to her stomach as her mind and body revolted at what she was about to do. Shannon, a mad man at home in a mad world, bent over his knees, groaning, his pants around his ankles as she paddled him.

And the man who caused all this was Shamus O'Brien, and she cursed him, cursed him to the deepest caverns of hell.

Him and all his vile brood.

"Is that Shade Shannon I hear hollering?" Luke Caldwell said.

"Dora is giving him a beating," DeClare said.

"He's a freak," Caldwell said.

"I know, but right now we need him." He looked at the tall, loose-limbed Texas gunman. "Is it done?"

"It's done."

"You made sure?"

Caldwell's lean, grim face didn't change expression. "When a man's got the hilt of a Green River knife sticking out of his throat, he don't need much convincing that he's dead."

DeClare smiled, a humorless grimace that didn't reach his eyes. "So, we wait until Patrick O'Brien swings, then Shannon will bide his time and jump the lovely Lorena first chance he gets." He clapped together his thin, blue-veined hands. "Our plans proceed apace, do they not?"

For a few moments Caldwell didn't speak, then he said, "All the O'Brien brothers are good with the iron, but the one you have to look out for is Jacob. He could spoil your plans pretty damn quick."

"I know that he's fast on the draw-and-shoot."

"Maybe the best there is. And he's as mean as eight acres of rattlesnakes, and he likes to shoot first and talk later."

"Can you take him, Luke?"

"Maybe. I don't know. But it would be close, and he'd put lead in me, count on that. Jake O'Brien won't die easy."

"Then we'll have to find a less dangerous way to dispose of him, won't we?" DeClare scowled in thought, then brightened. "I know, we'll talk to Shannon. He'll find a way."

"Talk to him yourself. If he takes down his pants to show us his *gage d'amour*, I swear I'll put a bullet up his ass."

DeClare shook his head. "Harsh talk, Luke, harsh talk indeed."

"Listen," the gunman said, "you want Shamus O'Brien ruined, right?" He saw DeClare nod and said, "Then let me ruin him for keeps. I can lay up on the mesa with a rifle and scatter his brains as soon as he sticks his head outside." Caldwell allowed himself a rare smile. "For sure, that'll spoil his day."

DeClare nodded. "Your suggestion is not without merits, Luke, but it's too easy. Dora and I want to rip O'Brien's heart out, destroy his soul, have him suffer the fires long before he reaches hell." The cripple's face was vicious. "A dead man can't suffer. I look forward to the day when O'Brien sits amid the ruin of Dromore and all his dreams and ambitions lie in ashes at his feet. Perhaps on that day he'll blow his own brains out, but before he does I will make him whimper the name DeClare. Damn him, he'll rue the day he first heard it."

"Josh, you and your sister make pretty powerful enemies," Caldwell said.

DeClare smiled. "Yes, and we place our trust in a pretty powerful friend."

Chapter Nine

"You're thin, Jacob, too thin," Shamus O'Brien said. He scowled as his disapproving eyes scraped from the crown of his son's uncombed head to the toes of his scuffed, down-at-heel boots. "What do you eat when you do eat? Lizards?"

Jacob smiled. "When there's nothing else around, Colonel. But Lorena made me such a fine breakfast this morning it'll more than make up for my missed meals."

"And you're dressed in rags, patched all together like a Dublin beggar," Shamus said, refusing to let go of the subject of his son's sorry appearance.

Samuel came to his brother's assistance. "Pa, not every man is like Shawn, always dressed up as though he's going to a wedding or a preaching."

"More's the pity," Shamus said. He shifted in his wheelchair and grimaced, the old Apache lance head in his back punishing him. "Jacob, your brother told you about Patrick."

"Yes, Colonel, he did."

"He won't hang," Shamus said.

"On that we both agree, Pa," Jacob said.

"I want you in Georgetown, keeping a watch on things," Shamus said. "I don't want those damned vigilantes to spring any surprises on us."

Jacob nodded. "I'll stay on the scout."

Shamus's probing blue eyes pinned Jacob to his chair like a butterfly in a display case. "What do you feel, son?" he said.

Jacob didn't hesitate. "The air is black, Colonel, hard to breathe."

"Where?"

"Here and in Georgetown. Other places."

"You have the gift, and your mother, God rest her soul, had it before you."

Jacob said nothing, and the colonel continued, "Ireland is a poor, oppressed country, but she freely gives her sons and daughters what little she has. Your portion was the gift of second sight and the love of music."

Jacob remained silent. The colonel would eventually get around to what he really wanted to say.

Then Shamus said it. "I feel someone wants to do Dromore great harm, and that the trumped-up charges against Patrick were just the start."

"Not everyone has reason to love Dromore," Jacob said.

"No, indeed," Shamus said. "But in the past our enemies have always come at us with guns. I sense— no, Jacob, tell me what you feel."

"I told you already, Colonel. The air is thick and black. I feel like I'm walking through the smoke of burning bodies."

Samuel was startled. "Hell, Jake, what does that mean?"

"It means he senses evil, as I do," Shamus said.

"What kind of evil?" Samuel said. "I swear, you two are making my skin crawl."

"I don't know what kind of evil," Jacob said.

"Lawyer Dunkley talked about evil, said he was afraid of it," Samuel said. "I didn't understand him, either."

The Dromore black butler stepped into the study. "Excuse me, Colonel," he said. "There is an officer of the law here to see you. His name is Sheriff John Moore."

"Show him in, and please ask Mr. Shawn to join us and Mr. Ironside."

"Mr. Ironside is still out with the herd, sir," the butler said. When Shamus waved a dismissive hand the man bowed and left.

"Moore must have some news," Shamus said.

Neither Jacob nor Samuel spoke, aware that news can be good but can also be bad.

The butler led John Moore into the study, and the lawman stood for a few moments in silence and turned his hat in his hand.

"Damn it, man, take a seat," Shamus said. "Samuel, give the sheriff a drink. He looks like he can use one."

Moore gratefully accepted both chair and bourbon. His face was gray with fatigue and his eyes were glazed with disbelief and fear, like a man who'd just received a death sentence.

"Well, speak up, Moore," Shamus said. "Don't keep us in suspense."

Shawn stepped silently into the room and sat near the window. He was wearing a gun, unusual for him when he was at home.

Watching him, Jacob drew his own conclusions from the Colt at his brother's hip. Shawn felt something, too, and it troubled him.

"I've got bad news, Colonel," Moore said. He took a gulp of whiskey.

"Out with it," Shamus said. "Is Patrick all right?"

"He's fine," Moore said. "And he's guarded by a man I can trust who has faith in scatterguns." The sheriff took a deep breath. "Colonel, Lucas Dunkley is dead. Murdered."

He talked into the stunned silence that followed. "Happened sometime yesterday afternoon, I reckon. A person or persons unknown stuck a knife in his throat."

"I spoke to Lucas yesterday," Samuel said. "He was afraid somebody would try to kill him, and he told me he'd pack a gun."

"He lied. Lucas didn't have a gun," Moore said. "And if he had, he wouldn't have known what to do with it." He caught and held Samuel's eyes. "The widow of the man you killed . . . Mrs. Harris?"

Moore had framed the statement as a question, and Samuel answered it. "How is she doing?"

"She ain't doing nothin', Sam. Her and her two kids are dead."

"But how . . . I mean . . . who?"

"There ain't no 'who.' The how is that her cabin caught fire and she and the kids burned to death," Moore said.

"An accident?" Samuel said.

"Seems like," Moore said.

The sheriff turned his attention to Shamus. "Colonel, I got more bad news. Captain Miles Shannon is dead."

Shamus jolted upright in his chair. "Jesus, Mary, and Joseph, how?"

"We think it was his crazy son." Moore blinked. "Bashed the captain's head in with an iron bar, then fled the scene."

"You're talking about Shade Shannon, right?" Jacob said.

"Yeah, I am, Jake. You know him?" Moore said.

"After he murdered his father, he stabbed a whore to death at a dugout saloon south of here."

"You were there?"

"Yeah. Another man and I went after him, but we lost him in the dark."

Shawn shook his head. "Well, this has been real pleasant. Bless you, John, you've got to visit more often. You're such a cheerful body to have around."

Moore sighed. "Sorry, it seems that in my line of work all I get is bad news."

Shawn rose to his feet. "All right, Sheriff, tell us again how Dunkley died."

"It ain't complicated, Shawn, a Green River knife to the throat."

"Hardly a self-inflicted wound then?"

"No, somebody else done it. A man wouldn't kill his own self like that."

"Now think carefully, John, before you answer. Do you think Dunkley was killed to stop him telling what he knew?"

"About what?" Moore said, his face wary.

"About who really raped and murdered Molly Holmes."

"It's possible," Moore said. "Anything's possible."

"Could Shade Shannon be Molly's real killer?" Shawn said.

Moore didn't hesitate. "Well, yeah, I guess he could be, but there's no way of proving it."

"Maybe Lucas Dunkley had the proof."

Jacob said, "John, did you search Dunkley's office?"

Moore shook his head. "No. I didn't reckon I'd any need to."

"He may have written something down," Jacob said.

"He might at that," the sheriff said. "I'll take a look when I get back to town."

"We'll take a look, you mean," Jacob said. "I'm going with you."

Shawn looked at his brother. "Samuel, when you spoke to Mrs. Harris, did she seem suicidal? Did she want to end it now her husband was gone?"

"No," Samuel said. "She was talking about how she wanted to leave the territory and make a life for her children somewhere."

"The night wasn't real cold, was it?" Shawn said.

"Of course not, it's summer."

"Then it's unlikely Mrs. Harris left a fire burning, and she'd damp down the stove, don't you think? I mean, it being hot and all. And she wouldn't leave a lamp lit the whole night, oil being as expensive as it is."

"You mean somebody set the fire deliberately?" Samuel said.

"To cover a triple murder. Yes, I do."

"Shade Shannon," Jacob said.

"It's a real possibility," Shawn said.

Jacob turned to Moore again. "Looks like we've got our work cut out for us, huh?"

"Hell, Jake, Shannon could be anywhere by this time," Moore said.

"I know, but we'll find him and make him confess to killing Molly Holmes. Your word will hold in Georgetown, John."

"Hell, we'll just drag him back and he can tell the whole town. If we find him, that is," the sheriff said.

"No, we'll find him and he'll confess in your hearing, John," Jacob said.

"And then?" Moore said.

"And then I'll put a bullet in his belly."

Shamus looked at Jacob, wondering at him. His son played Chopin with all the sensitivity of a poet and dreamer, a rare talent that displayed a certain beauty of soul. He was a man prone to bouts of deep depression as black as midnight, yet he could be a cold-blooded, ruthless killer. He was both sides of the same coin, something Shamus would've thought impossible before Jacob had showed him otherwise.

"Sheriff," Shamus said, "can you think of anyone who would want to harm Dromore badly enough that he'd commit murder to see us destroyed?"

Shamus expected a quick "no," but to his surprise Moore gave it some thought, then said, "Goin' back a few years, do you mind Jes Murphy, the black hoss wrangler you caught rustling your cattle up on the Santa Fe River that time?"

"He's in Yuma," Shamus said.

"He was," Moore said. "He got paroled six months ago."

"Hell, Jes had sand," Shamus said. "If he had any hard feelings he'd come looking for me with a gun."

Moore nodded. "Well, that's true. He did favor a Sharps right enough."

"I'm thinking more along the lines of somebody new in the territory," Shamus said. "Somebody that's down on me and mine but doesn't have the *cojones* to do his own killing."

"Could be a woman," Shawn said. He smiled, "Now that you've mentioned a lack of *cojones*, Pa."

"It's not a member of the fair sex," Shamus said. "A woman didn't order the rape and murder of Molly Holmes."

Moore's face creased in thought. After a while he said, "Colonel, I sure don't recollect seeing strangers around." He smiled, reared back in his chair, and slapped the top of his thigh. "Whoa there, John, you plumb forgot about Miss Dora DeClare and her brother."

Suddenly, Shamus's face tightened with interest. "Who are they?"

"Two young people, moved into a Mex village south of town," Moore said. "Josh, that's the brother, got crippled when a horse fell on him. He sits in a wheelchair, and he's a skinny little feller and there sure ain't much of him left." Moore drained his glass and stared sadly into its arid depths. After Samuel refilled it for him, he said, "Josh is trying to make a name for himself as an artist, a painter, and Dora says they moved into the territory for his health."

"What does she look like?" Shawn said.

"Pretty enough to make a man plow through a stump," Moore said. "I mean, she's got a fine figure, yeller hair, and the kind of big brown eyes guaranteed to keep a man like you awake o' nights, Shawn."

"She sounds real interesting," Shawn said, grinning.

"More to the point, a crippled painter and his pretty sister don't pose any danger to Dromore," Shamus said. "They're harmless."

Chapter Ten

He awoke, lit the lamp beside the bed, and grinned as the whore shrank away from him.

His voice sounded like the wind pummeling a rusty gate. "You don't like my face," he said.

The girl was sixteen years old, fresh off the boat from Ireland, and she attempted a smile. "No, no, it's just fine," she said. "Honest, mister, I hardly noticed. See, when I was sent to your room it was dark and—" She stopped, knowing she'd made a mistake.

"It's burned," he said. "Melted in fire. How could you not notice?"

The girl bit her lip and made no answer.

The man called Lum reached out, grabbed one of her breasts, and twisted hard. As the whore cried out in pain, he said, "How could you not notice?"

He twisted harder and the girl screamed, "I noticed! I noticed!"

"Kiss me," he said. His flat lips drew back in a

grin, exposing teeth as long and yellow as ivory piano keys.

Again the girl shrank from him, her eyes wide and frightened.

He turned onto his back and laughed, loud bellows of mirth that filled the hotel room. Finally, as his laughter receded, he said, "It was dark, huh? What am I to do with you?"

"Please, mister, don't hurt me," the girl said, her bottom lip trembling.

The girl was small, undernourished, and terrified. Her slender back arched as she fought against the ropes that bound her wrists to the bed's brass spindles.

"Are you trying to leave, and us just getting acquainted?" he said. Lum leaned on one elbow. "Did I ever tell you about Tom Scratcher of San Francisco town? No? Well, he was a rum one was old Tom. He'd always give you a fair go, no fears about that, but in the end he always came up trumps. Aye, many a lively lad rode Tom's bullet to the grave, and many a woman and child as well, if the truth be told."

The whore's eyes were as round as coins, damp with fear and dread.

"See, Tom took me under his wing, like," Lum said. "He taught me his ways, how to rob and kill and sleep sound o' nights after the deeds were done." Lum stabbed a stiff finger into the whore's chest. "Do you know what they were, the ways of Tom Scratcher?"

The girl shook her head.

"They were the ways of hell," Lum said. "Wherever he went, ol' Tom brought hell with him." He sighed deep and long. " 'Course, they done for him in the end. He was strung up by vigilantes and me alongside o' him. Damned hicks, they set fires under us, and Tom died in the flames, bold as brass to the end, a-cursing the hicks, seed, breed, and generation of them. As for me, I was burned, as ye can tell, but I fooled them. I was still alive when they cut me down and left me lying there for the buzzards."

Lum's wolf teeth gleamed in the darkness. "Oh, no, he didn't die, not ol' Lum. Leastways, his body didn't die. You know what died, missy?" He jabbed a thumb into his chest. "In here? No? Well, my soul died. It burned up in the fire, and I hauled it out as a cinder."

Lum laughed, as though he'd said the funniest thing that ever was.

"Please let me go," the whore said. "I have to make money to send to me mother."

"She won't get any money," he said. He shook his head. "Oh, no, no, no, not ever again."

"Please mister—"

"Be quiet!" He slapped the girl so hard her blond head rocked on the stained pillow. His hands, the skin scraped raw by flame, circled the whore's slim throat and he squeezed.

* * *

He called himself Lum because, the discarded son of a two-dollar-a-bang whore, he had no other name. Without sparing a glance for the dead girl on the bed, he hurriedly dressed and buckled on his gunbelt. As was his habit, he drew his Remington from the holster and checked the loads. The revolver's balance was excellent, as he knew it would be. An English gunsmith in Boston had fine-tuned the weapon's action and closely fitted its ivory grips until the Remington was in itself a work of art.

Lum had killed the man to make sure he'd never make another like it.

He reholstered the gun, then settled a gray plug hat on his bald, fire-scalded head and studied himself in the small dresser mirror. In the guttering lamplight, half his face in shadow, he looked almost human. He scowled. What a pity.

A fist pounded on the door, and Lum said, "What do you want?"

A woman's voice said, "Trippy is needed downstairs."

"Go away, she's busy," Lum said.

The fist pounded again. "Open up, mister," the woman said. "You've had your five dollars' worth of Irish ass."

Lum cursed and stepped to the door, his huge six-foot-four-inch, former prizefighter's frame filling the doorway.

The woman saw him and took a step back, her face frozen in shock.

"Trippy will be down in a minute," Lum said, enjoying the effect his features and size had on people.

The woman, plump, blowsy, showing six inches of sweating cleavage, couldn't take her eyes off the burned mask that was Lum's face. She thought his hairless skin looked like melting candle wax, and she wanted to cross herself and run away.

But she'd been a madam with her own stable of whores for twenty years, and she was made of sterner stuff. She tried and failed to look around Lum's shoulders, then said, "Let me talk to that lazy hussy."

"Come back in five minutes and you can have her," he said. He reached into his pocket, showed the woman a five-dollar coin, then dropped it down her cleavage.

"Five minutes," he said.

The woman fished between her huge breasts and recovered the coin. She smiled, "Hell, mister, so long as you're paying, take all the time you need." She leaned forward and, in a confidential tone, said, "Is she giving you value for money, doing little things for you? If not, I can send up a Chinese girl who'll do anything you want."

"Trippy is just fine," Lum said.

"Tell her to"—the door closed on the woman's face and she finished her sentence whispering to varnished timber—"do something nice for you."

* * *

Lum didn't hurry. He took a letter from the inside pocket of his black ditto suit coat and reread it for the fifth or sixth time since it had reached him in Fresno.

Brother Lum,

It is the decision of myself and the rest of the brethren that we assist Brother Joshua DeClare in his struggle against a papist murderer and oppressor he will make known to you. It is our wish that you summon the powers of the Master we all serve to assist you in this endeavor.

A map that will guide you to Brother DeClare's location in the New Mexico Territory is enclosed and the sum of five hundred dollars to cover expenses.

Needless to say, time is of the utmost importance and you will immediately leave on your quest on receipt of this dispatch.

The only outcome of this enterprise I will accept is the complete destruction of our mutual enemy, his spawn, and all his works.

Brother Lum, I warn you, fail at your peril.

Dr. William T. March,
Great Neck, New York

Lum folded the letter and put it back in his pocket. March's threat amused him. One day he'd break the little man's back like a dry twig and take over the coven himself. Still, the money was welcome because, like whiskey, whores came easy, but never cheap.

He had time and thought about banging the whore again, but he dismissed the idea. He felt as though the hick town was closing in on him, crushing the life out of him. Lum dashed sudden tears from his eyes. Nobody understood him, his needs, and his right to live as he chose and prey on whom he chose. The United States Constitution granted him that much, and he deserved to be protected from those who would do him harm.

Devils! They had taken his soul and now they wanted the thin brew that was left.

Feeling a deep sorrow for himself, Lum picked up his valise, eased the Remington into its holster, and stepped to the door. A few lamps burned along the hallway and cast shadows that crouched like black dwarves in the corners. The carpet under Lum's feet and the stained walls smelled of mildew, dampness, and coal-oil smoke overlaid by the pungent aroma of ancient human sweat.

Lum walked down the creaking stairs and past the desk. The clerk, a gangly, pimply youth with a shock of red hair and dull eyes, caught sight of the valise and said, "Hey, if you're leaving, drop off the damned key."

A length of fence wire attached the key to an inch-wide iron canister shot. Lum turned swiftly, and his right arm slung the key at the clerk's head with tremendous force. The shot hit the youth in the middle of the forehead and drove him back against the key rack and a large Chinese vase. Clerk, keys, rack, and vase clattered and shattered to the floor, and Lum grinned like a David who'd just overcome a diminutive Goliath.

"There," he said, "I dropped off my key."

But the drooling, eye-rolling clerk didn't hear.

Lum stepped into the town's only street, a dusty track flanked by rickety timber buildings on either side. Behind him, he heard a man yell. Lum stopped and turned, and the man, short, fat, and agitated, hollered, "Hey you, get the hell back here!"

The fat, blowsy madam stood beside the fat man and shook her fist, shrieking obscenities.

Lum smiled. Drew his revolver. He shot the man in the head and then put a bullet between the woman's huge breasts. He watched the pair fall, then resumed his walk to the livery stable, his Remington hanging at arm's length by his side.

He'd taken but a few steps when the door to the saloon burst open and a man wearing a lawman's badge stepped into the street. Lum had time to ponder why it was that the smaller the town, the fancier its lawman's badge, before the sheriff yelled at him to halt.

Without breaking stride, Lum's arm came up and he shot the lawman dead. Several men had followed the sheriff onto the boardwalk, and now they turned and bolted for the saloon door. Fists and

boots swung as they battled to get inside, away from
the death on the street. Lum smiled, fired again,
and dropped a big feller in the doorway, adding to
the yelling, cursing mayhem.

It was, to Lum, all uproariously funny, and he
tilted back his head and laughed his way to the
livery, dust from the street swirling around his legs
like smoke.

Lum led his horse out of the stable and stood in
the light of the lamp that glimmered on the adobe
wall. He looked down the street where a crowd had
gathered outside the hotel. A second, smaller group
clustered around the body of the dead sheriff.

"There he is!" a man yelled, pointing.

Nobody made a move toward him, remaining
still as painted figures on a canvas.

Lum drew his Remington, a move that made several people step out of his line of fire. He held up
the big revolver in the lamplight where all could
see it, rotated the cylinder, and let the spent shells
drop free. Then, slowly, deliberately, he reloaded.

"You damned hicks!" Lum yelled, "leave me the
hell alone!"

Cowed, the people in the street shrank back.
Skilled gunfighters who revealed a reckless readiness
to kill were rare in the West, and though there were
men in the crowd who did not lack courage or a

familiarity with arms, they did not step forward and cross the line that separates bravery from suicide.

Slowly, deliberately, Lum mounted his black and rode out of town. To the east, the bulk of Glorieta Mesa blotted out a vast rectangle of stars, and the sighing high country winds sang their requiem.

Chapter Eleven

"I won't choose your requiem just yet, Patrick," Jacob O'Brien said. "One way or another, we're getting you out of here." He studied his brother more closely. "You don't look well."

"I don't feel too good, either," Patrick said.

"What ails you?" Jacob asked.

Sheriff John Moore said, "He's burnin' up, so I'd say it's jailhouse fever. It can surely make a person feel right poorly pretty damn quick."

"What does the doctor say?" Jacob said. He laid the palm of his hand against Patrick's sweaty forehead.

"Nothing, on account of how he's out of town," Moore said.

"The Vigilance Committee can't hang a sick man," Jacob said. "And my brother is sick."

"Well, Jake, they've took a different stand on that. Hugh Hamlin, tall, skinny feller that owns the general store, told me, 'Sheriff, the sight of the gallows will soon restore the condemned to health. The rope is the sovereign remedy for fevers, agues, rheumatisms, the croup, and all derangements of the brain.'"

Moore shrugged. "Sorry, Jake, but you see how it is with me."

"My brother needs a doctor and care," Jacob said. "He's got a high fever."

"Sorry, Jake," Moore said. The lawman looked miserable and a tic twitched at his left eye. "There's nothing I can do."

"There's something I can do," Jake said. Suddenly a Colt was in his hand, the muzzle shoved into Moore's belly. "I never gunned a lawman before," he said, "but there's a first time for everything."

Moore took a step back. "Jake," he said, "you're crazy. Put the gun away."

"Unbuckle your gunbelt and let it drop, Sheriff," Jacob said. "I'm not taking any chances with you."

"Jake—"

"Do as I say, John, or I swear, I'll drop you right where you stand."

Moore read the warning in Jacob's eyes, and his gunbelt thudded to the floor of the cell.

Jacob turned and looked at Patrick. "Can you ride, Pat?" he said.

"No." One word, but its quiet feebleness conveyed the fact that Patrick was desperately ill.

"John, your horse is at the rail, so we're all taking a ride," Jacob said. "Pat will get up with me."

Moore was worried. "Jake, if any of the committee

members see you they'll raise the alarm, and you'll be dead before you can cover a mile."

"You'll be with us, so I'll take my chances," Jacob said. "If I leave my brother here, he'll have to be carried to the gallows." Jacob's eyes hardened into blue steel. "That isn't going to happen."

Moore shook his head. "Jake, if you go through with this, there'll be hell to pay."

Jacob said, "You weren't listening. If hell is the price of saving my brother's life, then I'm willing to pay it."

The noon sun hung directly over Georgetown, and the street felt as though someone had just opened the door of a blast furnace. The weeds that grew around some of the buildings were brown and shriveled, and the dust was powdered so fine even a faint wisp of breeze lifted it in yellow veils. The dust was everywhere. It lay thick in Georgetown's stores and homes and made its way inside everyone's clothing. Gritty, smelling faintly of horse manure, it made women hot and irritable and frayed the tempers of men as it abraded necks under high, celluloid collars.

The murder of lawyer Dunkley had set the town on edge, and in the relentlessly enervating heat men took quick offense at everything and anything.

It was a day made for a killing, and no one was more aware of that than Jacob O'Brien. Escaping from town without a shooting scrape depended on

Sheriff John Moore and his attitude. The big man had sand, and he could decide at any moment that he'd no longer be pushed. If that happened, the ball would open and men would die.

Jacob was prepared for that eventuality. If Moore raised the alarm, he would shoot fast and shoot to kill, wipe out this whole damned town if he had to.

There was no one in the street when Jacob stepped outside the sheriff's office supporting Patrick, who was now drifting in and out of consciousness.

Jacob's Colt on him, Moore helped to lift Patrick onto Jacob's mount, and then, without protest, he swung into his own saddle.

"Jake, I sure hope you know what you're doing," he said.

"Saving my brother's life is what I'm doing," Jacob said.

"Doc Cassidy will be back in a couple of days," the lawman said.

"My brother could be dead in a couple of days," Jacob said.

Moore shifted his bulk in the saddle. "Jake, Patrick was condemned to hang. There's nothing you can do to stop that."

Jacob stepped into the leather behind his brother. Patrick slumped against him, and he took the weight, adjusting his seat in the saddle. When he was settled he looked at Moore. "John, to get at Patrick you'll have to step over my dead body and two dozen others. Do you understand?"

Moore didn't flinch. "I understand this, Jake. Starting today, a hundred different kinds of hell will descend on Dromore."

"You figure the ball has opened, John?"

"It has."

"Then you'd better choose a partner," Jacob said.

"I dance with who I brung, Jake, and I brung the law." The big lawman kneed his horse into motion. "And don't you ever forget that."

Chapter Twelve

They crossed the Pecos two miles west of Starvation Peak, and Jacob told Moore he could now return to Georgetown.

"I reckon not, Jake," the lawman said. "I couldn't talk sense into you, but maybe I can make the colonel see the light."

They'd drawn rein in the thin shade of some pines, the rugged mesa and canyon country that stretched to the west promising hard going for Jacob's overloaded horse.

Jacob held a canteen to Patrick's lips, and his brother drank deep, parched by fever. When Jacob took the water away, his brother said, "My eyeglasses, Jacob. Did you bring my glasses?"

"Got them here in my pocket, boy," Moore said. He glared at Jacob. "More'n some would do for you."

"Thank you kindly, Ma," Patrick said.

And Moore said, "That boy should be resting, Jake. He's plumb out of his mind with the fever."

"He'll be in bed soon," Jacob said. "And I mean in his own room at Dromore."

Moore shook his head. "We done covered that already, Jake, and I won't say another word on the subject until I talk with the colonel."

He gave Jacob a belligerent, challenging glare, but the younger man was looking beyond him at a rider emerging through the shimmering heat haze. Moore turned and saw what Jacob saw. Horse and rider were strangely elongated in the rippling distance, as though they were twenty feet tall and thin as rails.

Gradually, as the rider came closer, he and his mount shrank to their normal size, which, as Jacob would recall later, was big enough. The man sat a black American stud that must have gone seventeen hands, and he was huge, the heavy muscles of his chest and shoulders apparent under the baggy suit he wore. He sported a plug hat that seemed a size too small for the enormous boulder of his head.

He was, Jacob decided, a man to be reckoned with.

Then Jacob saw his face.

His features had been burned away, no lips, no nose, hollow eye sockets, bereft of lashes and eyebrows, giving him the appearance of a skull. The skin was tight to the bone, white planes of scar tissue and scarlet ridges marking the places where his face had melted.

It was a visage that looms in a child's nightmares,

but Jacob passed no judgment. For all he knew this horribly disfigured man could be a good fellow.

Or he could be a monster.

The rider drew rein. His eyes had been spared the tragedy that had befallen his face. They were black, shot through with flecks of gold, the eyes of a snake.

The man looked at Moore, dismissed him, then at Jacob and Patrick. His stare lingered. "He sick?" he said.

"He's got a fever," Jacob said.

The rider grunted, then turned to Moore again. "Lawman?"

"I'm the sheriff of Georgetown," Moore said. "North of here, up in the El Barro country."

The rider's huge bicep bulged under his suit coat as he removed his hat and wiped the sweatband with his fingers. He replaced the hat and said, "I'm looking for a place. They call it El Cerrito."

"South of here on the Pecos," Moore said.

"How far?"

"Oh, ten miles, maybe less." Moore couldn't read the rider's face because all the text had burned away. But the man had the eyes of a carrion-eater, and that troubled the sheriff more than it should. "El Cerrito is a Mex village," he said. "They don't have a saloon."

The rider touched his hat. "Obliged," he said.

"What kind of business do you have in El Cerrito?" Moore said.

"My own," the man said.

* * *

As they rode out of the pines, Moore said to Jacob, "What do you make of that ranny?"

"He isn't pretty," Jacob said.

"Do you think he's on the scout?"

"Could be."

"I've got a bad feeling about him, Jake. Real bad."

Jacob smiled. "Funny you should mention that, John. So do I."

"I think maybe I'll swing by El Cerrito when my business at Dromore is done."

"You don't have a gun. Cross that man and you'll need one mighty fast." Moore lapsed into silence, thinking about that, and Jacob said, "I'll get you one at Dromore."

"What the hell is he?" Moore said.

"Trouble," Jacob said.

"Damn you, Moore, my son's got typhus, and he got it in your filthy, rat-infested cells," Shamus O'Brien said. "You're not taking him anywhere."

"It's the law, Colonel," Moore said.

"It's the law in your dung heap of a town," Shamus said. "But I'm the law here in Dromore."

Moore drank from his whiskey glass, taking his time, steeling himself for what he had to say. Finally he said it. "Colonel, when I come back here, I'll have a posse behind me."

"You mean those damned Georgetown vigilantes?"

"They're sworn to uphold the law," Moore said.

"They're a sorry bunch of trash," Shamus said.

"Those men will stand, Colonel."

"Then more than a few of them will be dead on the ground before this is over," Shamus said, his eyes blazing.

Moore opened his mouth to speak, but Shamus held up a silencing hand. "Why are you and your vigilantes not looking for the man who murdered lawyer Dunkley," he said, "instead of hounding a sick boy?"

"Colonel, Patrick was tried, convicted, and sentenced to hang," Moore said. "You must stand aside and let the law take its course."

Shamus's rage flared. "Dear God and his Blessed Mother, you know Patrick didn't rape and murder Molly Holmes."

"I know he was incapable of such a crime," Moore said.

"Damn it, man, then let him be."

"I can't, Colonel. It's the—"

"Yes, I know, it's the law. Moore, you spout that like a trained parrot. Is that all those damned vigilantes taught you to say?"

Moore was stung, and it showed. "Colonel O'Brien, I'm my own man."

"Well, you've a funny way of showing it," Shamus said. "Threatening me under my own roof you are, and be damned to ye."

The door opened, and Samuel stepped into the study, Luther Ironside behind him.

"How is he?" Shamus said.

"He's not coughing as much, but his fever is still high and he's complaining of a pain in his lower back," Samuel said.

"You sent a man on a fast horse for the doctor?" Shamus asked.

"Of course," Samuel replied.

Ironside, tall and terrible, walked up to Moore, his spurs ringing. "John, if that boy dies I'll put a bullet in your belly," he said. "Depend on it."

"The fever was none of my doing," Moore protested.

"He was in your custody," Ironside said. "That's blame enough for me."

Ironside was not making an idle threat. Everyone in the room knew he was deadly serious, including Moore.

Luther Ironside was well into middle age that summer, and Shamus referred to him as his segundo, though his actual status was friend and confidant. He'd served with distinction under the colonel during the War Between the States and later had helped him establish Dromore. Ironside had killed men in the past, though he made no count of them, and when he made a threat, it was no small thing.

"Luther," Shamus said, "Sheriff Moore is a guest in my house. We'll have no more talk of shooting."

Ironside nodded. "Just as you say, Colonel, no more talk."

Moore rose to his feet. "I'll be going, Colonel," he said. "Will you give me the road?"

"No one will harm you, John," Shamus said.

Moore turned his hat in his hands. "I'm sorry, Colonel."

"I'm sorry, too, John."

"You know I'll be back. I have to come back."

Shamus nodded. "And you know we'll be waiting for you."

Moore heaved a shuddering sigh. "Everything is in a mess, huh?"

"Seems like," Shamus said. He rolled his wheelchair to his desk, opened a drawer, and produced a blue Colt. "Take this, John," he said. "I won't leave a man to ride unarmed."

Moore shoved the revolver in his waistband. "I'll see you get it back, Colonel." He shook his head. "I mean when . . . after—"

"I know what you mean," Shamus said, smiling faintly. "Samuel," he said, "will you show the sheriff to his horse?"

"I'll do it, Colonel," Ironside said.

"No, Luther, you'll stay right here where I can keep an eye on you," Shamus said. "Now, let John pass."

Ironside gave an exaggerated little bow and swept his hand in the direction of the door. "This way, John," he said. "And remember what I told you."

Moore stepped past Ironside. He said nothing, but his face was stiff, his back stiffer.

After the sheriff rode out, Ironside said, "How do we play this, Colonel?"

"I don't know," Shamus said. He said to Samuel, "I hear Jacob playing the piano. Ask him to come here, and Shawn." Then, answering the question on his son's face, he said, "I want them in Georgetown. If need be we can defend Dromore with the vaqueros."

Samuel still looked puzzled, and Shamus said, "Don't ask me the why of it, Samuel. I just know that they have to be there."

The Irish gift of second sight was not to be discounted, and Samuel said, "What do you see, Pa?"

"Blood," Shamus said. "A great river of blood."

Chapter Thirteen

The peon would not look at Lum directly but kept his head bowed, aware that he was in the presence of a mighty demon.

"Where are the white people?" Lum said again.

The Mexican stared at the ground between his toes, silent.

"Gringos," Lum said.

His head still bowed, the peon moved a couple of feet to his right and pointed. Lum turned his head and saw that the man was indicating an adobe at the edge of the village.

"Gracias," he said.

The peon bowed lower but said nothing, afraid to speak to such a powerful evil spirit without a priest close at hand. His knees shook because he knew his tongue would burn to black cinders in his head if the demon engaged him in conversation.

To the Mexican's relief the demon swung his

horse away and rode toward the casa of the gringo artist and his sister.

Without looking back, the peon ran to his own house, where he told his wife about his meeting with the spirit. His wife immediately filled her husband's pockets with the basil herb to ward off the evil eye. Then, trembling, she said she'd heard an owl, the death messenger, hoot in the middle of the day, surely a dreadful sign.

Much afraid, the peon and his wife gathered up their children and bolted their doors.

Lum sat his horse outside the adobe and waited. Not for him the polite "Hello, the house." That was for rubes.

A couple of minutes passed, then the timber door opened and a man stepped outside. Lum's interest quickened. Was this Joshua DeClare?

The man was tall, lean, with careful eyes. He wore the black frockcoat and brocaded vest of the frontier gambler/gunfighter, his nickeled, ivory-handled Colt worn high and handy on his right side.

"What can I do for you, mister?" the man said.

"You Joshua DeClare?" Lum said.

"No. Mr. DeClare is inside, and he's not receiving visitors."

"He'll receive me," Lum said.

The rider's face was grotesque, and Luke Caldwell was appalled. What possible business could this gargoyle have with the DeClares?

"Come back tomorrow," Caldwell said. "Or the next day."

He turned to go back inside, but Lum's voice stopped him.

"Tell Joshua DeClare that the Brotherhood sent me," he said.

"Just that?"

"Just that. And I won't repeat myself."

Caldwell looked into Lum's eyes, and something died inside him. It was as though maggots curled and writhed in his belly and were suddenly eating all his courage and gunfighter's self-assuredness.

His mouth dry, he said, "I'll tell him."

"Yes, you do that," Lum said.

Caldwell went inside, and a few moments later Dora DeClare appeared outside. The Texan had obviously prepared her for what she was about to see because she didn't flinch.

"You said the Brotherhood sent you," the woman said. "I'm Dora, Joshua's sister."

"Dr. March sent me," Lum said, his eyes moving over Dora's body. He wanted this witch.

"You have a message?" Dora said.

She felt herself being stripped one garment at a time. Soon, after all her clothing was gone, she'd stand naked and the man's eyes would ravish her.

"No message. My name is Lum, and I've been sent to help you."

"How, Mr. Lum?"

"Any way I can. And it's just Lum."

"It's hot out . . . Lum," Dora said. "Please come inside."

"If it's hot for me, it's hot for my horse."

"Oh, yes, of course. There's a barn behind the house. You can put him there."

Lum smiled, showing his fangs, and Dora knew he'd finally stripped her. Something else dawned on her—she was deathly afraid of this man.

"So that's the story, huh?" Lum said.

"Yes," Josh DeClare said. "All of it."

"Then you seek a reckoning," Lum said.

"That sums it up," DeClare said.

"Then I will bring it about for you."

A glass of lemonade sat untouched at Lum's elbow, and Dora said, "The lemonade is not to your liking?"

"I drink whiskey or I don't drink at all," Lum said. He motioned to Shade Shannon, who sat in a corner, his eyes lost behind his dark glasses, his breath wheezing in his chest. "What is that?" Lum said.

Dora gave Shannon's name and said, "Like you, he is assisting us."

"He's a kindred spirit," Lum said. "I can sense that."

To allay her fears, Dora was determined to be cheerful. "Oh, really?" she said, smiling. "In what way?"

"He knows." Lum's stare settled on Shannon like

a swarm of flies, and the man squirmed. "Come here, boy," Lum said.

Reluctantly, Shannon rose to his feet and stepped toward the big man. Caldwell, tense and wary, stood with his back against the parlor wall.

"Take those glasses off, boy," Lum said. "When I talk to a man I like to see his eyes."

Shannon did as he was told, and Lum stared into their milky depths. He grinned. "I thought so. You've seen hell, boy, haven't you?"

"I don't know what you mean," Shannon said. "And my name is Shade, and I'm not your damned boy."

Lum's eyes flickered, but he said nothing for several moments. Then he said, "You like them dead, boy, don't you? Later you'll tell me about them. All of them, in detail."

"I don't know what you're talking about," Shannon said, but his voice was unsteady.

"Ah, but you do," Lum said. "Tell me about . . ." he looked at Dora. "What was her name?"

"Molly Holmes," Dora answered, her throat tight.

"Yes, her. Now, boy, tell me about pretty Molly. What did you do to her? Tell it open now, open and square."

Josh DeClare pushed his wheelchair toward Lum. "No! We told you Shade murdered her so we could pin the blame on Patrick O'Brien and begin the fall of the house of Dromore. Now let it go at that, Lum. My sister is not used to such talk."

"I'm a rough-spoken man," Lum said, "that's right enough. But when you invite hell into your home, don't expect polite conversation over tea and cake."

Lum reached out, grabbed Shannon by the shirt-front, and pulled the man's face close to his own. "You and I will talk later. You will tell me what you know, and I will tell you what I know. We will educate each other in many ways."

"Lum!" DeClare's shout edged on hysteria. "I thought you came to help us."

Lum pushed Shannon away from him. "Oh, but I have."

"We told you about Shamus O'Brien's sons. When the time comes, you will help kill them all."

"That will not be a difficult task," Lum said.

Luke Caldwell snorted. "In a pig's eye! Jacob O'Brien is a demon with a gun."

Lum grinned. "Ah, he's yet another kindred spirit. For am I not a demon with a gun?"

Dora gave a little peal of nervous laughter, but her brother's face was grim. Suddenly, DeClare realized that unleashing dark forces was one thing. Controlling them was quite another.

Chapter Fourteen

Jacob O'Brien sat in a rocker on the front porch of the Clementine Hotel in Georgetown and studied the street. "Not much moving, Shawn," he said.

Shawn brushed beer foam off the tip of his nose and said, "I can't figure it. I reckoned John Moore would have a posse mounted by this time."

"I haven't seen him since we rode in," Jacob said. "Where the hell is he?"

Shawn shrugged a silent answer and went back to his beer.

The long summer day had finally shaded into night, and a cool north wind off the Santa Fe Mountains strolled around town, smelling of high timber and dry grassland. Lamps glowed in the stores and saloons along the street, and the fashionable young belles who had appeared on the boardwalks looked at Shawn from under the fringes of their eyelashes. The only sound was the soft tap of lace-up boots on timber, the rustle of petticoats, and the high tenor voices of the lovesick beaus who wooed the ladies with snatches of song from Mr. Gilbert and Sullivan's latest operetta. The sporting crowd had already made the saloons rowdy, but of a hanging posse, there was no sign.

Jacob and Shawn were on their second beers when a small, thin man rode up on a rawboned mule and dismounted with all the grace of a first-time rider. He took a carpetbag and rectangular leather case from the saddle horn, dropped them at his feet, and vigorously rubbed his butt.

Shawn, an affable man by nature, smiled and said, "A Missoura mule will do that to you, mister."

The little man, dressed in black broadcloth, a derby hat of the same color on his head, said, "It's a horse."

"No, it's a mule," Shawn said.

"The man in Santa Fe who sold it to me told me it was a horse."

"Then he lied to you," Shawn said.

"Horse . . . mule . . . whatever the cussed animal may be, riding it is not an experience I wish to repeat any time soon," the little man said.

He picked up his bag and the leather case, then stepped onto the hotel porch. He looked at Shawn. "There are rooms to be had, I trust?"

"I reckon," Shawn said. He looked over the little man, who barely stood five feet tall, from the top of his hat to the soles of his elastic-sided boots. "What brings you to Georgetown?" he said. "Business or pleasure?"

"Are you a constable?" the man said.

"Nah," Shawn said. "In a manner of speaking we're just passing through."

"Well, in answer to your question, I'm here on business. I plan to kill a man."

Now the little fellow had the undivided attention of the O'Brien brothers. "Anybody we know?" Jacob said. "He could be kin."

"Hmm . . ." the man said. "Have you ever spent any time in an asylum for the criminally insane?"

"Not recently," Jacob said.

"Then you won't know him and he isn't kin. His name is Lum." The small man smiled. "Now, if I can take him into custody alive, then I will." He shook his head. "But I fear that won't be the case."

"Mister, you ain't even heeled," Shawn said. "This is a rough neighborhood."

"Oh, you mean my apparent lack of a firearm. Well, I've taken care of that." He lifted the leather case and showed it to Shawn. "In here I have a very fine twelve-gauge Hollis and Sheath shotgun, with the barrels cut back to twenty inches. It's all the firearm I need."

"That feller in Santa Fe who sold you the mule didn't tell you the scattergun was a Winchester rifle, did he?" Jacob said.

For a moment the little man seemed confused, then his mild, good-natured face brightened and he smiled. "Oh, I see, you're making a good joke," he said. "No, I realize that this is not a rifle. The Hollis and Sheath has been at my side for ten years, and during that time I've killed fifteen men with it. As weapons go, the shotgun at close range is a most efficient weapon."

A faint alarm bell rang in Jacob's mind, and with it the hazy remembrance of a man who'd long since passed into Western legend.

"Do you mind telling us your name, mister?" he said.

"Not at all," the little man beamed. "It's Ernest Thistledown, out of, if you'll forgive the rhyme, Boston town."

Jacob nodded. "I recollect now, you're called the Buggy Bounty Hunter."

"As ever was," Thistledown said, making a bow. "Now, if you gentlemen will excuse me, I must secure a room and a stable for my . . . whatever it is."

He moved to the hotel door, then turned and said, "How remiss of me. I didn't ask you gentlemen your names."

"I'm Jacob O'Brien. This is my brother Shawn."

Thistledown allowed that he was glad to make the brothers' acquaintance. "Perhaps we can talk later over a beer," he said.

"Fine by us, we're not going anywhere," Jacob said.

Shawn met the coy stare of a pretty girl who just walked past in a cloud of perfume, and he smiled. "Of course, that all depends."

"Keep your mind on business, brother," Jacob said. "We're here to head off a posse, remember?"

Shawn nodded. "All right, Jake, so amuse me.

Tell how that funny little man became the Buggy Bounty Hunter."

Jacob built, and then lit, a cigarette before he talked. "Ernest Thistledown hates riding, so he always travels by train, then horse and buggy."

"Or mule and buggy, huh?"

"I'd say that's likely," Jacob said, "since he don't know the difference."

"Has he really killed fifteen men, like he says?"

"Depends on who you talk to. Some say more, some say less. He only goes after outlaws who are worth at least five thousand dead or alive. They say he won't leave Boston for a penny less."

"How come I've never heard of him before?" Shawn said.

"Thistledown is discreet. Like you said, he's a funny-looking little man, so he goes unnoticed. But he can track like an Apache, and there's no backup in him. When Ernest Thistledown is on your trail, you pretty much know that you're already a dead man. Sooner or later he'll catch up to you and cut you in half with his scattergun."

Shawn smiled. "Jake, I'm not doubting your word, but I don't believe any of that. I reckon somebody's been telling you some mighty big windies. Hell, that little man's about as dangerous as a pug dog in a brothel."

"Did you look into his eyes, Shawn?" Jacob said.

"Of course not. I save that kind of thing for the women I like."

"He's got the eyes of a killer," Jacob said. "Don't

let his harmless act fool you, he's a mighty mean little feller."

Shawn laughed. "I'd like to see him try to take you, Jake. By the time he unlimbered that scattergun you'd have six bullets in him."

"Maybe so, but when he goes into a showdown with a man the shotgun will be in his hands. All he has to do is pull the triggers, and that's faster than I can draw."

"Oh, hell," Shawn said, looking over his brother's shoulder, "speak o' the devil."

Thistledown stepped toward the O'Briens, a smile on his lips and a waiter in tow bearing a tray and three steins of beer.

"My treat," the little man said.

"Thank you and take a chair," Jacob said.

Thistledown seated himself, and the waiter served the beers. The little man took a sip and said, "Ah, very good. Riding gives a man a thirst."

Jacob parked his glass and began to build a cigarette. "Tell us about this man you're hunting," he said.

"Lum? He's more animal than man, a vile creature spawned in a hell of his own making."

"How did he end up in the loco lockup?" Shawn said.

"He was tried for murder, rape, and robbery, but judged too insane to hang," Thistledown said. He made a face. "Lum had a good lawyer and a sympathetic jury, and he got a life sentence to a private asylum for the criminally insane." The little man waved a hand. "He soon escaped, of course, after killing half a dozen of the institution's staff."

"So now he's on the scout and you're after him?" Shawn said.

"That's not quite the way of it. Lum escaped years ago. He made his way to San Francisco's Barbary Coast, where he took up with a runner and all-around thug by the name of Tom Scratcher."

Shawn's handsome face was half in shadow, but, with a hunter's eyesight, Thistledown saw the question in the O'Brien brother's eyes. The bounty man said, "There are hell ships out of New York City commanded by captains under whom no sailorman in his right mind will sail." The man smiled. "Thugs like Scratcher shanghai poor drunken sailors and provide those crews."

Thistledown watched the flare of Jacob's match glow red on the hard planes of his face, then said, "For years Lum provided Scratcher's muscle, and he was reckoned to be the best man with the black-jack, brass knuckles, and slingshot along the whole Barbary Coast. He was also good with a gun and ready to use it. Later he did some prizefighting for Scratcher, winner take all. Lum killed eight men with his bare fists in prizefights and crippled twice as many."

"So how come he's here?" Jacob said.

"Vigilantes, with the blessing of the San Francisco Police Department, finally said enough was enough and strung up Lum and Scratcher from a walnut tree on the edge of town. Then they poured coal oil over the pair and set them on fire. Somehow Lum survived, and now he thinks he can't be killed, and that makes him even more dangerous."

The evening promenade of the belles and their suitors had ended, but the saloons still prospered, the street ringing with tinny piano music, the roars of men, and the high, false laughter of whores.

Thistledown looked at Shawn and smiled. "I'm boring you, Mr. O'Brien, and I do apologize."

Shawn shook his head. "No, you're not boring me. Thanks to my brother's sense of duty I've got nothing better to do this evening."

"The girls will be back tomorrow night," Jacob said.

"And I won't be here to see them probably," Shawn said. "By then we might be gunfighting a hanging posse."

Jacob saw interest quicken in Thistledown's face at that remark, but he headed off the little bounty hunter's question with one of his own.

"What's Lum doing in this neck of the woods?" he said. Jacob remembered the man with the burned face he and Moore had met on the trail, but he figured he wouldn't tip his hand just yet. Let Thistledown do some more talking. Slight as it was, there was always a possibility that all of this could affect Dromore.

"Lum belongs to a Satan-worshipping cult," Thistledown said.

"A what?" Shawn said, leaning forward in his chair.

"A Satan-worshipping cult," Thistledown repeated. "It's based in New York City, but it has chapters in other towns across the nation, and it's particularly big in San Francisco."

"I've never heard of such a thing," Shawn said. He hurriedly crossed himself. "The colonel would hang every damned one of them."

"I'd never heard of it, either," Thistledown said, "until I was asked to take this job."

He drank some beer and then lit a long, thin cheroot, something that Jacob thought was out of character for a man who looked more preacher than bounty hunter. "The cult is run, or I should say was run, since he's now locked up in a mental institution, by a man who calls himself Doctor William T. March." Thistledown spoke from behind a blue cloud of smoke. "March, probably in an effort to save his own skin, recently renounced all Satan's works and made a speedy conversion to Christianity."

"Good for him," Shawn said, grinning.

"And perhaps one might say, good for the people of the New Mexico Territory." Thistledown smiled. "You see, March said he'd recently been corresponding with one of his disciples in Fresno, California. He said he'd dispatched Lum to the Territory to help a brother Satanist destroy an enemy."

"Who's the enemy?" Jacob asked.

"I don't know," Thistledown said. "But he or she has got to be around here somewhere."

"How do you reckon that?" Jacob said.

"I'd been tracking Lum for a month when I got a lead in Santa Fe. The newspapers said that a local whore had been murdered by what an eyewitness described as 'a monster.' Then a second whore was killed in the same way in a town south of the city. A lawman was shot and killed that same night, and a couple of men were wounded. This time about a hundred people saw the killer, and the man they described could only be Lum. I figured he was heading south to join up with his fellow disciple, so my search brought me here." Thistledown paused, then continued, "I have a lot of territory to cover."

"Maybe I can help you out," Jacob said. "I met a man answering Lum's description on the trail west of here. He wanted directions to El Cerrito, a Mexican village on the Pecos."

"Is the village close?"

"Yeah, I reckon about ten miles south of here."

"Then that is where I'll go," Thistledown said. He leaned forward so his face was close to Jacob's. "Listen, my friend, you had a narrow escape on the trail, so thank your lucky stars Lum was not in a killing mood. Now, if you see him again, step wide of him and then come tell me. I'll deal with him. He's very dangerous, do you understand?"

Jacob suppressed a smile. "I sure will, Mr. Thistledown. I'll come right to you."

The little man nodded. "You can't go up against

Lum and live. Run from him." His eyes went from Jacob to Shawn and back again. "Both of you remember that. Your lives could depend on it."

"We've got it," Shawn said, but his smile was obvious.

"Then, gentlemen, I'll bid you good night," Thistledown said. "The damned mule horse has worn me out."

After the little man left, Shawn turned to his brother and said, "Aren't you glad that the gallant Mr. Thistledown is around to protect us?"

"I sure am," Jacob said with a straight face. He thought for a moment, then said, "I wonder who hired him to get this Lum character?"

Shawn shook his head. "Somebody in New York, I guess. Does it matter?"

"No, I guess not," Jacob said. He glanced up and down the empty street. "Where is John Moore with his damned posse?" he said.

Chapter Fifteen

Later, Jacob O'Brien would not wonder if fate brought the two riders to the hotel that night. But Shawn would. And he would marvel at it for the rest of his life.

Despite Thistledown's reputation as an efficient and deadly bounty hunter, neither Jacob nor Shawn rated him as a fighting man. Even his strange name worked against him. No one on God's green earth was called Thistledown except this one little insignificant man.

So when two tall riders wearing dusters and holstered revolvers drew rein at the Clementine Hotel and asked if a man named Thistledown was staying there, Jacob and Shawn expected the worst.

One of the men dismounted and entered the lobby. He appeared a short while later and said, "He's here all right, Dorn. I told the clerk to tell him the Wellstone brothers were calling him out."

The man called Dorn swung out of the saddle,

and his brother joined him in the dusty street. Rectangles of light from the hotel fell on the Wellstone brothers, tinting the hard, relentlessly grim planes of their faces with an orange glow. Both men pulled their dusters free of their guns . . . and waited.

Shawn, as always inclined to be sociable, said, "You boys rode far?"

"Far enough," Dorn said. His eye sockets were in shadow, but Shawn felt his stare. "You friends of Thistledown?"

Shawn shook his head. "Had a beer with him. Does that make us friends?"

"You answer that question your own self," Dorn said, and his brother, who looked to be still in his teens, nodded.

"Mr. Thistledown is in bed," Jacob said.

"By this time he knows we called him out," Dorn said. "He'll get up."

"Got a beef with him, huh?" Shawn said, smiling.

"He killed our brother," Dorn said. "Killed him for the five thousand bounty on his head."

"Must have been a real bad man, your brother," Jacob said.

"He was a Wellstone," Dorn said, as though that explained, and excused, everything.

"You're Texas boys, huh?" Shawn said, trying to talk down what was shaping up to be a shooting situation.

Dorn and his brother ignored him, their eyes on the hotel door.

The night wind had risen, and the Wellstone

brothers' dusters slapped against their boots. Dorn was wearing a soft black slouch hat, and the right brim continually flattened against the crown. The lamps on either side of the hotel door guttered and cast shadows that formed dancing circles on the timber deck of the porch.

"Where the hell is he?" the younger brother said. He kept flexing the fingers of his right hand, a movement that Jacob decided was caused by nervousness.

"He'll be out soon enough," Dorn said.

"Suppose he escapes out the back?"

"He'll be out, Clem," Dorn said. "A man in his line of work can't be branded a stinking, yellow coward, even though he is one."

Ernest Thistledown stepped out of the hotel door a few moments later.

Jacob, attuned to men who fought with a gun, noticed a telling transformation. Thistledown seemed to stand taller, and the man was relaxed, showing no fear. His shotgun hung from his right shoulder by a leather strap that was attached to the stock and barrel.

"You know why we're here and why we called you out," Dorn said.

"I believe so, Dorn," Thistledown said.

"We're here for Billy," Dorn said.

"Billy was a rapist and a murderer, Dorn. He was a piece of human filth. Don't die because of him."

"Damn you, he was a Wellstone," Dorn said.

And he drew.

* * *

Jacob had seen skilled gunfighters in action, and he'd come up against a few himself, but again and again he'd replay in his mind what Thistledown did that night and wonder at it.

As Dorn skinned his Colt, Thistledown was already diving to his right. Even as he fell, he swung the shotgun into play and cut loose. The heavy bucks hit Dorn square in the belly, and the man cried out in fear and pain as he fell on his back. Thistledown hit the porch deck hard, but he twisted his body, landed on his shoulder, and triggered the scattergun again. The younger Wellstone brother thumbed off a shot at the same time. It was a miss that splintered its way into the hotel wall. Clem Wellstone, eighteen years old, hit in the chest, didn't even have time to scream before he rode buckshot into eternity.

The fight was over in a couple of seconds, and the echoes of gunfire surrounded Georgetown as men and women spilled out of the saloons to see what the shooting was about.

Thistledown rose to his feet and, in a gunfighter's automatic response, reloaded his shotgun. He looked at Jacob. "They could've walked away from it," he said.

Jacob nodded. "I reckon they were notified."

Dorn lay on his back and now he lifted his head, black blood in his mouth. "Thistledown, you bastard. You've done for me."

"It would appear so," the little man said. "And it sorrows me, Dorn."

But the man called Dorn didn't hear. He was as dead as he was ever going to be.

The gawking crowd on the boardwalk in front of the saloon across the road from the hotel parted as a man forced his way through.

Short, portly, and belligerent, he stopped to look at the two dead men, then his eyes found Jacob and Shawn in the gloom. "If there's a shooting scrape, O'Briens are sure to be involved," he said.

"Not this time," Jacob said. He nodded toward Thistledown. "Meet Mr. Ernest Thistledown from Boston town."

The portly man glared at Thistledown. "You did this?"

"I'm afraid so. Who the hell are you?"

The portly man puffed up, self-importance swelling the brocade vest under his frockcoat. "I am James Wentworth, Chairman of the Georgetown Vigilance Committee and proprietor of the Lucky Seven Saloon and Dance Hall across yonder." He stabbed a finger at Thistledown. "Explain yourself and the dead men."

"Not much to explain," Thistledown said. "Those two called me out."

"Why?"

"Because I killed their brother Billy. He was low down, but I don't know if Dorn and Clem were the same way. It doesn't matter a hill of beans now, one way or the other."

"Who were they? I mean last names."

"Lying there at your feet are the Wellstone brothers, out of west Texas," Thistledown said. "They were cattlemen."

Wentworth was now flanked by a couple of hard cases from his saloon, skull-and-knuckle fighters wearing white aprons and scowls. He shifted his attention to Jacob and Shawn. "Did you see this?"

"Sure did, and it was a clear-cut case of self-defense," Jacob said. "Like Thistledown says, those two rannies called him out, then drew down on him. He didn't have much of a choice."

"Will you two put that in writing, said documents to go before the entire committee?" Wentworth said.

Jacob answered that question with one of his own. "Where's the sheriff?"

"You tell me."

"I don't know where he is," Jacob said.

"Moore took your brother from the jail," Wentworth said. "Nobody in town saw him leave, and since then he's been missing. The committee has men out hunting him. They will also search Dromore, of course."

Shawn smiled. "Good luck with that."

"You've got no authority outside of this town, Wentworth," Jacob said.

"In or out of town, twenty rifles pack a lot of authority, Mr. O'Brien." Wentworth turned and said to his men, "One of you two get the undertaker."

After the man left, he addressed Thistledown again. "The Vigilance Committee is hereby confiscating the horses, saddles, and firearms of the dead men, the proceeds to pay for their funerals."

"Gonna bury them in high style, huh, Wentworth?" Jacob said.

Mr. Wentworth, his eyes suddenly hard and penetrating, said, "Mr. O'Brien, a word of warning, sir. I don't yet know what your business is in Georgetown, but I should tell you that it is the Vigilance Committee's suspicion that you and your brother may have aided and abetted the removal of one Patrick O'Brien, rapist and murderer, from jail and were then involved in Sheriff John Moore's disappearance. Therefore I strongly advise you to remain here at the hotel until the committee's investigation is complete." His face ugly, he continued, "In other words, don't even think about leaving town for the next few days."

"Wentworth," Shawn said, anger flashing in him, "you're true blue, a stand-up fellow."

"You have been warned," Wentworth said, "and you'll be watched." He turned the full force of his authority on Thistledown again. "Once I get the O'Briens' affy-davy that these killings were in self-defense, you will get out of Georgetown and never come back." He scowled his authority. "Do you understand?"

"Perfectly," Thistledown said. "A pity because this is such a nice, friendly burg."

Chapter Sixteen

For the hundredth time that day, Sheriff John Moore wondered if he was doing the right thing. Now, as the moon rose higher in the sky and bladed the hill country around him with mother-of-pearl light, he sat his horse and tried to think the thing through.

He figured he was about two miles west of the Pecos and the village of El Cerrito. He'd spent the previous night on the trail, riding in circles before he'd bedded down, but confused thoughts had clamored in his head and given him no rest.

He should already have led a Georgetown posse to Dromore and taken Patrick O'Brien back into custody, instead of following a hunch that had as little substance as a will-o'-the-wisp.

Was it because he feared a showdown with tough old Shamus O'Brien? Moore sat his saddle, stared hard at the moon, and allowed that was a possibility. As was his way, Shamus would not back off. He'd protect his son and men would die.

"You among them, John," Moore said aloud. "And that's why you're skulking out here in the long grass. Damn it, man, you're a low-down yellow dog."

The sound of his own voice lashed Moore, flayed him with remorse.

Was he using the burned man only as an excuse to run away?

"Damn it! No!" he yelled. His face in his hands, he listened to the echoes of his voice, mocking him again and again.

Moore reached into his shirt pocket under his vest and found his next-to-last cigar. He stuck it between his teeth and lit it. The familiar, musk-perfume odor of the smoke helped soothe and settle his reeling brain.

He'd been a lawman a long time and knew from experience how to read a man. Years back, when he met John Wesley Hardin for the first and only time, he looked into his eyes and pegged him for what he was—a born killer. He'd pegged the burned man as well. Only, when he'd looked into his eyes he'd stared into *hell*.

That's why he was here, Moore told himself. He wasn't afraid of Shamus or any man, but the burned man had made him shrink inside, as though he was looking at death come for him.

Yes, that was why he was here—to face his fear and overcome it.

Moore drew deeply on his cigar. The tip glowed crimson, then faded to an ashy, ruby glimmer.

He had worked it out, and that pleased him. He was a rational man facing an irrational fear; that was all.

But then, wasn't it wise to be afraid in the presence of evil?

And the burned man was evil. He had no doubt about that. Evil surrounded the grotesque figure like a vile stench.

Moore nodded. Yeah, he was doing the right thing. Patrick O'Brien could wait. Hell, the kid was innocent anyhow. It was time to talk to the burned man and find out what had brought him to the territory.

Perhaps it was he who'd murdered Molly Holmes and maybe lawyer Dunkley.

Stranger things had happened.

The Mexican peon was a night traveler like himself, and by his smile, inclined to be friendly. The man sat a donkey and had a rooster in a cage balanced precariously behind him.

"Is El Cerrito close?" John Moore said.

The Mexican nodded. "Not far. I go there."

"Then we'll ride together," Moore said, happy to hear a human voice besides his own.

The peon said, "There is a cantina in El Cerrito. It has mescal." He shrugged and made a sad face. "But no whores." He smiled. "Of course, I'm a respectable married man, so I do not think of such things."

Moore grinned. "Whores are all right. At least they're honest. They give you the bill right up front."

"*Sí,* this is true," the Mexican said. He waved a hand to the north. "The bandits who come down from the hills are very good to their whores." He shook his head. "But very bad to their wives."

The Mexican seemed to be a talking man, and Moore decided to press him. "Señor," he said, "have you seen a man in the village, a big Americano with a—"

"Burned face," the peon said.

"Yeah, that's him."

The peon made a cross on his chest, and when he looked at Moore his black eyes were haunted. "He lives with the crippled artist and his sister. Do not go near that house, señor, it is the abode of el Diablo." The Mexican hurriedly crossed himself again. "It is a gate to hell."

"What goes on there?" Moore said.

"Do not go into that house," the peon said. "Be warned. You will be taken down to the fires of hell."

For a while the two men rode in silence, the only sound the creak of Moore's saddle and the back-and-forth yips of a pair of hunting coyotes.

The moonlight had grown brighter, and now it sculpted the landscape into sharp edges of silver and black. The wind spun around the big lawman, and his horse tossed its head, the bit chiming, as it smelled the river and the shoaling fish in the shallows. Behind the peon the rooster flapped in its cage and squawked.

"There is the house, señor," the Mexican said. "By the cottonwood." A small man on a small donkey, he turned and looked up at Moore. "Turn back now," he said.

Moore smiled. "I figure I'll take a look, maybe talk to the burned man."

Horrified, the peon said, "*Que Dios te proteja, señor.*" He threw Moore one last fearful glance, then kicked the burro into a shambling trot. Alarmed, the rooster squawked louder and beat frantically at the wicker cage.

Sheriff John Moore dismounted and tied his horse to a dead skeletal juniper that was lost in shadow. He drew his long-barreled Colt and walked toward the adobe on silent feet, surprising in a man of his girth.

The breeze rustled in the cottonwood as Moore made his way to the back of the house. Behind him the two-story barn loomed like a black cliff, and ahead he saw a rectangle of light spill on the ground from a window hidden by a brick chimney stack.

Moore had no plan, no aim in mind, other than spying on the burned man. He had the vague hope that he would catch him doing something illegal, but he was also aware that the man might be sitting in an easy chair, a-reading the Book of Psalms, the odors of his pipe and his sanctity mingling in the room.

Well, there was one way to find out. He stepped toward the window, his feet quiet on sand. If Moore had been on talking terms with God, he would've prayed that he'd catch the burned man cutting off a virgin's head or something.

But in the event, he saw something much different . . . something that both chilled him to the bone and stirred his manhood.

The window was covered with a black roll-up blind that had not been pulled down all the way, leaving a three-inch gap at the bottom. Moore kneeled, removed his hat, and peered inside.

He looked into a small kitchen, but the door that separated the kitchen from the dining room was wide open. Moore took in everything in his first, stunned glance.

A woman, wearing nothing but candlelight, lay on her back on a dining table that was covered in a purple sheet of some glossy material. The burned man, huge and naked, chanted over her. The woman joined in the chant, drowsily, as though she was in a deep trance. Her hair spread around her head like a golden halo, and her scarlet lips were wet and parted.

Two men watched, one in a wheelchair. The

other wore a blanket that covered his head and made him look like a praying monk. Both onlookers chanted strange words that Moore didn't understand, and then he looked from them to the wall beyond the table where a large crucifix hung upside down from a nail.

The burned man tilted his head and raised his arms, his soft chant now a frenzied series of shouts. It seemed to Moore that the woman rose from the table and hung in the air, but he figured his eyes were deceiving him.

. . . The blow seemed to come out of nowhere. Moore felt something hard whip across the back of his skull. He tried to rise, his Colt coming up, but a second, crashing blow hit him on top of the head and forced him to the ground. He heard grunts, saw the silhouette of a tall man, his arm rising and falling as the blackjack hit him again and again.

Moore, a strong, game man, could no longer struggle to get to his feet. His head reeled, pain bursting his skull open, and he let darkness take him. The ground yawned open around him and he fell, tumbling into darkness shot through with streaks of scarlet, into a pit that had no bottom . . .

Chapter Seventeen

Shawn O'Brien tumbled off the bottom step of the hotel porch, but, after an ungainly little dance, regained his balance before he fell.

"Too much beer, Shawn?" Jacob said, smiling.

"Seems like," Shawn said, his chiseled features set in a frown. "Damned step is warped. That's dangerous."

Jacob nodded. "For a beer-drinking man, I guess it is."

"Brother," Shawn said, falling into step beside Jacob, "I don't know if you realize it or not, but sometimes you can be a real pain in the ass."

Jacob smiled as they stepped onto the boardwalk and headed in the direction of Lucas Dunkley's office.

As they walked past a general store, the clock inside chimed twice. One of the saloons had already closed, and only a few stalwarts held out at the second. Shawn reckoned aloud they must have ugly wives at home, and Jacob allowed that was probably true.

"What do you expect to find, Jake?" Shawn said.

"Nothing," Jacob said, "that's what I expect." He turned and looked at his brother. "But you never know."

The street was in darkness, and a lone coyote had come in close and was sniffing around in the shadowed alley next to the Bon-Ton restaurant across the street. Occasionally a man laughed in the saloon, but the town was quiet enough that the O'Brien brothers' spurs rang on the boardwalk like silver coins.

The shades were drawn in the window of the lawyer's office, and to Jacob's surprise when he tried the door it was unlocked.

"So much for John Moore's efficiency," Shawn said.

"Yeah," Jacob said, "but good for us."

He opened the door, stepped inside, and Shawn followed. Jacob thumbed a match into flame and risked lighting the oil lamp on Dunkley's desk. The shades were heavy, and only someone passing by would see the light, unlikely at this hour. Just in case, Jacob turned down the wick until only a soft glow illuminated the office.

"What are we looking for?" Shawn said.

"Anything at all that might give us a clue to what Lucas knew," Jacob said.

His brother eyed the dusty stacks of files and heaped-up law books and said, "That's a tall order."

"Then get to work," Jacob said. "And don't sit on Lucas's chair. It looks like he bled out pretty good after he was stabbed."

The desk and chair were thickly covered in dried, black blood. Shawn shook his head. "Poor guy didn't know what hit him."

"He knew all right," Jacob said, head bent, thumbing through a file. "A knife in the throat takes its time to kill a man. He nodded. "Lucas knew all too well what hit him."

An hour's search turned up nothing. Solemn as a courthouse clock, a night rain ticked on the law office roof, and the lamp flickered as the oil ran low. An errant wind gusted raindrops against the window, the loudest sound in the room.

"We're wasting our time, Shawn," Jacob said. "Let's get out of here."

"I guess whatever Lucas knew, he kept in his head," Shawn said.

"Seems like," Shawn said.

Shawn picked up a notepad that had fallen off the desk to the floor. After he studied it for a few moments, he said, "Lucas was quite an artist."

"What do you mean?" Jacob said.

"Take a look for yourself." Shawn handed his brother the notepad.

Jacob studied the pad for a few moments, then asked, "What does *Nemesis* mean?"

"No idea," Shawn said. "Is the hanging man supposed to be Patrick?"

"Georgetown has a gallows," Jacob said. He tapped the notepad. "This ranny is hanging from a tree."

"Who's the woman?"

"Just . . . some woman, I guess," Jacob said.

"Maybe her name is Nemesis."

"Maybe. But the word is nowhere near her. It's under the tree."

"Hell, Jake, what does it mean?" Shawn said.

Jacob looked at him just as the oil lamp fluttered, then died. "It means Lucas liked to draw scary pictures."

"Let me have it," Shawn said. "I want to ask Patrick what that word means."

"If he's well enough."

"Yes, of course, only if he's well enough." He tore the page from the notepad, folded it, and shoved it into his shirt pocket.

When the O'Brien brothers stepped out of the law office the rain had come and gone. But the air smelled fresh now that the dust had settled, and to the south heat lightning flashed, illuminating the edges of the retreating clouds with tarnished silver.

When they reached the hotel, Jacob got pen, ink, and paper from the desk clerk, then he and Shawn sat in the empty parlor and wrote out what they'd witnessed before, during, and after Thistledown's gunfight.

"How the hell do you spell *Thistledown?*" Jacob asked, chewing on the end of his pen.

Shawn told him, and his brother said, "Heathen name if ever I heard one. What is it—Hindoo?"

"I don't know," Shawn said. "You take O'Brien, now. That's a good Christian name."

"Damn right," Jacob said.

"It's English actually." Thistledown stepped out of the shadows. "I believe my family was named for a village where thistles grew."

"Why are you out of bed?" Jacob said, the late hour making him surly. "The only reason we're awake is because we're trying to save your damned neck."

"I can't sleep after I kill a man," Thistledown said. "I can't eat, either. But I drink. That's why you may detect that I'm half-drunk."

"Helluva thing to kill a man," Shawn said.

"Yes, it is," Thistledown said.

"If a man needs killing, it doesn't bother me too much," Jacob said. He sat back in his chair, held up his affidavit, and admired the paper at arm's length. "Perfect," he said. "Thistledown, this could get you into heaven."

The little man smiled. "I reckon it'll take more than that." He laid a half-empty bottle of Old Crow on the table and pulled up a chair. "Help yourself to a nightcap, gentlemen," he said.

Shawn signed his paper with a flourish, took a long swig from the bottle, and then removed from his pocket the page he'd torn from Dunkley's notepad.

He pushed the oil lamp closer to Thistledown and marked the word *Nemesis* with his thumb. "Know what that means?"

"Well, the simple answer is that it means an opponent who can't be beaten or overcome," Thistledown said. "For example, Sitting Bull was the gallant Custer's nemesis, as Pat Garrett was Billy the Kid's."

Jacob took the paper. "See this woman watching the hanged man, could her name be Nemesis?"

"She's crying over the hanged man," Thistledown said. "See, those drops falling from her eyes are tears. She's badly drawn, but those are definitely tears." The bounty hunter slurred his words slightly. "I doubt her name is Nemesis. Jane or Florence or Martha maybe, but not Nemesis."

Jacob grinned. "There, Shawn, I told you that wasn't her name."

"As I remember my reading—" Thistledown began.

"My brother reads books this thick," Shawn said, four inches of space between his forefinger and thumb. "He's real smart."

The beer and bourbon were working on Shawn, and Jacob threw him a look.

"My business often entails long train rides," Thistledown said to Shawn. "And on those occasions books are a great comfort to me. I'm very fond of Mr. Dickens, and I've quite fallen in love with young Mr. Thomas Hardy to be sure."

Shawn opened his mouth to speak again, but Jacob shut him down. "What were you about to say before my brother interrupted you?" he said.

"Ah, yes," Thistledown said, "about Nemesis." He picked up the Old Crow bottle, then said, "She was one of the Greek goddesses, and she brought swift and terrible retribution to those who committed crimes without punishment or enjoyed good fortune they didn't deserve." The little man took a drink from the bottle. "In other words, Nemesis was an avenger, and her justice was swift and fearful."

"Look at the picture," Jacob said. "What the hell does it mean?" He took the bottle from Thistledown. "I need a drink," he said.

The little man stared at the crude drawing for several minutes before he spoke. "Someone was hanged, that much is obvious," he said. "The woman, possibly his wife, stands under the hanging tree and grieves for the dead man." He looked into Jacob's eyes. "As I interpret it, the female is vowing vengeance on those who hanged her loved one. She's determined to be the nemesis of the guilty party."

"Then it's Patrick in the drawing," Shawn said. "Maybe the gal is meant to be the ghost of Molly Holmes."

"I told you before, Shawn," Jacob said, "you've seen the gallows that was specially built for Patrick. Lucas would've sketched that, not a tree."

Shawn leaned back in his chair and raised his hands. "Then it's a mystery." He smiled. "Hell, maybe Lucas didn't mean it to be anything but a stupid drawing."

"It troubles me," Jacob said. "Disturbs me a lot."

"Is that old Irish sixth sense nagging at you again, brother?" Shawn said.

Jacob sat in silence for a while and then took a swig of bourbon. He wiped his mouth with the back of his hand and said, "Lucas told Samuel there was a great evil behind Patrick's getting railroaded for rape and murder."

Jacob's eyes moved to Shawn, but his stare was unfocused, distant. "I believe the woman in the drawing could be the source of the evil Lucas was talking about," he said.

Shawn smiled. "A woman doesn't scare me none."

"Right now," Jacob said, "she scares the hell out of me."

Chapter Eighteen

Sheriff John Moore woke to pain. When he moved, the red-hot spikes that rammed into his skull were worse than anything he remembered, even the morning after the two-whore, two-bottle bender in Denver long ago.

He opened his eyes a crack, and the morning light sharked into his eyes. He groaned, trying to remember.

Dora DeClare helped him.

"Pour soul," she said, "how are we feeling this morning?"

"We feel like hell," Moore said.

"I'm afraid you took a nasty knock," Dora said. "You gave all of us a fright, you know."

Moore slowly realized two things: that he couldn't open his eyes without pain and that his wrists were shackled above his head.

"What the hell have you done to me?" the sheriff said, his furious face displaying the lawman's traditional outrage at disrespectful treatment.

Dora smiled. "A minor inconvenience, Sheriff Moore, to one destined for glory."

"What the hell are you talking about?" Moore said, yanking on his chains. "And who hit me?"

"That would be me."

The sheriff followed the sound of the words, and his glare came to rest on Luke Caldwell. "Damn you, Caldwell, I always pegged you for a sorry piece of Texas white trash," Moore said. "I should've gunned you that time in Abilene when I had a chance."

"You tried," Caldwell said.

"Yeah, but I never was one to shoot a running man in the back, especially a no-good yellow dog like you." Moore tried to kick out at the gunman, but his chains held him back. He settled for, "What did you hit me with, a brick?"

Caldwell drew with lightning speed. His Colt came out of the leather, spinning, and then the ivory butt thudded into his palm. "With this," he said. The gunman spun the revolver again, then let it drop into the holster.

"You're just full of those cheap, tinhorn tricks, ain't you, Caldwell?"

The gunman stepped to Moore and kicked him hard in the ribs. "Keep a civil tongue in your head."

"Please, Luke, don't do that," Dora said. "You'll spoil the picnic."

The woman looked as fresh as a spring morning, blond, brown-eyed, and pretty in a pale pink gingham dress, bows of the same color in her hair. Dora looked nothing like the creature he'd seen through the kitchen window.

"Lady, we're in a barn," Moore said, angry at Caldwell, angry at this strange woman.

"So what?" Dora said. "I like to have picnics in the barn."

"Are you on the menu like you were last night?" Moore said.

The woman shrugged off the insult. "We all have to do things we think are repugnant, Mr. Moore. I mean, when it's for the greater good."

"Whose good? Yours?"

"Yes, mine, yours, my brother's, all of us," Dora said. She gave Moore a sweet Jane Austen smile that the lawman thought had been practiced. "You'll see."

Moore tugged on his chains again, then saw they were looped through iron rings that had been driven into a huge granite slab. Suffering a world of hurt from his head and the kick Caldwell had given him, he said, "Let me go now and I'll mention it in your trial."

"That's quite impossible, Sheriff," Dora said. "You are needed here."

"For what?" Moore said.

The woman ignored him. "Luke, get the picnic hamper and tell Lum to bring my brother." Now she looked at Moore again. "Then we'll all settle down and enjoy ourselves." Dora's hand flew to her cheek. "Oh, I do hope you like fried chicken and lemonade cake. If not, well, quite frankly, I just don't know what I'll do."

She's a lunatic, John, humor her, Moore thought.

"Sounds just fine," he said. He hoped that between the fried chicken and cake he might have a chance to grab a gun.

Caldwell returned with the picnic hamper, followed by Lum pushing Joshua DeClare's wheelchair. Dora spread a red-and-white-checkered cloth on the dung-encrusted floor of the barn and then told everyone to sit.

Shade Shannon arrived late and Dora chided him for being tardy, then told him to sit next to Lum.

Again Moore made a few futile tugs on his chains. Then he retreated into bluster. "Shannon," he said, "I'm placing you under arrest."

"Shade," Dora said, smiling, "help yourself to food. And pour wine for everyone."

"This is good, Dora," Lum said, chewing on a chicken leg. "You cook as good as you look. Damn right."

Dora looked as though she'd been slapped. "Please, Lum, no profanity, and certainly not within the hearing of a lady of breeding."

"Sorry, Dora," Lum said. He elbowed Shannon, winked, and both men smiled.

"Shannon," Moore said, "I'm arresting you for

the murder of your father, a prostitute, and possibly others. What have you to say for yourself?"

"Only that you're a pompous windbag, Moore," Shannon said. "And if you don't shut your trap I'll get up and piss all over your face."

Lum thought that hilarious, but Joshua DeClare frowned and said, "Shade, that's quite enough. As Dora said, there is a lady present."

Dora looked at Moore and smiled, revealing white teeth in a pink mouth. "Enjoying the picnic, Sheriff?"

"Hell, lady, I haven't been offered anything to eat yet," Moore said.

"I'm so glad," Dora said, as though she hadn't heard.

The sheriff watched the giggling picnickers for a while, then closed his eyes and rested his head against the stone slab. He thought there was something familiar about this grotesque feast, as though he'd seen it all before. Then he remembered and, in pain though he was, smiled.

Back in the fall of 1882 he'd attended an Oscar Wilde lecture at the El Paso Club in Colorado Springs. Wilde, dressed in velvet, mentioned that the novel *Alice's Adventures in Wonderland* was a particular favorite of old Queen Vic. He'd then read a passage from the book about Alice's visit to the Mad Hatter's tea party.

He'd seen it before, when Wilde painted vivid

word pictures with his fine Irish lyricism, and now he was seeing its likes again—the Mad Hatter's picnic.

After an hour, Dora rose and began to pack the leftovers into the hamper. She folded the cloth and said, "Now, shoo-shoo everyone, back to the house. We have plans to make."

She looked at Moore. "Did you enjoy that, Sheriff?"

Moore said nothing, and the woman smiled at him. "I'm quite sure you did." She followed the others out of the barn, but stopped in the doorway. "You'll be sacrificed tonight at midnight. Isn't that exciting?"

The lawman's anger flared. "Crazy lady, you go to hell."

Dora's smile grew almost beatific, and her beautiful hand flew to her slender throat. "Oh, Mr. Moore," she said, "I do hope so."

Chapter Nineteen

Ernest Thistledown stopped his rented buggy on a treed rise, a black silhouette against the amber glow of the lowering sun. The beautiful Hollis and Sheath hung from his shoulder, two red shells in the chambers. The scattergun's hammers were cocked, ready to go, because the little bounty hunter knew that his fight with Lum would be a mighty quick thing.

Thistledown shaded his eyes with his hand and studied the village.

This had to be the place Jacob O'Brien had mentioned, a Mexican settlement on the Pecos River that served as a gateway to the East and miles of nothing. The bounty hunter was not impressed. El Cerrito was a dung heap, an ideal spot for a crowing rooster like the man called Lum to hide out.

Suddenly, Thistledown was alert as he watched a tall man who'd just stepped out the front door of an adobe at the edge of the village. The man stopped, adjusted his gunbelt, and then walked into the barn behind the house.

Thistledown swore under his breath. This was a complication he didn't need. He was willing to bet the farm that the tall, lanky man was Luke Caldwell, the Texas draw fighter. It sure looked like Caldwell, even to the way he wore his gun, high on the waist, horseman style.

Luke was fast on the draw-and-shoot, and there were maybe ten or twelve hard cases planted in Boot Hills across the country that had made him prove it.

Was Caldwell in cahoots with Lum? Thistledown pondered that and reached the logical conclusion: Why would two named killers be in the same fly-speck of a village at the same time if they weren't partnered-up?

Thistledown clucked the Morgan into motion and drove the buggy farther into the cover of the trees. He'd no desire to go against Caldwell to get at Lum. The Texan was not a man to trifle with, and besides, as far as he knew, Caldwell didn't currently have a bounty on him.

Ten minutes passed and Thistledown, by long habit a careful man, kept silent vigil. Then Caldwell left the barn, followed by a volley of curses that bombarded him all the way to the house.

Thistledown waited, watched. Another ten minutes went by, then fifteen, and then twenty. Nothing moved but the wind and the falling sun behind him.

Whoever was in the barn was a cussing man with a real talent for the profane. Could it be Lum?

Thistledown made up his mind. He wasn't about to ride up to the front of the adobe, not with Luke Caldwell around, so a check of the barn was his obvious choice. If it wasn't Lum inside, then he'd silence the man who was there and gain entrance to the adobe from the back. That way, he'd kick for the moon and take the occupants by surprise.

It wasn't a great plan, not even a good one, but right then it was all the little bounty hunter had. But first he needed darkness.

Thistledown drove the buggy off the rise and into a small meadow surrounded by juniper and a few boxwoods. He didn't intend to be long, so he kept the Morgan in the traces and led it into the trees. The horse was old and apparently didn't mind, because it dropped its head and immediately fell asleep.

Thistledown sat, lit a cigar, and watched the sun, with agonizing slowness, lower over the Manzano Mountains to the west. The coyotes were already out, but the sky was still banded with scarlet and jade, and the night birds were yet to peck at the first stars.

Then, as the daylight faded the air grew cooler, and a drift of sage and pine fleeted in a night breeze that stirred the trees and tied bows in Thistledown's blue cigar smoke.

Finally, as darkness started to crowd close to him and the Morgan and its buggy could no longer be seen among the junipers, Thistledown rose to his feet. He had laid his shotgun aside, and now he again hung the weapon from his right shoulder, barrels down, so when his hand slapped on the stock they would lift up and level on the target.

He hoped that target would be Lum.

Thistledown made his way back to the rise, stopped on the crest, and looked down at the adobe, where every room showed light. An oil lamp burned in the barn and cast a pale orange glow on the dirt outside. The little bounty hunter thought he heard the faint clank of a chain and a man's muttered curse.

Keeping to shadows, Thistledown scrambled down the slope and then stepped into a patch of darkness as he studied the barn. To his surprise, his heartbeats pounded in his ears and his breath came in short, quick bursts. Thistledown's mouth tightened. The unexpected and unwelcome sight of Luke Caldwell had unnerved him. Angry with himself for what he perceived as cowardice, he strode toward the barn with more purpose.

This was no time to be lily-livered. Timid men were too easy to kill.

* * *

"Is there anyone there?" Thistledown said in a low voice. "And be warned, I've got faith in this here scattergun."

"Yeah, damn it, I'm here," a man's voice answered.

"And who are you?"

"Sheriff John Moore of Georgetown, and be damned to ye."

"Hell," Thistledown said, "I heard you were dead or missing or something."

"I'm missing all right," Moore said, his voice edged. "If I ain't in Georgetown, then I'm missing."

Thistledown walked deeper into the barn and caught sight of Moore, who was chained to a huge slab of rock.

"Just don't stand there gawking, man, help me get loose," Moore said.

"I'm not, in the main, much inclined to assist lawmen," Thistledown said.

"Then make an exception, damn your eyes," Moore said. "I'm to be sacrificed at midnight."

"To what?"

"Hell, I don't know, maybe some pagan god or something. How the hell should I know?" Moore looked hard at the diminutive bounty hunter, seemingly unimpressed. "What in the name of creation are you?"

"If it's my name you seek, then it's Ernest Thistledown, out of Boston town, if you'll forgive the rhyme."

"I've heard of you," Moore said. "The Buggy Bounty Hunter."

Thistledown gave a little bow. "As ever was."

"What are you doing here?" Moore said.

"I'm tracking a man I know only as Lum."

"The burned man?"

"That would be him."

"Hell," Moore said, "so am I."

"And you're making an excellent job of it, I see," Thistledown said.

"Luke Caldwell—you heard of him?"

"Yes, I have."

"Well, he crept up and buffaloed me," Moore said. "When I woke up, I was chained up in this damned barn. Then they had a Mad Hatter's picnic, right there where you're standing, and the woman, Dora, told me I was to be sacrificed tonight."

"If I recall the novel correctly, that should be a Mad Hatter's tea party," Thistledown said.

"I can read as good as you—"

"I doubt it," Thistledown said.

"But this was a picnic. Every one of them is damned loco, and the woman is the craziest." Moore yanked on the chains. "Now, see if you can get me loose."

"I told you," Thistledown said, "that I don't help peace officers." He made a face. "And besides, all this is most inconvenient. I'm here to kill a man, not play nursemaid to you."

Moore's anger flared. "Thistledown, if I get my hands around your scrawny neck, I'll—"

"Sheriff, your hands are shackled to great iron staples," Thistledown said. "Or haven't you noticed?"

"All right, all right," Moore said, letting his breath go, "please help me."

"No."

"Why the hell not?"

"I have a man to kill."

"Hell, you can't go up against those crazies by yourself. A murderer by the name of Shade Shannon is with them, and he's as bad as they come." Moore looked at the shotgun. "Three bad men, two shells. You're bucking a stacked deck, mister."

"I've managed before."

"You've never come up against Luke Caldwell before. He won't stand around and whistle Dixie while you reload."

Thistledown made a tut-tut sound, then said, "This is most bothersome indeed. I just don't have time for this kind of thing."

"You mean saving my life?" Moore said, outrage rouging his cheeks.

"Yes," Thistledown said. "Exactly that, my fettered friend."

Anger tightened Moore's voice. "Little man, I swear I'll . . ."

But Thistledown was already examining the staples driven into the stone slab, and the sheriff let his threat fade away.

"Can you do anything?" Moore asked.

"I can shoot you," Thistledown said. "Put you out of my misery."

"There's a crowbar over there in the empty stall," Moore said. "Use that to pull the iron rings free." He couldn't bear it that his words were almost civil, and, as an afterthought, he added, "And be damned to ye for threatening an officer of the law."

"And the same to you," Thistledown said. He stepped to the stall and brought back the crowbar, a hefty chunk of steel about three feet long. He looked at Moore. "You know when you're freed you're going to clank like Jacob Marley, don't you?" he said.

"Who's he?"

Thistledown sighed. "No matter. Somebody you don't know."

"Quit gabbing and get them damn rings out," Moore said, suspecting that he'd just been slighted.

To the surprise of both parties, when Thistledown used the crowbar as a lever, the iron staples broke free of the stone easily. The rings had been fixed in place with local cement of low quality that crumbled under pressure.

Moore groaned in pain as he brought down his stiff arms. Then, with Thistledown's help, he managed to get to his feet. "Thank you," he said, grudging each word.

But a split second later Moore dropped to the ground again, felled by the bullet that slammed into him, accompanied by a noise like thunder.

Chapter Twenty

"No thunder, just lightning flashes to the south," Shawn said. "It's kinda pretty."

Jacob nodded. "Usually means it'll be a hot one tomorrow."

"Where you figure Thistledown went?" Shawn said.

"Probably after that Lum character," Jacob said.

"So why aren't we doing the same thing? Lum is high on our suspect list."

"I'm not interested in Lum for the moment," Jacob said. He grunted as he jammed a knee into his horse's belly, then tightened the cinch. "But I do want to talk to Miss Nemesis."

"We don't even know if she's in El Cerrito," Shawn said. "And we don't know if she's Nemesis. I do know that if Wentworth's vigilantes catch us sneaking out of town they'll string us up for sure."

"They're all in bed," Jacob said, "sleeping like babies."

"Where we should be," Shawn said.

He and Jacob led their horses to the door of the livery, and Shawn said, "Brother, I think we're off on a wild-goose chase. You really want to do this?"

Jacob thought for a while before he answered. He took out the makings and without looking up from tobacco and paper, he said, "Remember when I brought John Moore to Dromore with Patrick?"

"Sure, I remember."

"Moore said that young people, a brother and sister, had moved into a Mex village south of here."

Shawn said, "Yeah, the brother is a writer or something."

"Painter."

"And his sister is a beauty by the name of Dora DeClare."

Jacob smiled. "You never forget a pretty woman's name, do you, Shawn?"

"No, never."

"Tell me this," Jacob said, "why would a woman and her talented brother choose to live in a jerkwater village like El Cerrito?"

Shawn grinned. "To be close to me, of course."

Jacob was lifting his cigarette to his lips, but his hand froze midway. He turned his head slowly and stared at his brother. "Yes, to be close to you," he said.

The strange expression on Jacob's face startled Shawn. "Jake, I was only joking," he said.

Again Jacob lapsed into a taut silence. Then he said, "Here's another suppose."

"Let me hear it," Shawn said.

Jacob thumbed match into flame and lit his smoke. "Suppose Lum was headed for El Cerrito to meet the lovely Dora?"

Shawn laughed. "Jake, now you're trying to sweep sunshine off the porch, going from improbable to impossible."

"Suppose Dora DeClare is Nemesis, and suppose she's the fellow Satanist Lum was sent to help?"

"To help her get revenge on somebody?"

"Exactly."

"Who?"

"I don't know. But I have a suspicion."

Shawn held up a hand. "Whoa, Jake, you're not thinking about Dromore?"

"How many men has the colonel hanged?"

"You're talking about Lucas's drawing again."

"Suppose the hung man was really Dora's father or husband? In that case, she stood under the cottonwood and vowed to be Dromore's nemesis, her and her brother."

"The crippled artist?"

"Yeah. He's crippled, and that's why she needs Lum's help."

Shawn blinked slowly a couple of times and then said, "Jake, I'm putting you to bed. You need to rest."

"Shawn, think about it," Jacob said. "Tell me it's possible."

"It's preposterous."

"Is it possible?"

Shawn hesitated. "Anything is possible," he said.

Jacob swung into the saddle and looked down at his brother. "And that's why we're headed to El Cerrito."

"Let's talk to the colonel first," Shawn said. "Ask him to reason it out for us."

"We don't have time for that. A few hours from now a hanging posse will be riding out of here to drag Patrick back to jail and the gallows."

A silence stretched between the two men. A horse kicked its stall, and rats rustled in the shadowed corners of the barn.

Finally, Shawn mounted and then looked at his brother. "God help me," he said, shaking his head. "I must be as loco as you are."

The man who stood in the shadows watched the O'Brien brothers ride out of town, heading south under a black sky shimmering with lightning.

Now he had to hurry.

He crossed the empty street and took the outside staircase that led to the cribs above the General Lee saloon two steps at a time. He opened the half-glass door and stepped into the hallway. There were two rooms on each side, where his men lay with whores and snored off the night's whiskey.

One by one, Joe Aiken woke up his cursing warriors, pulling them out of bed to the distress of their wailing, kicking whores.

When he had all four of his men assembled and dressed, he said to his bleary-eyed crew, "The O'Brien brothers just rode out of town. Get saddled up; we're going after them."

Hiram Post rubbed his belly and yawned. "Hell, Joe, them two looked like a pair o' thirty-a-month punchers to me. What's the damned hurry?"

"They're O'Briens, you idiot," Aiken said. "They're sitting three-hundred-dollar saddles on American studs that cost at least six hundred apiece. Throw in their guns and what they have in their pockets, and we'll have enough money to keep us in whiskey and whores until winter."

"Hey, Joe," a tough-looking towhead said, his holstered Colt and cartridge belt over his shoulder, "them O'Briens is mighty gun handy."

"Damn you, Dixie, there's five of us," Aiken said. "So we lose a couple of men, that means a bigger share o' the spoils for them as are left." Aiken scowled, his eyebrows meeting on the battered bridge of his twice-broken nose. "I'll smooth it out for you, Dixie. I'm talking better whiskey and prettier whores for them as is still on their feet when the smoke clears."

"Joe's talking sense," Post said. "Let's go get them. And I want that arrogant swine they call Jacob."

"You're welcome to him," Dixie Foster said.

Chapter Twenty-one

"It's like an itch between my shoulder blades and it's driving me crazy," Jacob said. "Recollect that time when we were boys and the Kiowa stalked us and Pa down on the Chavez Draw?"

"I remember," Shawn said.

"Well, I had the itch then."

"And the colonel said we should pay mind to you because you had the Irish gift. Worked out you were right and the damned Kiowa jumped us."

"Shawn," Jacob said, "somebody's riding our back trail. I'm certain of it."

"Who?"

"Damn it, Shawn, I don't know. I don't have that much of a gift."

Shawn's eyes were on the moon-shadowed darkness ahead of him. Then he turned to his brother and said, "Talking about the colonel, I remember him saying that cavalry should never charge through a clearing bounded by woods."

"Sounds like something he'd say," Jacob said.

"Well, there's a clearing just like that ahead of us," Shawn said.

"Hell, Shawn, where? I don't see it."

"About a hundred yards in front of us, a hump-back ridge with pines on either side of a clearing."

Jacob leaned over the saddle horn and peered into the gloom. "How can you see that? I can't see that," he said.

"Jake, I guess you're not a night-seeing man, is all," Shawn said.

More than a little irritated, Jacob said, "Well, let's take a look." He turned in the saddle and glared at his brother. "Probably it's a damned wall of rock anyway."

But it was a low saddleback as Shane had described, thick stands of ponderosa pine and a few piñon on either side of a grassy clearing.

"You were right," Jacob said as they topped the rise.

Those three words were all the grudging recognition Shawn was going to get, and it made him grin, though he was careful to keep his face turned away.

"How do we play it?" Jacob said. "One of us on either side of the clearing?"

Shawn shook his head. "No. We're liable to shoot each other that way. We'll stay together." He leaned over and patted his horse's neck, then turned his head toward his brother. "Pick a side, Jake."

Jacob pointed to his left. "In there. It's as good a place as any."

"Are you sure?" Shawn said.

"Yeah, I'm sure."

"Suppose it's the Georgetown posse or a whole passel of Apaches?"

"Then we'll hide out and let them ride past."

"Give me a number, Jake. Whoever it is will be here pretty quick."

"A number for what?"

"How many we're prepared to fight."

"Damn it, Shawn, you're asking me conundrums. I'll know when I see them."

"How will I know?"

Jacob bit his tongue, let his annoyance settle, and then said, "I'll nudge you."

"Got it," Shawn said, enjoying himself. "Nudge means fight. What means don't fight?"

"How about a kick up the ass?" Jacob said.

Shawn smiled. "Just wanted to get it right, Jake. Nudge—fight. Kick up the ass—no fight." He nodded. "Yeah, I think I can keep it straight." Shawn made to dismount, then stopped, one foot in the stirrup. "What if you're wrong, Jake, and the only thing on our trail is your imagination? Suppose you're like an old maid hearing a rustle in every bush?"

"Then, brother, you get a kick up the ass anyway, because I'll be so sorely disappointed," Jacob said, feeling testy.

* * *

Jacob and Shawn led their horses well back into the trees and then returned to the clearing, rifles in hand.

Moonlight shone on the grass atop the ridge like a hoarfrost, an illusion because the night was warm, heavy with the scent of pine and night-blooming wildflowers. Somewhere in the woods coyotes called, and a startled owl asked a question of the darkness.

Five minutes passed . . . then ten . . .

The soft thud of a walking horse froze the O'Brien brothers into a crouch, and their eyes scanned the night. The quiet around them was so profound Jacob heard Shawn swallow his tension, his throat bobbing.

A lone rider rode to the top of the ridge, then vanished from sight over the rim. A few moments later he reappeared piece by piece, starting with his hat, ending with the hooves of his horse as he again crested the rise from the far slope.

Jacob saw the man's face, framed by shoulder-length black hair, and silently cursed. He'd seen the man before, a French-Cheyenne breed by the name of Frenchy Petite. The last Jacob had heard, Frenchy, good with a gun and an expert tracker, was running with the Tewksbury brothers and that wild crowd down Arizona way. But now he was right there, within spitting distance, and it was the worst possible news.

Shawn put his mouth close to Jacob's ear and whispered, "Want me to gun him?"

Jacob shook his head. If Frenchy was scouting, there would be others behind him, none of them model citizens, and a rifle shot would bring them running. But how far behind were they?

Frenchy swung out of the saddle and jerked his rifle out of the boot. To Jacob's relief the breed stepped slowly toward the opposite line of trees, his moccasined feet making no sound, silent as a silk nightgown dropping on carpet.

Jacob reached into his pocket and dug out his knife, a Buck folder, its carbon steel blade honed to razor sharpness. He held up an open hand to Shawn, warning him into silence, then, crouching low, he left the trees.

Keeping Frenchy's horse between himself and the breed, Jacob covered ground, staying to patches of thin darkness. The moonlight gleamed on his open knife as he rounded the rump of Frenchy's mustang and stepped into full view. Ten yards separated the two men, and Jacob made a run at Frenchy's back.

The breed turned like a striking snake, his rifle coming up fast. Jacob left his feet and dived for the man. Jacob's right shoulder hit the stock of Frenchy's rifle hard, and it jolted him with a sudden stab of pain.

Both men hit the ground and rolled, teeth bared, growling like animals. Jacob was on top of the breed, looking for a chance to use his knife, but

Frenchy was strong and he clamped Jacob's wrist in a bone-breaking grip. The breed brought up his right knee, trying for his opponent's groin. Jacob rolled away, and the knee hit him in the thigh, numbing his leg for a moment.

Lithe as a panther, Frenchy scrambled to his feet. Snarling his anger, he went for the holstered Colt at his side. Jacob saw the danger and dived at the breed again. He grabbed the man's right hand, pushing the revolver up and away from him. But the right side of Jacob's face was momentarily un-protected. Frenchy hit him with a pair of hard lefts that opened up the tight skin of Jacob's cheek-bone. Blood splattered over both men as they again wrestled to the ground. Jacob wrenched Frenchy's Colt from his hand, tossed it away, and got a hard left hook to the chin for his pains. Jacob's head snapped back, and the breed tried to roll away from him. Too slow. Jacob half-rolled, half-fell onto him. Whipping his shoulder, arm, and thick wrist into it, Jacob smashed the bolsters of the big Buck squarely into the bridge of Frenchy's nose. Bone shattered and blood splashed onto the front of Jacob's blue shirt.

Frenchy, his glassy eyes rolling in his head, was out of it, at least for a moment. But the breed was half-cougar and all game. The bottom half of his face a scarlet nightmare of blood, snot, and shards of bone, he tried to struggle to his feet.

"You murdering devil!" Jacob yelled, no longer

human, possessed by the fighting madness that made him lose all reason.

He crashed the toe of his boot into Frenchy's face, and the breed screamed and fell on his back. Jacob straddled the man, and his right arm crossed his chest, ready for a backhanded slash across Frenchy's exposed throat.

Suddenly, Shawn grabbed his arm. "Jake," he yelled, "no! He's had enough!"

Jacob tried to wrestle free of his brother. "Get away from me. I'm gonna gut this bastard!"

"Jake!" Shawn shoved the muzzle of his Colt against his brother's temple. "Damn you, leave him be."

Jacob's face was twisted in rage, flecks of white foam on his battered lips, but he hesitated just a moment. Shawn took advantage of the pause. "Jake, he's done." He put a name to the unconscious man, knowing that in his mind his brother was no longer battling the breed but one of his own faceless demons. "Frenchy Petite is done," he said.

It took a tense minute before Shawn saw the stiffness leak out of Jacob's shoulders. Another few moments passed, and when Jacob turned his head and looked at his brother the madness had fled his features.

"We'll drag him into the trees with us," Jacob said. He rose to his feet and looked around. "Where is his horse?"

"When the fisticuffs started it took off over the rise—thataway," Shawn said, pointing south.

Jacob nodded. "Good, it's probably still running and in the right direction."

"Maybe we should follow it," Shawn said. "If you don't mind me saying so, Jake, you look like hell."

Ignoring that, Jacob said, "Frenchy was scouting for somebody, probably a bunch of somebodies. I don't want them to catch us out in the open, even in darkness."

"Why do you reckon they're after us, Jake?"

"I don't know. Robbery, maybe."

"Nemesis, you think? Hired herself some guns to do us in?"

"Maybe, but that's stretching things mighty thin." He motioned to the groaning Frenchy. "Pick up his gun while I drag him into the trees. If he gives me any trouble, I'll bash his brains in with a rifle butt."

Shawn smiled. "You're not a forgiving man, are you, Jake?"

"Devil near broke my jaw," Jacob said. "Hell, only a saddlebag preacher would be that forgiving."

Shawn looked at the sky where clouds had swept the stars aside. "I smell lightning in the air," he said. "It could be fixing to storm."

Jacob wiped off his knife on Frenchy's buckskin shirt, then got behind him and started to drag the man toward the trees by the armpits.

"Maybe if it storms, the boys who are tracking us, whoever they may be, will turn back," Shawn said.

Jacob paused and looked at him. "You believe that?"

"No," Shawn said.

"Neither do I," Jacob said.

Chapter Twenty-two

Ernest Thistledown doused the oil lamp, and lightning flashes shimmered in the darkened barn.

He took a knee beside John Moore and said, "Where are you wounded?"

"Here," the lawman said. He touched the front of his left shoulder, and his fingertips came away bloody. "Feels like I got hit with a big fifty."

Thistledown said, "Every bullet that hits a man feels like a big fifty."

"I guess the shot came from the house, huh?" Moore said.

"I would say that is likely."

"Then we got to get out of here," Moore said.

Thistledown got to his feet and stood in the shadows at the corner of the barn door. All the lamps in the adobe had been extinguished, and the house was in darkness. Out in the village, a Mexican voice yelled, "*Quién es?*" Thistledown understood that, but he couldn't make anything out of the chorus of voices that answered. Probably, "*The hell if we know,*" he figured. But he wasn't sure.

A star of fire appeared at the window of the adobe kitchen, and another bullet rattled through the thin timbers of the barn.

Thistledown threw his shotgun to his shoulder and slammed two shots at the window. He heard the sharp shatter of breaking glass, but no cry of pain.

He turned his head and said to Moore, "At least they know I'm not sitting on my gun hand."

The lawman got to his feet, and Thistledown told him, "You stay right where you're at. A big target like you will get plugged for sure."

"I already got plugged," Moore said.

"Just proves what I'm saying," the little man said. He took two shells from his jacket pocket and fed them into the Hollis and Sheath. "These are my last," he said. "So we have a situation here."

Thistledown let a silence stretch as he tried to think his way out of this fix. Finally he said, "Moore, do you have any strength left or are you bleeding out too fast?"

"Damn you," the sheriff said, "I swear, you'd mock a dying man."

"Answer the question," Thistledown snapped.

"Yeah, I've got strength left," Moore said. "I ain't quite dead yet."

"Then get to the back of the barn and pull some boards free. We're going out that way."

"You mean just cut and run?"

"Do you have a better idea?"

"I might have, if I had a gun," Moore said.

"Well you don't, and that's one of the reasons we're beating our feet out of here," Thistledown said. "Now get back there and tear down timber. Take the crowbar with you; that'll help."

After Moore cussed his way to the rear of the barn, Thistledown saw the kitchen door open and a shadow step into the moonlight. He shouldered the scattergun and triggered off one shot. The shadow quickly disappeared inside, and the door slammed shut. Immediately, a couple of bullets chipped through the barn, high and harmless.

Thistledown reckoned that Lum and the others were keeping the shooting to a minimum because they didn't want to hit their horses. Come daylight, when they could see better, that would change.

"How are you doing back there?" he whispered to Moore.

"I'm shot through and through," the lawman said. "How the hell do you think I'm doing?"

"Then try harder," Thistledown said. "It'll be daylight in a couple of hours." He heard boards splinter and said, "That's the way, Moore. Are you putting your back into it?"

The sheriff's reply was to exhaust his repertoire of curses and invent a dozen more. Delighted, Thistledown smiled.

* * *

Regularly spaced shots from the adobe kicked up V's of dirt just outside the barn doors. The warning was clear: *Don't even think of trying to break out. If you try, we'll kill you before you've taken a couple of steps.*

The only way of escape was through the rear wall. Thistledown reckoned that once clear they would try their chances in the dark hill country and make their way to his horse and buggy.

But time was running out. Dawn was not far off and then the shooting would start in earnest.

"Moore," Thistledown said, "I don't hear you back there."

He was greeted with silence. The half a dozen horses in the stalls dozed and made no sound, and even the rats seemed to have ceased their scurrying.

"Damn it, Moore," Thistledown said, "I'm coming back there with a stick."

He propped his shotgun against a stall and made his way to the rear. There was no thunder, but inside the barn lightning flickered like a magic lantern show.

"Where are you, Moore?" Thistledown said.

"Over here."

The little man followed the voice. The sheriff sat on the floor, his back fetched up against a sack of oats. Blood stained the front of Moore's shirt, and under his mustache his lips were pale.

Thistledown saw where the crowbar had chewed splinters out of a few pine boards, but Moore had not managed to remove any.

"I swear," the sheriff said, his voice thin as mist,

"that the Mex who built this damned barn used a bushel o' tenpenny nails on every plank." Moore's head lifted to Thistledown, his eye sockets shadowed. "I'm weary."

Thistledown tried to budge the boards, but they were stiff and unyielding.

"Looks like we're done for, huh?" Moore said.

Thistledown nodded. "Come first light, I reckon."

"I don't know how to die well," the sheriff said. "Do you?"

"Never really thought about it," Thistledown said. Then after a while, he remarked, "No, I guess I don't."

"You've got one shotgun shell left," Moore said.

Thistledown nodded. "I'll take one of them with me. I want Lum because I've never taken money for a contract I didn't honor."

"Use the shell on me, Thistledown."

The little man was surprised, and Moore read the look on his face.

"I don't want to fall into their hands wounded and helpless," the sheriff said. "Come first light, put the scattergun to my head and do for me."

Thistledown thought about that last, then said, "Moore, that's a lot to ask of any man."

"Then I'll do it myself." The sheriff grabbed Thistledown's pants leg. "Hell, man, I'm hurting here. And those insane devils will hurt me a lot worse." A long, painful silence, then Moore said, "I've never begged anything of any man, but I'm a-beggin' this of you."

Thistledown glanced up at the shadowed rafters of the barn where the spiders lived. He stayed like that for a long time. "All right," he said finally.

"Thank you, I—"

"Don't say another word, Moore," the little man said. "Just . . . let it go."

A moment later, a voice, male, low, accented, came from the doorway.

"Are you in trouble, my son?" the voice said.

Thistledown turned, and a fleeting thought flashed through his brain that he should make a dash for the shotgun. Then he saw the man and stayed where he was.

The man in the doorway, silhouetted by lightning, wore the dark brown robes of a monk. Beside him a small boy led a donkey, a canvas-covered bundle on its back.

"Are you in trouble?" the man asked again.

"Seems like, padre," Thistledown said. "There are men in the adobe who plan to kill us."

"My name is Brother Benedict," the monk said. "The people of El Cerrito are part of my flock. I heard the gunfire."

"I suppose," Thistledown said, "that you don't have any shotgun shells about your person."

"No. I am armed only with God's grace."

"Too bad," Thistledown said. "A box of shells would've come in real handy."

The monk smiled. "I will take you and the wounded man out of here."

Moore was lost in shadow, out of sight from the door. "How did you know—"

"I see blood on the floor. You are not wounded, my son, so there must be another man here."

"He's a lawman and he's badly hurt," Thistledown said. "How do you plan to get us out of here, padre? I'm surprised they haven't plugged you already."

"The people in the house won't fire on me," Brother Benedict said. Under his cowl his hair was yellow and his eyes were startling blue. "They're afraid of me."

"Why?"

"They worship evil, but they fear the wrath of God. Since time began, this has always been so." The monk waved a hand, encompassing the village. "They've brought bad luck to El Cerrito, and their very presence has polluted the river. The fish don't swim there anymore, nor do the antelope come to drink."

Thistledown said, "You should ask God to strike them down, especially a man called Lum."

Brother Benedict smiled, showing white teeth. "That's up to God. He doesn't need any help from me. Now," he said, "let's help your wounded friend."

Thistledown woke Moore from sleep, and when the big lawman saw the monk his eyes widened. "Well, I'll be . . . I always figured I'd end up in hell," he said.

"Moore, you're still in El Cerrito, and that's close enough," Thistledown said.

He and Brother Benedict helped the big man to his feet, and together they manhandled the sheriff to the front of the barn. Moore continued to stare at the monk, as though he couldn't believe his eyes.

Brother Benedict took the canvas-wrapped bundle from the burro's back, then said to the boy, "Get the sheriff onto the donkey."

With Thistledown's help, Moore managed to straddle the animal. His was a heavy weight for so small a donkey, but the burro stood four square on its legs and seemed to willingly accept its burden.

The monk opened the canvas and revealed a large crucifix as tall as the peasant boy. Like a man showing off a priceless relic, Brother Benedict said, "The wood of the cross is black because it was made from a charred timber taken from the ruins of a mission burned by Apaches. The Christ crucified was hammered from the melted silver chalices that were found in the chapel." The monk kissed the cross. "It is a very powerful crucifix."

"Yes, but will it stop bullets?" Thistledown said.

Brother Benedict smiled. "We'll see, my son, won't we?"

"Sorry for doubting you, padre," Thistledown said, "but I'm a Presbyterian myself."

"Ah, then I can give no guarantees," the monk said, smiling, and Thistledown worried that the padre wasn't making a joke.

"Get my horse and saddle," Moore said.

"You're not fit to ride," Thistledown said.

"I know, but I don't want to leave him with those damned heathens," he said.

"Pedro," Brother Benedict said, "please saddle Mr. Moore's horse. Then we'll leave."

The boy did as he was told and led the horse to the front of the barn. Thistledown grabbed his shotgun and then took the animal's reins while Pedro stood by the donkey's head.

"Are we ready?" the monk asked.

Thistledown looped the shotgun's strap over his shoulder. "As we'll ever be, padre," he said.

"Then we'll be on our way," Brother Benedict said.

It was still full dark, but far to the east in the star-studded sky above the Great Plains, a slender fissure of pale blue light appeared, heralding the coming dawn. Insects stirred in the grass, and the gray coyotes had ceased to yip.

Brother Benedict led the way out of the barn, holding the cross up in front of him. He whispered in prayer. Behind came Pedro with the donkey and its heavy burden, and Thistledown brought up the rear, leading Moore's horse.

Suddenly the chapel bell in the village began to toll, its slow *clang . . . clang . . . clang . . .* ringing loud, clamoring into the shattering darkness.

The back door of the adobe opened and Dora DeClare stepped outside, the others with her. Her brother sat in his wheelchair in the doorway, Lum just in front of him.

Brother Benedict stopped, then turned and held the cross high, its elongated shadow falling across the open ground between him and the house. The bell clanged and clashed louder, faster, and the monk's prayers grew in volume to an intense, terrible shout. Pedro urged the donkey to walk faster, and Moore, fevered and only half-conscious, roared and demanded to know if he was in heaven or hell.

Thistledown, his nerves unraveling, held the shotgun up and ready, his finger on the trigger. But no shots came his way.

One by one, like roaches scuttling into a hole, Lum and the others fled inside the house, driven by stark, supernatural fears of their own making. Soon only Dora remained.

The scream cut through Thistledown's brain like a blade and turned his insides to water. A shrieking, screeching, piercing cry of fear and rage, it sounded like nothing he'd ever heard in his life. It was the dreadful, hellish, scream of the newly damned.

And it clawed from the beautiful throat of Dora DeClare.

Chapter Twenty-three

"Where the hell are they?" Shawn O'Brien said. "Be light soon."

Jacob glanced at the sky. A narrow band of mother-of-pearl sky showed to the east, but the night was still ablaze with stars.

"They'll be here," Jacob said. "Count on it."

Frenchy Petite groaned, and his hand went to his battered face.

Jacob shoved the muzzle of his Colt into the middle of the breed's forehead. "You lay still and keep your trap shut or I'll scatter your brains," he said.

"Frenchy, how many men are with you?" Shawn said.

The breed opened his swollen eyes, and his split lips curled in a smile. "More than you can handle, O'Brien," he said. "Joe Aiken leads them, and he'll cut your heart out."

"Is that so?" Jacob said. Way too quiet, a thing Frenchy should've noticed.

"Yeah, it's so, you bastard," the breed said.

"Good night, Frenchy," Jacob said. The barrel of his revolver came down hard in the middle of the breed's skull, right where his long hair parted. Frenchy went out as though an anvil had dropped on his head.

"Damn it, Jake, did you have to do that?" Shawn said.

"Yeah, I did," Jacob said. "Frenchy is a talking man. He could've yelled out to Joe Aiken."

"Who is he, this Aiken feller?" Shawn asked.

"I've never met him, but I seem to recollect some talk about a small-time outlaw by that name."

"Why is he after us?"

"Because he wants to be a big-time outlaw."

The eastern sky was turning from black to lilac when a rider approached the rise. The man sat his horse, stood in the stirrups, and looked around. Shawn, his breath caught in his throat, whispered, the words coming out like an old man's asthmatic wheeze, "He's damned careful."

Jacob nodded but said nothing.

A long minute passed, then the man turned his horse broadside to the ridge and waved his hat. After a few moments three riders joined him. One of them said, "Where the hell is Frenchy?"

"Scouting ahead, I guess."

The man who'd spoken last was Joe Aiken, and

now he swung his horse around, ready to ride over the ridge.

Jacob knew he was fast running out of room on the dance floor. Gun in hand, he jumped to his feet and charged into the clearing, Shawn following behind.

It had never crossed Joe Aiken's mind, as it had Dixie Foster's, that two gunfighting men are a handful. As fate wrote the last line of the last chapter of his life, Aiken would come to realize it. But by then it was way too late.

There was now enough shooting light, and Jacob and Shawn cut loose.

Bullets cut into Aiken's men, and the first couple of volleys emptied a couple of saddles. All Aiken's sand ran out of him. He tried to swing his horse away from the ridge, but he collided with a riderless mount. His horse reared, and Aiken tumbled over backward and hit the ground hard.

Dixie Foster, showing more backbone than his boss, fought to control his frightened mount, his Colt leveling on Shawn. Both men fired at the same time, and a scarlet rose blossom appeared under Dixie's hat brim. The outlaw toppled off his horse, dead before he hit the ground.

Hiram Post, big-bellied and pig-eyed, the whore smell still on him, kicked his mount toward Aiken. "Get up, Joe," he yelled.

But Jacob eyed him. He thumbed off two fast shots, and Post took them both in the chest. The outlaw threw up his arms and cartwheeled over the head of his galloping mount. He screamed when he hit the ground, from pain or a glimpse of hell, Jacob didn't know or care.

Aiken tried for Post's horse, but it ran past him, stirrups flying.

He heard footsteps and saw Jacob, Colt in hand, striding toward him. "O'Brien, I'm all through," he yelled. His fingers opened, and he let go of his gun as though it had suddenly become red hot.

"You Joe Aiken?" Jacob said.

"Yes, yes. Joe Aiken as ever was."

"You picked the wrong men to rob, Joe."

Aiken looked contrite, smiling. "I know that now, Mr. O'Brien."

The outlaw shoved his hands in his pockets in a boyish, "*Aw shucks*," kind of way, and Jacob shot him between the eyes.

Shawn stepped through a drift of gun smoke and looked from his brother to the dead man. Without a word, Jacob kneeled and searched the man's pockets. He came up with a Remington derringer.

"I figured ol' Joe for a man who'd pull a sneaky gun," he said.

"Wherever he is, I bet he's regretting it now," Shawn said.

"That would be my guess," Jacob said.

Joe Aiken had made one mistake, now Frenchy Petite made another.

On silent feet, the breed stepped out of the trees, a skull-crushing rock raised above his head. He was only a yard from Shawn when the sound of his moccasins shuffling through dry grass betrayed him.

Shawn turned and at spitting distance fanned three fast shots into Frenchy's belly. The man's face twisted in pain, and the rock fell to the ground. The breed tried to walk away, but after a couple of staggering steps he stretched his full length on the ground and lay still.

Jacob smiled at his brother. "Regrets all around, I reckon."

"We laid out five dead men on that ridge," Shawn said. He shook his head. "I find it hard to believe."

"Helluva thing," Jacob said, head bent, rolling a cigarette.

"We'll have to see they get buried decent, Jake," Shawn said.

Jacob lit his cigarette and then said, "Maybe they got an undertaker in El Cerrito."

"Suppose they don't?"

"Then the coyotes will do the burying for us."

"You don't care, do you, Jake?" Shawn said, a cool anger building in his eyes.

"When I kill a man who's trying to kill me, no, I don't give a damn."

"They all had mothers, wives maybe," Shawn said.

Jacob smiled. "Aiken and that crowd? They probably murdered their mothers for the old ladies' sewing money and spent it on whiskey and whores."

"Damn it, Jake, when did you get so hard?"

Jacob tapped the Colt on his hip. "Around the time I started to sell this. A soft-natured man doesn't live long in this territory."

"You think that's what I am, a soft-natured man?" Shawn said.

Jacob inhaled deeply, and then he let the smoke trickle from his nose. "No, I don't. Patrick, now, is a soft-natured man; that's his way. But Shawn, you're like Samuel and the colonel, killers both, and again like them you put a gloss on it." He stared at the blue morning sky. "I don't."

"Pa's not a killer, Jake, nor is Samuel," Shawn said. "They've killed men and hung their share, sure, but it was all for Dromore."

Jacob turned to his brother and grinned. "Glossing it again, ain't we, Shawn, huh?"

Chapter Twenty-four

The village of El Cerrito lay under a haze of wood smoke as the women lit breakfast-cooking fires. The morning was hot, and the few trees that stood among the casas looked limp and still, as though already exhausted from the heat. The smell of tortillas and strong coffee scented the air, and Shawn said his belly was rumbling.

"We'll get something to eat after we track down Dora DeClare," Jacob said, "and ask her about the Nemesis drawing."

"Right, like she'll tell us if she has plans to hurt Dromore," Shawn said.

"She won't, but we can beat it out of Lum," Jacob said.

"If he's even here."

"If not, we'll beat it out of her brother," Jacob said.

Shawn turned his head, a wan smile on his lips. "Jake, you're one hard-hearted feller."

"Maybe, but it's for Dromore, remember? So that makes it right."

The peon with a hoe over his shoulder listened patiently to Jacob's question, his eyes full of concentration, as though he was translating each word one by one in his head.

Finally he said, "The Americanos have gone, señor." He crossed himself. "By the grace of God."

"Do you know where?" Shawn asked.

"No. But in the casa over there, see, with the cactus outside the window?"

"I see it," Shawn said.

"A boy named Pedro lives there, and he can tell you more, I think."

The O'Brien brothers nodded their thanks, then dismounted and walked their horses to the cactus house. Immediately, the rug that served as a door pulled back and a woman stepped outside.

"*Buenos días, señora,*" Shawn said. "We'd like to speak to Pedro. Is he your son?"

Fear flashed in the woman's black eyes. As the man had done earlier, she crossed herself. "Are you demons?" she said.

Shawn smiled. "Not so you'd notice, ma'am."

The woman looked baffled, and Jacob said, "We're . . . vaqueros. And we need to talk with Pedro." Under his mustache, Jacob stretched his lips in what he hoped was a winning smile. "We're trying to find the Americano lady who lived here with her crippled brother. We're friends . . . *amigos.*"

The woman threw Jacob a horrified look, screamed, and ran into the house. A moment later the rug drew back a few inches and she yelled, "*Vayase! Vayase!*"

"What does that mean?" Jacob said.

"It means she wants us to get the hell away from here," Shawn said.

Jacob sighed. "Damn it, now what?"

"Well, it seems your birds have flown," Shawn said. "Let's see if we can find a cantina around here."

"Shawn, I'm convinced Dora DeClare could be Nemesis, and somebody must know where she's gone."

"I don't think she's Nemesis," Shawn said. "I figure she's nothing but a pretty girl with a crippled brother." He looked around him. "Do you see anything that looks like it might be a cantina?"

"We'll go scout," Jacob said. "Maybe once you get some tortillas and frijoles in your belly you'll be more inclined to listen to reason."

"Maybe," Shawn said, "but I still won't believe a slip of a girl and a cripple are trying to bring down the house of Dromore."

Jacob looked over the rim of his coffee cup at his brother. "You've eaten a dozen tortillas and two bowls of frijoles, Shawn. Had enough?"

"I reckon."

"You know what happens to men who eat too many beans, huh?"

"Speak for yourself, Jake. I'm much too refined to fart."

"We'll see. I recollect the time when—"

Jacob stopped in midspeech as a small Mexican boy with a shock of black hair and huge brown eyes stepped to the table.

"My name is Pedro," he said. "You wanted to talk to me?"

"We sure do," Jacob said.

"About the Americanos who lived in the house with the barn?" Pedro said.

"Yeah, I guess that's right," Jacob said.

"They've gone."

"We know that, Pedro," Jacob said. "But where did they go?"

The boy looked over Jacob's patched and threadbare shirt and his scuffed chaps and boots and seemed less than impressed. He stepped to Shawn and gave him the once-over. "You are the one with money, señor?" he said.

"How much money are we talking about, and why?" Shawn said.

"Five dollars American for what I can tell you."

"Let me see your neck, kid," Jacob said.

The boy pulled down his poncho, and Jacob said, "I knew it, made for a rope."

"Five dollars," Pedro said.

"Shawn, give the boy five dollars," Jacob said.

"Hell, give it to him yourself, Jake."

"You know how long it's been since I had five dollars all at the same time?" Jacob said.

"Kid," Shawn said, "we ran into some of your kind back on the trail." He reached into his pocket and stacked five silver dollars on the table. The boy grinned and grabbed for the money, but Shawn covered the coins with his hand and said, "Uh-uh, tell us about the Americanos first."

"A padre came through our village and saved two men from the fiends," he said.

"What kind of men?" Jacob said.

"One was small and thin, the other big and fat," Pedro said. "The fat one wore a star on his shirt and was wounded."

"John Moore," Shawn said, looking at Jacob.

"Yeah, and I'm willing to bet the farm that the other one was Ernest Thistledown."

"How did those two meet up?" Shawn said.

Jacob shook his head. "Beats me." He said to Pedro, "How did the padre save the Americans?"

"They were in the barn and the fiends were shooting at them from the house," Pedro said. "The padre came and took the two men away. He carried a cross and I led a donkey." He smiled. "The fat man was on the donkey because he was wounded and bleeding."

"Did they shoot at the padre?" Shawn said.

"No, they were afraid of him," Pedro said. "That's why they left."

"They were afraid of the padre?" Jacob said.

"*Sí*, a holy monk. They were afraid of him, and the woman screamed when she saw the cross he carried."

Jacob and Shawn exchanged looks. Then Shawn said, "Are you telling us a windy, kid?"

The boy shook his head. "No, señor, what I tell you was what happened. They were afraid of the padre, and they stayed away from him."

"Jacob, are there any named guns in our neck of the woods?" Shawn said.

"You mean a fast gun could've dressed as a monk, but the DeClare brother and sister recognized him and he scared them off?"

"It's as good an explanation as any."

"I heard that Pat Garrett was gambling in Santa Fe a month ago, and Roscoe Burrell is around," Jacob said. "But neither of those gents is the type to dress up as monks and go a-rescuing folks."

Shawn said to the boy, "Where is the padre now? We'd like to ask him a few questions."

Pedro shrugged his thin shoulders. "I don't know."

"Does he live in a mission near here?" Jacob said.

"I don't know," Pedro said. He saw Jacob hard-eye him and said, "He was never in our village before. The padre came that night, and then he left with the gringos. After we led them to their horse and wagon, the padre told me to take the donkey and the cross back to the village." The boy spread his hands. "After that, I never saw him again."

"Where is the cross now?" Shawn said.

"I left it in the chapel, but our village priest told me he'd never seen it before," Pedro said. "He said it is a very beautiful cross and a great and holy mystery."

"So where did the gringos go?" Jacob said.

"I don't know, señor. When I got back to the village, they were already gone and the house was empty."

"You think it's worth looking over the house?" Jacob said to Shawn.

"I doubt it," his brother said. "The last time we searched a place we found a drawing that sent us on this wild-goose chase. God forbid that we'd find another. We'd end up in China or somewhere."

"We'll take a look anyhow," Jacob said. "They might have left a clue about where they're headed."

"Sure, Jake," Shawn said. "Anything to get this thing out of your system."

"My God, what's that smell?" Shawn said.

He and Jacob stood in the adobe's living room. The furniture was still in place, but wide-open cupboards and desk drawers suggested the DeClares had left in a hurry.

Jacob sniffed his great beak of a nose. "Damned if I know what it is."

"Like something dead," Shawn said. "And I mean long dead."

A search of the house revealed no bodies, animal or human. But the stench pervaded the entire adobe, the sweet, sickly smell of decay. And something else the O'Brien brothers couldn't identify. Something vile.

The air was thick and hard to breathe as though all the oxygen had fled the casa, to be replaced by . . .

"Damn it, Shawn, it's sulfur," Jacob said. He glared at his brother. "Them frijoles getting to you?"

"Hell no, it isn't me. A man would have to eat a bushel of beans to produce a smell like this."

"Then where's it coming from?" Jacob said.

"Didn't Ma tell us one time that hell stinks of sulfur?" Shawn said. "She said that it's the smell of the damned."

"Now how would Ma know that?"

"She said a priest told her that at confession one time."

Jacob said, "Yeah, probably one of them old Irish priests that try to put the fear of hell into everybody." He looked into a drawer. "Empty," he said. Then he asked, "What sin could Ma possibly have committed?"

"I recollect she said she was too lazy to bring the milk in from the byre and it curdled. The priest said it was the sin of sloth, a terrible affront to God and the industrious Blessed Virgin. That's when he told her about sulfur and the damned an' sich."

Jacob slammed the drawer shut. "What do priests know?"

"Jake, they go to school to study these things," Shawn said. "A priest knows what hell smells like."

Shawn did two things that revealed his agitation: he crossed himself, something he hadn't done since he was a kid, and he adjusted the position of his holster on the cartridge belt.

Jacob, an attentive man, noted both actions and said, "Let's get out of here. We'll check the barn."

"I'm with you," Shawn said, and hurried to the door.

"Back here, Jake," Shawn said. "They tried to get out through the barn wall. Didn't succeed though."

Jacob stepped beside his brother and studied the chipped boards. "Seems like," he said. "And there's bloodstains all over the floor." He held up a spent shotgun shell. "Thistledown was here all right."

"All we can do now is get back to Dromore," Shawn said. "We'll be needed there."

"I want to ride to Georgetown, see if John Moore is still alive," Jacob said. "You go on to Dromore, and I'll catch up later."

"You reckon that hanging posse has left yet?" Shawn said.

"I don't know. But Moore's the only one who can stop them, if he's still on his feet."

Shawn nodded, but his face was troubled. Without looking at Jacob, he said, "In the house, Jake, you think that was really the stink of hell?"

"I think, like you, they ate too many frijoles," Jacob said.

But he didn't smile. He didn't smile at all.

Chapter Twenty-five

"Colonel O'Brien! Colonel Shamus O'Brien! Show yourself!"

James Wentworth sat his horse in front of the big house of Dromore, ten riders strung out behind him, all armed with Colts and rifles.

"You know why I'm here, Colonel," Wentworth called out. "Surrender Patrick O'Brien into my custody or face the consequences. The choice is yours."

Luther Ironside looked out of the living room window.

"How many?" Shamus said.

Ironside took time to count, then said, "Eleven. The one doing all the shouting is James Wentworth. He owns a saloon in Georgetown and heads up the Vigilance Committee. I see Tom Harkness, owns the hardware store. He's on the square, deals honest and says what's on his mind up front."

"And the rest?"

"Wentworth scraped the bottom of the barrel," Ironside said. "Looks like every grifter, pimp, and dancehall lounger in town signed up to earn their ten dollars."

"Will they stand, Luther?" Shamus said.

"Maybe, for the first volley. But then they'll break and run."

"How many vaqueros are here at the ranch?"

"Three. All the rest are out on the range." Ironside turned and looked at his boss. "It's enough with Samuel and me."

Shamus nodded. "Bring the vaqueros here. But before you do that, get me my crutches. I'll be damned if I'll meet that scum in a wheelchair."

Shamus had been holding his baby grandson on his knee, and when Ironside brought him his crutches and gunbelt, he passed the infant to Lorena.

"Shamus, you shouldn't go out there on crutches," the woman said. "A breath of wind could knock you over."

"I'd like to see the wind that will knock me over on my own ground and in the presence of my enemies," Shamus said. He waved a dismissive hand. "Now, away with you, woman."

Lorena looked helplessly at her husband. "Sam, tell your father to stay inside."

Samuel shook his head. "Lorena, you should know by this time that when the colonel makes up his mind to do a thing, he does it."

"Damn right," Shamus said. He rose unsteadily to

his feet, buckled on his gun, and positioned the crutches under his armpits. "Come, Samuel," he said, "let us read the book to the riffraff outside."

"Shamus O'Brien, you know why I'm here," Wentworth said. The man had dismounted and stepped toward the colonel. He stopped when he was just five feet away and said, "Your son will hang today before sundown."

"No, he won't," Shamus said, his eyes full of blue fire.

"He was found guilty in a court of law of murder and rape," Wentworth said. "You are shielding a fugitive."

"I'm shielding my son," Shamus said.

Wentworth watched Samuel, Ironside, and the three vaqueros line up behind the colonel. All five were good with a gun and were not men to be underestimated. Wentworth didn't make that mistake.

"I have ten deputies with me, Colonel," he said, "all well-armed and determined men. Now, I must take Patrick O'Brien into custody. Will you let me pass?"

"Deputies? Is that what you call that hired scum?" Shamus said.

"Wentworth," Ironside said, "by all means pass, but I'll drop you before you reach the door."

The saloon owner half turned his head. "Stand to your arms, men," he said.

"Wentworth, tell your deputies that at least half

of them won't live to spend the money you're paying them," Samuel said as the posse's rifles rattled into position. "Ask them! Ask them if they want to open the ball."

Uncertainty showed on the faces of the posse. The colonel had made a show of force, but where were the two fast guns? Were Jacob and Shawn O'Brien somewhere inside the house, waiting?

"Don't listen to O'Brien's bluster, boys," Wentworth said. He waved a hand. "Wilson, Forbes, dismount and come with me."

The sudden snick of revolvers skinning from leather stopped Wentworth in his tracks. Now he faced five Colts, all pointed at his belly. He glared at Shamus. "By God, sir, you wouldn't dare shoot me."

"The colonel might not," Ironside said, "but I sure as hell will. And them two yellow-bellied skunks skulking behind you as well."

Wilson and Forbes didn't look like they had sand enough to stand and fight at a distance of a few feet. In fact, both were green around the gills. It takes a certain kind of courage to engage in a belly-to-belly gunfight, and these men were lacking.

The two posse members realized that Colonel O'Brien and the rest of his men might be willing to die for a cause, saving the life of the boss's son. But Wilson and Forbes were not willing to die for a ten-dollar posse fee.

The two men eased back, putting distance between themselves, the guns, and Ironside's death glare.

One of the posse members, a grizzled old-timer with mean eyes, spat a stream of tobacco juice over the side of his horse and said to the man beside him, "This ain't goin' too good." Then he called to Wentworth, "Hey, Jimmy, are we gonna fight or just sit here pissin' our pants?"

But Wentworth wasn't listening. He'd dug himself a hole and didn't know how to get out of it. He'd believed that the men he'd brought with him would intimidate Shamus O'Brien. Now he realized that none of the Dromore hard cases, including the colonel, intimidated worth a damn. Worse, he knew that most of the rabble he'd hired would not stand.

Ironside eyed the man, and his voice sounded like a threat made in a sepulcher. "No matter what happens, Wentworth, you get it first." He smiled. "I never did cotton to that rotgut you sell as whiskey."

Shamus, never a man to hang back and let things happen, hobbled forward on his crutches and stopped when he and Wentworth were separated by inches.

Then he did something that brought grins to faces, including the faces of a few members of the posse. Balancing precariously on one crutch, Shamus used the other to scrape a circle in the dirt around Wentworth's feet.

"Wentworth," he said, "don't move out of that circle until you've ordered your men to retreat."

Without a shot being fired, Wentworth knew he was beaten.

Drawing the remains of his dignity around him like a ragged cloak, he said, "I'll be back, and there will be more of us."

"If they're the same stripe as the ones you got here, better bring a regiment," Shamus said. His eyes hardened. "Now, order the retreat and scat."

After Wentworth and his crestfallen bunch rode out, Samuel said to his father, "Suppose he'd moved out of the circle?"

Before the colonel could answer, Ironside said, "Then I would've shot him in the head and scattered his brains."

Samuel smiled. "Luther, sometimes you sound just like my brother Jacob."

"I should," Ironside said. "I taught that boy all he knows."

Chapter Twenty-six

"They're leaving," Lum said. "Riding away."

"Good," Dora DeClare said. "We don't want anyone else doing our job for us."

"Do you see the woman?" Shade Shannon said. "I want to see the woman."

"She's inside," Dora said. She smiled the smile that so often transformed her beautiful face into the evil caricature of a witch. "You'll see a lot of her soon enough."

Shannon giggled and Lum said, "Share and share alike, remember."

"Even you two won't be able to wear out what she's got," Dora said. Her hand flew to her suddenly hot cheek. "Oh, how unladylike," she said. "I can't believe I said such a thing."

"You should know about wearing it out, eh, Dora?" Lum leered.

And the woman blushed prettily again and fluttered her long lashes.

Dora, Lum, and Shannon lay on the edge of Glorieta Mesa, hidden by rocks and a few wind-twisted junipers. Joshua had been tied to his horse for the journey from El Cerrito. But now he sat in a small meadow a mile west of the Pecos with Luke Caldwell and waited while the others spied on Dromore.

Dora DeClare, dressed for the trail, wore a man's hat, a white, tight-fitted shirt, and a split canvas riding skirt. A pair of English-made riding boots encased her lovely legs.

"I think we've seen enough," she said. "Josh will be pining for me."

Lum rolled on one elbow and said, "How do we play it, Dora? I counted eleven men down there who couldn't get inside Dromore."

"Leave that to me," the woman said. "I'll find a way."

"When we get Lorena O'Brien," Shannon said, "how long do we play with her?"

"For as long as it takes, Shade. I want her to be a raving lunatic after you and Lum are finished with her."

"Caldwell might want a taste," Lum said.

Dora smiled. "What's the old saying? Ah, yes, of course, 'the more the merrier.'"

"What did it look like to you, Shade?" Dora said. She and her brother sat beneath a leafy tree, Joshua small, pale, and frail as a bisque sailor doll.

"Looked like a posse to me," Shannon said. He'd only been half-listening, looking at Dora, remembering her naked body in the casa at El Cerrito.

"Why wasn't the sheriff, what's his name?"

"John Moore," Joshua supplied.

"Why wasn't he leading it?"

"I don't know," Shannon said. He wore dark glasses against the sun glare. "Maybe he's dead. There was blood in the barn."

"With or without Moore, why was a posse at Dromore in the first place?" Dora said.

"Don't know that, either," Shannon said.

"Maybe we should find out," Caldwell said. He stood tall and rangy by the fire, a tin cup of coffee in his hand. "Could be there was something or somebody in the house they wanted real bad."

Dora thought about that. Around her crickets sawed fiddle tunes in the grass, mockingbirds sang, and jays quarreled in the juniper and wild oak trees. The high sun scorched the sky and the day was hot.

"There are forces gathering against us, powerful forces," Dora said. "That was revealed to me in a vision. The damned monk that chased us out of El Cerrito is a part of those forces."

"Dora, you should've let me gun the gospel-grinding SOB," Caldwell said.

"That would have been a mistake," Dora said. "I sensed that he was protected, and he might have called destruction down on us."

"Hell, he was a hick Mexican monk," Caldwell

said. "A bullet in the belly would've dropped him like any other man."

Dora shook her head, her corn silk hair tangled with sunlight. "I couldn't take the chance, Luke. Not while my father frets in hell because he is still unavenged."

"My sister is right, Luke, we can't take any chances until Dromore lies in ruin," Joshua said.

Caldwell shrugged. "You pay my wages, so you call the shots."

"Shade," Dora said, "ride into Georgetown and find out what you can about the posse and why it was at Dromore. If John Moore is dead, then that is one enemy less. If he's not, then perhaps you can question him and then get rid of him. But be discreet."

Shannon smiled. "When I get back will you get naked again and lie on a table, Dora? Can we do some more of that there worshipping, huh?"

Dora's anger rose. "Shade, that is not an act of worship, it's a sacrifice, and my maidenly modesty is the victim. After the sacrifice comes the worship. Remember that."

"Oh, never fear, Dora, I will," Shannon said, grinning. A trickle of saliva ran from the corner of his wet mouth.

"Now listen to me," Dora said. "I suppose Patrick O'Brien is hanged by now. If he's not, ask around and find out why. It could be that his father used his money and influence and saved his son from the gallows. But I suspect that's not the case. Get the truth of it. And ask about the posse we saw. I feel that might very well concern Patrick O'Brien."

"You can count on me, Dora," Shannon said. "I'll get to the bottom of all this."

"Be back here no later than sundown tomorrow, you hear?" Dora said.

"And if there are any O'Briens in town, stay clear of them," Caldwell said.

"Those damned micks don't scare me," Shannon said.

Caldwell smiled. "Yeah? So how come you ran a hundred miles from one of them not too long ago?"

"You've got a big mouth, Caldwell," Shannon said. "One day somebody's going to shut it for keeps."

"You want to be the one to shut it?" the gunfighter said.

Shannon thought about it, his hand close to his gun.

"Shuck it, Shade," Caldwell said, standing relaxed and easy. "Find out what a bullet in the belly feels like."

Suddenly Shannon wanted no part of this. He turned to Dora, his voice rising to a whine. "Caldwell is threatening me," he said.

"Luke, back off," Dora said. "There are few enough of us as it is. We can't afford to lose anybody."

"Especially an officer and a gentleman," Lum said. He hid a grin behind the palm of his hand.

"Ignore them, Shade," Dora said. "Now ride out and do what I told you to do."

"Everybody hates me," Shannon said, dashing a tear from his eye, "and it's not my fault."

He spun on his heel and walked toward his horse.

Behind him Luke Caldwell shook his head. He very much wanted Shannon to bump into an O'Brien in Georgetown, preferably Jacob.

He smiled. Now that was something he'd pay admission to see.

Chapter Twenty-seven

"I'm sorry to see you so low, John," Jacob O'Brien said.

"How did you know where to find me?" Moore said.

"The sheriff riding into town with a bullet in him attracts a lot of attention, even in a burg like this," Jacob said.

"The whores are taking good care of me," Moore said.

Jacob looked around the frilly pink and white room that smelled of lavender water and said, "I'm sure they are."

"Damned butcher that calls himself a doctor near killed me taking the bullet out," Moore said. "That's why Thistledown brought me here. He said I needed round-the-clock care." With a dramatic flair Jacob didn't know the man possessed, Moore laid the back of his hand on his forehead and whispered, "I'm just so weak and fevered."

Jacob grinned. "John, you're a damned liar. You're as strong as an ox, and it's plain to see you're faking it."

Moore raised a hand in alarm. "Shh . . . Jacob, somebody might hear you. The Vigilance Committee is paying for this, you know. I can stretch it into a week, maybe two."

Jacob sat on the bed, took a bottle of bourbon from the side table, and studied the label. "Old Fitzgerald," he said. "They are treating you well." He poured himself a drink and raised the glass. "Your good health, John."

"Don't say that too loud, Jake," Moore said. "And go easy on the whiskey. That bottle's got to last until tomorrow. The whores ration me." He tried to smile. "Bless their hearts."

"Tell me about the posse that challenged the colonel this morning," Jacob said.

"You heard about that, huh?"

"How could I not? The whole town's talking about it."

"They came back with their tails between their legs."

"So I understand. Anybody shot?"

"Not a one. The colonel ran them off, and that was that." Moore punched his embroidered pillows into shape and sat up. "Wentworth wants to bring in the army, but I don't know if and when that'll happen. The soldiers are still trying to round up a few bronco Apaches, and that might keep them busy for a spell."

"You were in El Cerrito," Jacob said. "So were me and Shawn. We spoke to a Mexican kid named Pedro, and he told us about the monk."

Moore's expression changed. He looked confused, like a schoolboy who doesn't know the answer to a question.

"Jake, I'm not a man who believes in ghosts and ha'ants an' sich, but that whole business was mighty strange," he said.

"You and Thistledown met up in El Cerrito while you were both hunting that Lum character," Jacob said.

"Well, that ain't exactly how it come up, Jake," Moore said. "You might say Thistledown saved my life."

Moore told how he'd been captured and how the little bounty hunter saved him. He described the Mad Hatter's picnic, and then said, "And you know what I saw through a back window before they put my lights out and dragged me into the barn?"

The sheriff glanced around, as though he suspected there was a spy in the room. He leaned closer to Jacob and whispered into his ear, a cupped hand to his mouth. When he finished talking, he said, "So what do you make of that?"

Jacob shook his head. "John, that takes a heap of figuring. And that thing about the upside-down cross is mighty strange."

"Told you it was," Moore said. "But it got stranger

when the monk showed up; called himself Brother Benedict."

Moore described how the monk had led them out of the barn, holding on to a huge crucifix.

"Not a shot fired at us, even from Luke Caldwell, and he's a shootin' fool. And the scream Dora De-Clare let out"—the sheriff's eyes were haunted—"Jake, I never heard anything like that in my life. She's a pretty little blond gal, Dora is, but she sounded like a wild animal. No, louder than that. Hell, she sounded like a whole pack o' wild animals, and different kinds at that."

"You sure that was her on the table?" Jacob said.

"I don't mistake something like that. It was Dora all right, and she was naked as a jaybird."

Jacob poured whiskey for himself and Moore, and then he said, "I can't figure it. Lum, Shade Shannon, and Luke Caldwell, all gathered in that house, I mean. It's strange."

"Damn strange if you ask me," Moore said.

"John, did you hear anyone call Dora by the name Nemesis?"

"No, never did," Moore said. "What is it, a fancy back-east name?"

Jacob didn't feel like pursuing a dead end. "Yeah," he said, "something like that."

"They called her Dora," Moore said. "Just plain Dora."

"What happened to the monk?" Jacob said.

"He took us to Thistledown's buggy. You know that they call him the Buggy Bount—"

"I know what they call him, John. What about the monk?"

Moore spread his hands and shrugged. "Damned if I know. He just walked away and vanished into the dark."

"And Thistledown?"

"No idea. Out hunting Lum again, I guess."

The door opened and a woman walked inside, wearing a robe, a smile, and nothing else. "Visiting time is over," she said. "Sheriff Moore must rest now."

"I'm very tired, Trixie," Moore said in a weak voice.

"Yes, I know you are, poor thing," Trixie said. She rounded on Jacob. "Out! Out! Do you see what you've done? The sheriff is overtired."

"Yes, I am, Trixie, overtired," Moore said. "Even lying here all shot to pieces, people still come to me with their little problems."

"Later I'll bathe you, Sheriff," Trixie said. "And then get you something light to eat."

"Yes," Moore said, "maybe a steak and half a dozen fried eggs." He moaned. "That's all I can face today."

Trixie plumped Moore's pillows. "You rest now. I'll look in later, between my gentlemen callers."

Jacob rose to his feet. "I hope you feel better soon, John," he said. "You've been through a terrible ordeal."

"He's very brave, isn't he?" Trixie said, beaming at the stricken lawman.

"Oh, yes he is," Jacob said. "Makes a man proud just to shake his hand."

"We must leave him now," Trixie said.

Weakly, Moore said, "You can stay, Trixie. I get so lonely when you're not here."

The woman smiled at Jacob. "Perhaps you'd better leave now."

"Yes, I will. But if the end comes suddenly," Jacob said, "you'll let me know."

"Of course," Trixie said.

"Good-bye, old friend," Jacob said. He sniffed and pretended to wipe a tear from his cheek. "If we don't meet again in this world, wait for me in the next."

"Jake," Moore said after a weak little cough, "leave me now—and don't let the door hit you on the ass."

Jacob asked around town, but no one had seen Dora DeClare and her crippled brother. He decided to stay in Georgetown overnight and checked into the hotel. After dinner, he stepped into the Lucky Seven saloon for coffee and brandy, determined to spend the money he'd borrowed from Shawn, even at the cost of a lecture on fiscal responsibility from his younger brother.

There were only a half-dozen men in the saloon, and a tired and disinterested ten-cents-a-dance girl who glanced once at Jacob and dismissed him.

The girl showed more interest when he proved he had the wherewithal to buy a Hennessy and coffee. After Jacob sat at a table she joined him.

"Passing through, cowboy?" she said.

"Seems like," Jacob said.

"Like to dance?" the girl asked. "We don't have a piano player tonight, but if you name a song I know, I'll sing it."

"Now my brother Shawn can cut a dash at a cotillion and dance real fancy," Jacob said. "But I've got two left feet."

"Mister, everybody I dance with in here has two left feet." The girl took off a high-heeled shoe and wiggled her toes. "Get a load of them."

Jacob smiled. "Looks like every one of them has been broken at one time or another."

The girl slipped on her shoe again. "Every one of them has been broke at least twice at one time or another."

"I can buy you a drink, if you want," Jacob said. "I'm spending borrowed money."

"The best kind," the girl said. She turned in her chair and yelled to the bartender, "Hey, Lou, fix me a rum punch, will ya?"

Jacob waited until the girl had her drink and then said, "How long have you lived in Georgetown?"

"Too long, if you consider this living." The girl smiled. "All right, two years come the fall."

Jacob took the makings out of his shirt pocket,

and the girl took them from him. "Never met a man yet who could roll a smoke tidy."

She built the cigarette, held it out to Jacob to lick, and then handed it to him. "See how neat that is?"

"You've done that before," Jacob said, smiling.

"Only about ten thousand times. My name's Sarah, by the way, Sarah Elizabeth Walker."

Jacob lit the cigarette, then said, "All right, then Sarah it is. Tell me, Sarah, you ever hear of a gal by the name of Dora DeClare?"

"Sure, until recently she used to come into town now and again; had a crippled brother, I recollect," the girl said. "She came across as a real lady, pretty as a picture and always dressed nice. But I heard that her pa got hung for a cattle rustler when she was just a kid, so who knows, huh? You can't judge a book by its cover, I guess."

"Who hung her pa?" Jacob said, straining forward in his chair.

"I don't know, some rancher probably. Ranchers don't take kindly to folks who lift their cattle." She smiled. "Hell, you're a puncher, you know all about that."

Jacob nodded. "I guess I do. I've seen a few men hung. Never liked to watch it, though." He waited until Sarah sipped her drink, then said, "You ever hear that DeClare gal call herself Nemesis?"

Sarah looked surprised. "No, I never did. What kind of name is that?"

Jacob shrugged. "French, maybe."

"All I ever heard her called was Dora or Miss DeClare," Sarah said. "I don't recollect that anybody called her . . . what was that name?"

"Forget it," Jacob said. "It doesn't matter."

"What happened to her, that gal?" Sarah said. "Her brother kept right poorly, I remember that."

"She's around," Jacob said. "Travels a lot."

"What I said about her pa being hung," Sarah said, "I don't know that for sure. But it was the gossip around town. Seems that some old-timer, who's dead now, remembered the hanging; said the pa died real hard, cussin' God." Sarah shivered. "Can you imagine that, cussin' our Maker with your last gasping breath?"

"Hard to believe," Jacob said, shaking his head. "You sure the old-timer didn't say who hung DeClare?"

Sarah shook her head. She wore lilac eye shadow that Jacob thought looked real nice. "I don't know if he did or not," she said. "It was quite a while ago."

"People forget things," Jacob said.

"When it's not family," Sarah said.

"Yeah, I can see that," Jacob said.

"But if it really was Dora's pa who got hung, she won't forget."

"No, I guess not," Jacob said.

The saloon door swung open, and a man strode inside, arrogant enough to grin a challenge and occupy more space than he needed.

And Jacob knew right there and then that he would kill him.

Chapter Twenty-eight

Shade Shannon looked around the saloon, and then his white eyes met Jacob's. Held, clashed, panicked. "O'Brien, by God!" he yelled.

Shannon turned and made a dash for the door. Jacob drew, fired, and heard a yelp of pain as the man charged outside.

"Down!" Jacob yelled. He grabbed Sarah and dragged her to the floor.

Three shots in rapid succession slammed into the saloon, splintering wood. One hit an oil lamp that fell to the floor, spread its fuel, and burned with a blue flame.

Jacob got to his feet, aware of the bartender swatting at the flames with a corn broom, yelling at the girl to get the hell out of the way. When Jacob rushed outside, Shannon was already mounted, flapping his chaps as he galloped south out of town. Jacob stepped into the middle of the street and cut loose. He thumbed off three fast shots at the fleeing rider, but as far as he could tell, none took effect.

Feet thudded on the boardwalks, and men raised their voices and demanded to know what was going on. James Wentworth, breathless, a supper napkin tucked under his chin, skidded to a halt beside Jacob and said, "O'Brien, what the hell's all the commotion?"

Jacob nodded at the dust that still clouded the street. "Firing at a skunk," he said.

"Damn it, man, what skunk?" Wentworth said. "There are plenty of them in this town."

"A skunk by the name of Shade Shannon," Jacob said, thumbing fresh shells into his Colt.

"He's wanted for murder," Wentworth said.

"He is that," Jacob said.

"Hey, Mr. Wentworth!" a man yelled from the settling dust, "Lookee here!"

Jacob holstered his revolver and walked to the man, and Wentworth followed.

"Blood," the man said, pointing at his feet. "A lot of it." He motioned in the direction where Shannon had disappeared. "It goes quite a ways."

"Well, O'Brien, you winged him at least," Wentworth said.

"Seems like."

Wentworth watched his bartender pound a flaming broom on the boardwalk. "Lou," he yelled, "did the savage set my place on fire?"

"It's out, boss," Lou called back. "No damage done." He stomped on the still burning broom, gave up, threw it into the street, and went back inside.

Wentworth turned and stared down the street, his mind working.

"Don't even think about it, Wentworth, unless you got a full-blood Apache handy," Jacob said. "With those white eyes of his, Shannon can see in the dark. I've taken that trail before."

"Then we'll wait until sunup and go after him," Wentworth said. "He can't shoot up my saloon and get away with it. By God, I'll hang him myself."

Jacob remembered what Moore had told him about Wentworth's last attempt at a hemp posse, but he figured it would be ungracious to mention it.

"O'Brien, I'll need you to write a report of the incident, including the parties involved, times, locations, number of shots fired and at whom, et cetera," Wentworth said. He pulled his napkin away from his neck, as though he'd just now remembered it. "Triplicate will be fine."

"Sure thing," Jacob said without the slightest intention of writing a word.

"And you'll join the posse, of course. Ten dollars a day and grub is the committee rate."

"Of course," Jacob said. He had no intention of doing that, either.

Suddenly the man's eyes hardened. "I don't know if you've heard yet, but your father defied a lawful posse in the pursuit of a condemned criminal, and now there will be repercussions, serious repercussions."

"Yeah, I heard," Jacob said.

"You were not present when this, ah, act of defiance took place, so I'm absolving you of blame."

"Wentworth, that's true blue," Jacob said.

"When the army gets involved it will become a federal matter, and I intend to play hob," the man said. "You understand?"

"You've laid it out."

"Good. I just wanted you to know and to advise you to stay away from what's coming down."

Jacob nodded. "I'll surely consider what you've said."

"Well, see that you do. There's no reason for us to become enemies." Wentworth tried a smile that faded instantly. "Until tomorrow then. The posse mounts at first light."

"Yeah," Jacob said, "until when."

If Wentworth heard that last, he didn't let it show.

Jacob O'Brien stood in the middle of the suddenly empty street and pondered his next move. Shawn was a good tracker, but Shawn wasn't here. One thing Jacob didn't want to do was join Wentworth's posse. He and his rubes would wander around in ever-diminishing circles until they rode up their own horses' rears.

Jacob nodded to himself. All right, there was only himself. He had it to do.

He decided not to cancel his room at the hotel. Desk clerks were notorious spies, and word could quickly get back to Wentworth that he was leaving town.

Instead, Jacob walked to the livery and saddled his horse. He was about to step into the leather when a voice stopped him.

"Mister," Sarah said, "take me with you."

Jacob turned his head and smiled. "Kinda sudden, isn't it?"

"I think you're my only hope," Sarah said. "My last hope."

The girl wore a threadbare gray coat over her dress, a black hat with dusty imitation flowers above the turned-up brim, and she held a carpetbag in her right hand.

Jacob's smile grew into a grin. "Hell, lady, why me?"

"You saved my life in the saloon, and you were very brave," Sarah said. "I admire that in a man."

"I didn't save your life," Jacob said. "None of Shade Shannon's bullets even came close to you."

"But they could've done, so you saved my life."

Jacob figured there was some kind of female logic at play, and he let it go. "I'm going after Shannon," he said. "He's a killer, and you could get yourself shot."

"Mister—I don't even know your name—there are worse things than getting shot," Sarah said.

"Staying in Georgetown and getting pawed by every drunk who has ten cents is one of them."

"The name's Jacob."

The girl dropped the carpetbag and opened her arms. "Look at me, Jacob. How old do you think I am?"

"I can't judge women's ages, Sarah," Jacob said, caught flat-footed. "I'm no good at it." The girl was looking right through him. "All right, about thirty," he said, taking five years off what he really thought.

"I'm twenty-two," Sarah said. "I started whoring when I was thirteen, and I've been dancing for the past two years." She picked up her bag again. "You know, I tried to sign on with the cathouse down the street, but they threw me out. You know what the madam said?"

"Sarah, I—" Jacob began, floundering.

"She said I looked too worn out, too used up, and that her gentlemen wouldn't like that. She said maybe I could find a hog farm someplace that would take me, or a soldiers' brothel near one of the army posts."

Sarah smiled. "So that's my tale of woe, Jacob. Now do you pity me enough that I can tag along with you for a spell?"

"Sarah," Jacob said, "I'm a wandering man, and my life is hard and violent. I can't be slowed by a woman."

"You're Jacob O'Brien of Dromore ranch," Sarah said. "The bartender told me so."

"I'm the black sheep," Jacob said. "I go my own way, and it's not a way for a woman."

"Even a whore?"

"For a woman, Sarah. Any woman."

The girl nodded. "I understand." She turned and headed toward the livery door, a small girl, very thin, walking on broken toes.

"Wait," Jacob said, cussing his own weakness. "I'll take you with me until I figure there's enough git between you and this town. Then we part ways. How does that set with you?"

"It's better than nothing," Sarah said.

"Yes, it is," Jacob said. He swung into the saddle. "Climb up behind me and don't jibber-jabber," he said. "If there's one thing I can't abide it's a jibber-jabbering female."

Chapter Twenty-nine

There were three of them, Warm Springs Apaches who'd once been part of old Nana's band, and they'd been hunted like animals since the shaman Geronimo's surrender at Skeleton Canyon ten months before.

Before the winter came, the warriors had traveled north with two women and four children. One of the women was killed after she fell from a canyon wall two hundred miles to the south, and the others had died of starvation during the December blizzards.

The three Apaches were tired and hungry, their anger and hatred against the white man burning inside them like a disease.

They'd tracked the wounded man's blood trail from near the white settlement, almost all the way west to the summer-dry Pecos. Now, their black eyes glittering, they watched him.

Biding their time . . .

* * *

Shade Shannon knew he was hit hard. He was carrying Jacob O'Brien's lead in his right thigh, and the pain was a living thing that gnawed at him with teeth.

Once he crossed the Pecos he'd swing north toward Glorieta Mesa and Dora. She would take care of him, tend to him, kiss his wound, and tell him about all the wonderful things, female things, that lay in store for him.

Moonlight slanted through the pines, and a cool breeze fanned Shannon's cheeks. His eyes, white as milk, searched the trail ahead, anxious as he was for his first glimpse of the river.

Despite his pain, the rocking motion of his horse and the silken quiet of the evening lulled Shade Shannon into a drowsy twilight between wakefulness and sleep. He remembered nights like this when he wore yellow officer's straps on his shoulders, drinking coffee by the campfire after the day's patrol, listening to the night birds, smelling . . .

Shannon's head snapped up, and he stifled the scream that sprang to his lips. An odor came to him on the wind, a smell like no other, as distinctive and unique as that of the wolf—the feral, musky scent of the Apache warrior.

His mouth wide open in a soundless shriek, Shannon raked spurs along his horse's flanks. The startled animal kicked into a fast gallop, heedlessly crashing through pine branches that lashed at

Shannon's face. Terrified, his eyes as round and white as the moon that hovered above him, he heard the Apaches behind him, their nimble little ponies coming closer.

Shannon squealed in fear and drew his revolver. He thumbed shots into the menacing darkness. Momentarily blinded by muzzle flash, he never saw the tree limb that swept him from the saddle.

Winded, Shannon lay on his back, his revolver still in his hand. He twisted his head back and forth, searching for a target, his shrieks now giving way to a whimper.

Shannon had seen what Apaches can do to a man, and visions seared, flashing into his memory . . . the blood, the guts, the open mouths, the agonized screams echoing through eternity. He remembered men who'd taken way too long to die.

Babbling his fear, talking nonsense to dead soldiers only he could see, Shannon raised his gun to his temple. The Colt was kicked out of his hand roughly, and then he saw a flat, brown face close to his, the eyes as black and emotionless as an obsidian knife blade.

"Dora!" Shannon screamed. "Help me!"

He felt hands on his, and he was dragged, shrieking, into shadow.

"Jacob! My God, what is that?"

"A bobcat," Jacob said. "Just a bobcat."

"No, it's not," Sarah said. "It's a man, a man in pain."

Jacob drew rein. "We'll rest up here," he said. "Over there among the pines."

"He needs help," Sarah said. "Maybe he's broken a leg or something."

"That man is beyond help," Jacob said. "There's nothing we can do for him."

He threw his leg over the saddle horn and dismounted. Then he helped the girl to the ground. "I've got a pint of good rye in my saddlebag," he said. "I'd say this is an excellent time to share it."

The agonized cry of a man in mortal agony shattered apart the crystal night, followed by another and another. The serene moon glowed in the sky, and an uncaring breeze played among the trees.

Sarah put her hands to her ears. "I can't bear to hear it," she said. "Jacob, help him."

Jacob grabbed the girl by the arm and then led both her and his horse into the sheltering pines. He forced Sarah to sit at the base of a tree, took the rye from his saddlebags, and put the bottle to her mouth. "Drink deep," he said.

The girl shook her head, avoiding the bottle.

Jacob said, "Damn you, drink."

Sarah violently shook her head. "I don't want to drink! I don't want to hear that man scream! Why won't you help him?" She covered her ears again, rocked her head back and forth, and wailed, "Make it stop! Make it stop!"

Jacob slapped her then, his big, work-hardened

hand slamming into the side of Sarah's head. The girl cried out and fell to her right, but Jacob grabbed her and pulled her face close to his, staring into her unfocused eyes.

"It's Apaches, do you understand?" he said. "They're working on the man you saw at the saloon."

The left side of the girl's face was already showing bruises, but her eyes were quieter, less hysterical. "Apaches?"

"Yeah, and do you know what they'll do to you if they find us?" Jacob said.

Sarah startled to struggle, and Jacob laid it out for her. "You'll meet your Maker missing your tits, and maybe more."

Shannon's frantic screams were coming very close together now, and in the distance Jacob saw the glow of a fire in the tree canopy.

The girl lifted her bruised face to Jacob. Tears ran down her cheeks, mixed with streaks of lilac, the eye shadow that Jacob had thought so appealing earlier. "Give me the damned whiskey," she said.

Jacob handed Sarah the bottle, and she took a long swig. She handed the whiskey back and Jacob did the same.

The girl laid her head against the pine trunk and whispered, "Oh, God, please make it stop." She was calmer now, all too aware of what Apaches did to women captives.

But it didn't stop. Shannon screamed, by Jacob's

estimate, for six hours, until the long, venomous night shaded into a bright morning.

Somehow Sarah had managed to sleep, helped by a combination of rye whiskey and Jacob's slap. When he shook the girl awake and daylight revealed just how bruised her face was, he cursed himself for a violent, woman-beating brute.

"I'm going to take a look-see," he told the girl. "If you hear shooting and I don't come hightailing it back here, point my horse south and don't stop riding until you reach Georgetown."

Sarah nodded, and Jacob said, "Sorry about your face. I didn't mean to hit you that hard."

After her fingertips strayed to her cheek and she winced, the girl said, "Men have hit me harder."

"I don't go around striking women," Jacob said. "Or children, old people, or animals."

"Yes, I'm sure you don't," Sarah said.

"I mean, really I don't."

"Then I'll take your word for it."

Sarah touched her cheek again and winced for a second time, only her grimace of pain was more pronounced.

"Damn it, Sarah," Jacob said, "I've never hit a woman in my life. But you were hysterical and Apaches were out there, and maybe they're still around. I had to do something pretty damn quick."

"So you say, Jacob."

"You don't believe me?"

"I don't know what to believe, do I?"

Jacob groaned. "I'll never do anything like that to you or any other woman again."

"So you say, Jacob."

"I promise you, I won't."

"So you—"

"Damn it, Sarah, stop repeating that 'so you say' stuff," Jacob said.

"And if I don't, what will you do? Haul off and beat me again?"

Jacob recalled the only two pieces of advice he'd gotten from Luther Ironside that ever stuck with him. The first was, "Don't joke with cooks or mules, as they have no sense of humor." The second, and now he realized the most important, was, "Boy, there's two theories to arguin' with a woman, and neither one works worth a damn."

"Well, like I said, I'm going to take a look, make sure the Apaches are gone," Jacob said. He smiled sympathetically, he hoped. "You just rest there a spell."

"I'll try," Sarah said. "It's difficult for a woman to rest when she's in pain from a beating."

Jacob bit his tongue. But he managed to say, "Remember what I told you. If I'm not back within an hour, or if you hear shooting that ends with Apaches hollering, get on the horse and ride."

"I'll try," Sarah said.

Figuring that a woman who nurses her wrath to keep it warm was worse than Apaches any day of the week, Jacob drew his gun and stepped into the trees.

Shade Shannon had died hard. He hung by his ankles from the limb of a wild oak, his head inches above the ashy embers of a small fire. All his hair had burned away, as had his eyes, and at some point near the end, his skull had split and his brains had spilled out.

Jacob knew the man was a vicious animal who needed killing, but even a ruthless monster didn't deserve to die like this. His death had been painful and long in coming.

The Apaches were gone, and Jacob holstered his Colt and wondered what a man thinks when he's dying like that. Does he think only of the pain and nothing else, or does his mind go back to the events of his life—at least until his head cracks open and he hears his brains sizzle?

He had no way of knowing, and he never wanted to find out from firsthand experience.

Jacob took out his Barlow and cut the man down. He left him where he lay. The coyotes would find him soon enough.

Chapter Thirty

"Shade's not coming back," Dora DeClare said. "Something's happened to him."

"I suspect an O'Brien brother happened to him," Luke Caldwell said.

Lum spat. "He wasn't much. Who the hell cares?"

"I do," Dora said. "Now there are only four of us to get the job done."

Lum grinned and waved a hand toward Joshua DeClare. "Three and a half, if you're counting him."

The Colt New House .38 appeared like a striking snake from under the blanket that covered DeClare's legs. "You want me to make it two and a half, Lum?" he said, the belly gun pointing at the big man's head.

If Lum was intimidated, he didn't show it. "Suppose I shove that itty-bitty up your crippled ass and pull the trigger?" he said.

"Stop that at once," Dora said, stepping between

the two men. "We're all on edge, but we need to put our plan in motion. We can assume that Patrick O'Brien was hung and that his father now grieves for him, so part of my revenge is complete. Now it's time to rub salt into the colonel's wounds, and that means we must get hold of Lorena O'Brien."

Joshua DeClare put the pocket revolver away. "How do we play it, Dora?"

"We'll keep watch on Dromore for the next few days and see if the woman ever rides out alone," Dora said.

"And if she doesn't?" Caldwell said. He reached for the coffeepot.

"If she doesn't," Dora said, "well . . . watch this!"

Dora made a play of limping, then knocking on a door.

"Oh, kind sir," she said, making a little curtsy, her forefinger under her chin, "my horse threw me on the trail and I'm quite undone." She fluttered her eyelashes, and the men present laughed. "I fear I am badly bruised in places I can only show another lady. Is there a lady within?"

Dora pretended to drink tea. "Oh, my dear Mrs. O'Brien, I am but a young convent girl and not accustomed to the rough company of men."

This drew another laugh.

"So, could you please help me find my horse, dear, dear Mrs. O'Brien, pretty please?"

The men applauded, and Dora made another curtsy.

"Dora, do you think it will work?" her brother said.

"It's got to work," Dora said. "I'll make it work."

"I think it's inspired," Lum said. "A plan worthy of the master we serve."

Dora smiled. "Yes, I think our prince likes it. I can feel his hands on me, telling me he does." She looked at Lum. "Once I get the O'Brien woman alone, I'll hand her over to you, Lum. I want her so that she'll never again bear the touch of a man. Rape her until she screams for mercy, then rape her some more."

The woman pointed in the direction of Dromore. "From then forth, there will be a pall over the damned O'Brien house that will never lift. The colonel will sup sorrow with the spoon of grief, and then and only then will he feel the full measure of my own lamentation."

Dora smiled and clicked the fingers of her right hand. "Here's a wonderful thought. Our prince has just added to my plan and made it foolproof. All praise to our dark master!"

"All praise," Lum and Joshua said in unison. Caldwell smiled but said nothing, drinking his coffee, enjoying the fresh smell of the morning.

"Luke," Dora said, "you will give me your knife when I go to call on dear Mrs. O'Brien."

"You gonna stick her?" Caldwell said.

"Only if my initial plan fails," Dora said. "But think of it, brothers, if the bitch prefers to be a stay-at-home, I will pull my knife and gut her son, the dear, baby boy I was so anxious to see!" Dora raised her arms and tilted back her head. "All praise to our prince!" she yelled.

"All praise to our prince," Lum and Joshua repeated.

"Dora, they'll gun you for sure," Caldwell said.

"So?" Dora said. "Then all that happens is that my soul flies to hell and I join my father and my master." She kneeled at her brother's wheelchair. "Joshua, which is the more exquisite, to gut the son and let the mother live, or gut them both?" She smiled. "Now, out with it, I depend on your advice."

"Just the son," Joshua said. "I think it will destroy the mother and kill the colonel with grief."

Dora sprang to her feet, laughing. "Then that is how it will be."

"But releasing the woman to me is still our first choice, is it not?" Lum said.

"Of course," Dora said. "Having you rape the O'Brien wench until she goes out of her mind is still the most exquisite and, I must say, most wonderful plan of all."

Joshua DeClare grinned. "Then let's open the ball, sister. Who takes the first watch?"

"Luke, you will," Dora said. "Lum will relieve you in four hours. Now, be careful you're not seen, and take plenty of water with you. I'll have a pot of bacon and beans simmering on the fire all day. Big, strong men like you and Lum do get hungry."

"If I see Lorena O'Brien riding out, do I fog it back here or grab her myself?" Caldwell said.

"Come back for Lum," Dora said. "I want to be sure we capture her. If we don't, we won't get a second chance."

"Then we move on to your little lady in distress plan, huh?" Lum said.

"Yes. But I'd rather get my hands on the woman and take her into the mountains where she'll never be found. That is, until I want her found."

Lum's voice softened and his eyes hazed, like a man about to recall a fond memory from his schooldays. "We could send her back skun," he said. "One time up on the Barbary Coast I skun a Chinese whore who sassed me, strung her up from a roof beam and went at her with a razor. She never sassed anybody else again, I tell you that."

A silence descended on the group, and Dora's smile froze into a grimace. Caldwell just stared at Lum, his coffee cup halfway to his mouth, and Joshua looked even sicker than he already was.

"Lookit," Lum said, a man with all the sensitivity of a grave robber. He dug in his pocket and held up a small brown pouch, closed with a piece of blue silk ribbon. "This is one of her tits and a ribbon from her hair. I'm not a smoking man, but I made me a tobacco pouch of it, should I ever feel inclined to take up the habit."

Again, the big man's pronouncements were met with silence, and again he unheedingly stomped right over the stunned quiet. "I can slice up the O'Brien gal and make a tobaccy pouch for her husband," he said. Then, laughing, he added, "Wouldn't that be a kick in the ass?!" Lum looked around him, grinning. "Huh? Huh?"

"Yes, Lum," Dora said, "yes it would." She turned to Caldwell. "Luke, shouldn't you get on watch?"

The Texan nodded. "Yeah, I'm going. Just don't let that damned lunatic get behind me with a knife."

"It could happen, gunfighter, one of these days," Lum said, his face ugly.

"Then after you've made your brags, come at me straight on and true blue," Caldwell said.

Lum shook his head. "That's not my style, boy."

"Please, Luke," Dora said, "go on watch." She was very pale, her lips drained of color.

Caldwell hesitated, then said, "Dora, what are you going to do when this is over? I mean, how long has it been since Shamus O'Brien hung your pa?"

"Ten years ago this Christmas Eve," Dora said. "I was sixteen at the time."

"You've planned your revenge on the old colonel for so long, what will you do when he's dead and Dromore lies in ruins?" Caldwell said.

Joshua answered for his sister. "A gallery in London plans an exhibition of my landscapes next spring. We'll be there for opening night."

Dora raised her eyes to the tall gunman. "Does that answer your question?"

"I guess so," Caldwell said. He smiled. "Maybe I'll tag along. You might need my gun."

Joshua said, "I doubt if your kind would be

welcome in Europe, Caldwell. Texas gunfighters aren't needed in an art gallery."

"Too genteel for a man like me, huh?" Caldwell said.

"Exactly," Joshua said.

"But Satan worshippers like you and Dora are welcomed with open arms?"

"Let's just say that the Europeans, especially the English, appreciate the artistic temperament," Joshua said. "If a painter is talented, they'll overlook much."

"Hell," Caldwell said, "I don't want to go to London anyhow."

He turned on his heel and headed for his horse, and behind him, Joshua said, "Lum, you really will have to get rid of that lout one day."

"The pleasure will be all mine," Lum said.

Chapter Thirty-one

"You'll like Dromore, Sarah," Jacob O'Brien said. "It's a peaceful place. Well, most of the time. Right now my brother Patrick is in a heap o' trouble."

The girl leaned forward over the cantle of the saddle and said, "I met Patrick a few times when he came into the saloon, and I grew quite fond of him. He was kind and gentle with women, not like you."

Jacob didn't follow where Sarah was leading. Instead he said, "He was found guilty of raping and murdering Molly Holmes. It seems the Georgetown vigilantes are determined to see him hang."

"Patrick didn't kill Molly Holmes," Sarah said. "If you ask me her husband did it, crazy old Elijah. He was a woman-beater, too."

The "too" didn't go unnoticed by Jacob, but again he stepped lightly around Sarah's mantrap. "Elijah and two witnesses said they saw Patrick leaving the barn after Molly was killed," he said. "That was pretty damning evidence."

"I know, I heard them say that at the trial," the girl said. "The witnesses were a couple of raggedy-assed drifters who rode into town, then rode out again. I reckon somebody, maybe Elijah, paid them to say what they said because right after the trial they suddenly had double-eagles to spend."

"Could be," Jacob said. "But reckoning on a thing and proving it are different things."

The two rode in silence for a while through the forested high country south of Glorieta Mesa. The noon sun hung directly overhead, and dusty beams of light filtered among the pines and scattered stands of aspen. They paused briefly when a black bear got up on its hind legs and watched them pass, then shambled back into the trees.

Finally Jacob said, "Sarah, did you ever see Elijah Holmes talking with Dora DeClare?"

"No," the girl said. "I can't say it never happened, but I never saw them talk."

Jacob felt Sarah start behind him. "What was that?" she said.

"What?"

"I saw a flash of light on top of the mesa. It was there for just a second." She pointed. "Look, it's there again!"

"I see it," Jacob said.

"Is it the Apaches?" Sarah said.

"Maybe. They might be looking for a chance to steal horses or a couple of beeves."

"What was the flash, Jacob?"

"Sunlight on a gun barrel or the lens of a telescope," Jacob said. "Or Mexican silver jewelry hanging around an Apache buck's neck."

"What do we do?" Sarah said, a spike of fear in her voice.

Jacob slid his rifle from the boot and laid it across the saddle horn. "We ride careful and keep our eyes open," he said. "This is no place to tangle with Apaches."

"Jacob," Sarah said, hugging close to his back, "I'm scared."

"Hell, girl," Jacob said, "so am I."

The next couple of hours were tense as Jacob's eyes constantly searched the terrain around him, but he saw no sign of Apaches, and the ride to Dromore passed without incident.

Samuel stepped out of the house when Jacob rode in; Lorena followed behind him, baby Shamus in her arms.

"Welcome home, Jake," Samuel said. He looked beyond his brother to the girl and smiled. "What do you have there?"

As he leaned from the saddle and helped Sarah slide from the back of the horse, Jacob said, "This is Miss Sarah Elizabeth Walker, and right now she needs a job. I was kinda hoping you could find something for her at Dromore." He passed the girl her carpetbag.

"We always need help at Dromore," Samuel said. He stuck out his hand. "I'm Samuel O'Brien and that there is my wife, Lorena, and our son, Shamus."

Sarah dropped a little curtsy. "Right pleased to meet you, I'm sure," she said.

"Sarah, what happened to your face?" Lorena said.

"Jacob hit me," Sarah said.

"He did what?" Lorena said, very loud and tinged with outrage.

"Hit me, ma'am," Sarah said.

"Oh, you poor child," Lorena said. She passed the baby to her left arm and circled Sarah's thin shoulders with her right. "You come inside at once and let me attend to those bruises. And by the look of you, a little sherry would not go amiss."

Lorena glared at Jacob who still sat his horse, fearing to dismount onto female-held ground. "Jacob," she said, "how could you do such a thing?"

"Well, see, Lor—"

"Yes, explain yourself," Lorena said. "Explain, if you can, this . . . this . . . oh, it's so disgusting I can't even think of a word to describe it. Look! Just look at the wounds on this poor girl's face."

"There were Apaches, Lorena, and—"

"Come now, explain yourself!"

"Damn it, Lorena, I'm trying," Jacob said.

"Oh, when profanity enters into it, I don't want

to hear another word," Lorena said. "Sarah's bruises explain all, and in a singularly unpleasant manner, let me tell you."

Much moved by Lorena's words, Sarah began to sob as she was led to the house, and, as the women reached the door, two pairs of eyes turned on Jacob, raking him like talons.

Once the females had flounced inside, Jacob said to Samuel, "When I rode into Dromore today I was over six feet tall. Now I'm shrunk to about half that."

"Hell, why did you thump her?" Samuel said.

"There were Apaches about a hundred yards away, and a man was being tortured and she got hysterical and I had to stop her and—"

"You hauled off and socked her."

"Yeah. I did. I backhanded her. Too hard, I reckon."

"Well, it's one way to shut up a woman, I suppose."

"Flog me, flay me, but it was all I could come up with at the time," Jacob said.

"Who'd the Apaches get?" Samuel said.

"If you'd invite me inside and offer me a drink, maybe I'd tell you," Jacob said, testy as all hell and feeling more than a little trail worn.

Samuel grinned. "Step down, Jake, it's your house as much as mine."

Grumbling, muttering under his breath, Jacob let a Mexican boy take his horse, and he followed Samuel into the parlor.

* * *

"Be warned, Jake," Shawn said, "the colonel's real mad that you beat up on a woman."

"I didn't beat up on her, I hit her once," Jacob said. Then listening to himself, he groaned and buried his face in his hands.

"There were Apaches close by and the girl was hysterical," Samuel said. "It could be argued that Jake was justified."

"Could be argued!" Jacob said. "She was wailing and crying and she could've brought those bucks right down on top of us."

"He has a case," Shawn said, nodding. "There might have been justification."

Jacob's sharp retort died on his lips when the door opened and Shamus rolled inside, tall, grim Luther Ironside walking behind him.

The colonel nodded. "Jacob."

"Pa," Jacob said.

Shamus slowly, deliberately, and silently poured himself a drink, then he stared at the parlor's pink hearthstone and said, "There are people who believe that the foundation of this great house was a rock. It was not. The foundation of this house was a woman." He looked at Jacob. "That woman's name was Saraid, the Gaelic for Sarah, and she was my wife and your mother."

Jacob nodded. "That is true, Colonel."

As though he hadn't heard, Shamus said, "Imagine then, how I felt, when another Sarah came to my door today, showing all the signs of a vicious beating perpetrated by one of my sons."

Shawn pretended to cough as he suppressed a laugh. Samuel remained stone faced, like an ancient Roman procurator sitting in judgment.

Slowly, Shamus's head turned until he was looking at Jacob. "Explain yourself, boy," he said.

Again Jacob talked hysterics, Apaches, imminent danger, and, as he put it, "the slap heard round the whole territory."

After his son finished speaking, Shamus sat in silence for a while, gathering his thoughts. But Ironside said, "Damn it all, Jake, if you'd hit her where it doesn't show we wouldn't have this problem and Lorena wouldn't be demanding your head."

Jacob said, "Colonel, I'd say to Luther, 'I'll remember that the next time,' but I won't. I don't go around beating up on women, no matter what Lorena thinks."

"And Sarah thinks," Shamus said. "And remember, she's the innocent victim in this case."

"There is no 'case,' Pa, and there's no victim. I'm not on trial here," Jacob said. "If I hadn't shut her up, she'd be chewing buckskin in some Apache's wickiup by now, or worse, and I'd be hanging head down over a fire."

Shamus looked around the room. "Samuel, Shawn, what are your opinions on this matter?" he asked.

"Hell, guilty as charged," Shawn said, grinning. "A hundred lashes less one."

"Now tell me what you really think, Shawn, and without the profanity and levity this time," Shamus said, his face stern.

Chastened, Shawn said, "Sorry, Colonel. I reckon Jacob did what he had to do. He didn't have all day to think about it."

"Samuel?" Shawn said.

"I wasn't there, so I'm not going to judge," Samuel said. "Jacob did what he thought was necessary."

"Luther?" Shamus said.

The segundo grinned. "Jake did the right thing. That's how I taught him."

"You taught him," Shamus said, "a great many things, Luther, not all of them right or even decent. But I won't go into that now." He rolled his wheelchair to the window and looked outside at the shadow-slanted land. "Jacob, all agree that you did what was required of you at the time. I won't fault any man for that. The matter is now settled and forgotten."

Shamus turned his shaggy gray head and smiled, and in that moment he looked like an ancient Irish king who had just heard a minstrel who pleased him. "Go see your brother, Jacob," he said. "He's asking for you."

Jacob rose to his feet. "One thing, Colonel," he said, "When I was riding in I saw a flash on top of the mesa. It could be nothing, but after I visit with Patrick I'd like to take a ride up there and scout around."

"Apaches you think?" Shamus said.

"Maybe an Apache. Maybe somebody else."

"Luther, Shawn, you will go with Jacob," Shamus said. He thought for a moment, and added, "Take a couple of vaqueros with you. I don't like the idea of Apaches up there on the mesa pointing rifles at my front door."

Chapter Thirty-two

"So what did you think of Patrick?" Luther Ironside asked.

"He's looking a lot better, getting stronger," Jacob said.

"Lorena spoils him," Ironside said. "A man shouldn't be coddled like that."

Shawn laughed. "Luther, last time you had the rheumatisms, who sat in a chair all day while Lorena put mustard and brown paper plasters on your knees, and glasses of the colonel's best Irish whiskey in your hand?"

"That was different," Ironside sniffed, looking dignified. "A man of a certain maturity needs coddling now and then. Young whippersnappers like you don't."

Samuel drew rein and raised a hand. "Jacob, do you think this was the spot?"

"Looks like," Jacob said. "Except it was up there on the rim."

The switchback trail they'd taken was shielded from prying eyes by thick stands of ponderosa pine and juniper. A thunder sky misted iron gray on top of the mesa, and a few drops of rain gusted in a rising wind. The late afternoon shaded darker, and shadows pooled among trees that were already ticking raindrops.

Samuel pointed to a wall of rock that overhung a narrow, grassy ledge. "We'll leave the horses there and go on foot the rest of the way," he said.

Hunched against the rain that was now falling steadily, Shawn said, "Jake, are you sure you saw something up there?" He looked miserably through the tree canopy at the sky. "I still haven't forgotten your wild-goose chase to El Cerrito, or whatever that dung heap was called."

"I saw a flash, and that's all I saw," Jacob said.

"No matter," Samuel said, "we have to check it out."

He swung out of the saddle and led his horse to the ledge, and the others did the same, except for one young vaquero who held back, his mouth open as though he was gasping for air.

"Salazar, what ails you?" Ironside said.

The man shook his head. "I don't know. I can't breathe." His hand went to his throat. "Jesus, the air is foul."

"Juan, do you feel sick?" Samuel said.

The other vaquero answered for him. "Patron, Juan is a man of God, and he wishes one day to be a priest." The man lifted his nose and tested the air. "He is right, the air is foul."

"There's nothing wrong with the air. Now you two split-ass up the damned mesa," Ironside said, shrugging into his slicker. "Or you'll feel the toe of my boot."

But Salazar was slumped over in the saddle and he had rosary beads in his hand, his gasping, open lips moving in prayer.

"Juan can go no farther," the vaquero said. He shook his head. "Nor can I."

"Right," Ironside said, striding toward Salazar. "Then it's time for some ass-kicking around here."

"Leave them be, Luther!" Jacob said. "The vaqueros are telling the truth. The higher up the mesa we rode, the more rotten the air became. I've smelled that stench before, in El Cerrito."

"Jake," Ironside said, "those men are malingering in the face of the enemy. In the great Army of the Confederacy that was a hanging offense."

Samuel looked hard at Jacob, his eyes speculative. He said, "Luther, Jacob's right. I'm sending the vaqueros back."

"But Sam—"

"Let it go, Luther. If Jacob says the air is bad, then it's bad."

Jacob stepped to the vaquero. "Rodrigo, help Juan back to the ranch. Take him to the chapel and stay with him until he recovers."

The man called Rodrigo looked miserable. He turned to Samuel. "Patron," he said, "you will be without two guns."

"It's all right, we'll manage just fine," Samuel said. "Now go with Juan before he suffocates to death."

Ironside watched the vaqueros ride back along the trail. "Damned mollycoddling is what I call it," he said to no one in particular. "If you ask me, which you won't, of course, all them two needed was a good kick in the balls."

Jacob smiled. "Luther, how lost we'd be without your wise counsel."

"Damn right you would," Ironside said.

Shawn and Ironside were the best with rifles, so they led the way up the switchback. Thunder rolled through the Santa Fe Mountains to the north as though massive boulders were bouncing among the peaks. Lightning flashes accompanied the dragon hiss of rain as a wild weather system, ugly and mean, raced toward the mesa.

Samuel, breathing a little heavily on the slope, said, "I didn't smell it."

"But it's here," Jacob said. "All around us."

"What the hell is it? A dead animal?"

Jacob turned and looked at his brother, rain-water cascading off the brim of his hat. "Nemesis," he said.

"All right, Jake, give me another name for it."

"Evil," Jacob said. "Somewhere on the mesa there's evil. The vaqueros sensed it, smelled it, and so do I."

"What is it, this evil?" Samuel said. The confusion in his eyes told Jacob that he didn't understand any of this.

"It's in the shape of a beautiful woman," Jacob said. "And it's coming closer to Dromore."

"Why, for heaven's sake?"

"Because her name is Nemesis, and she's a destroyer," Jacob said.

Samuel shivered. "Enough, Jake, you're spooking the hell out of me." He looked ahead of him and called out, "Shawn, Luther, step careful there."

The warning wasn't needed because the pair had already stopped. Their rifles up and ready, they eyed the twenty yards of open ground that separated the trail from the rim of the mesa.

"See anything?" Jacob said.

"Not a damn thing," Ironside said. He peered into the distance. "All I see is rain, mist, and more rain."

Jacob took a step ahead of the older man and drew his Colt from under his slicker. He passed his rifle to Shawn. "I'm going up alone to take a look," he said. "No point on us all getting bushwhacked."

"No, I'm coming with you," Shawn said. His eyes scanned the rim. "You're such a trusting soul, Jake, an Apache could take advantage of your good nature."

"Then give my rifle to Sam, and let's go," Jacob said.

"Hell, boys, you're not going up there without

me," Ironside said. "Liable to get your fool heads blown off."

"All right, then, we'll all go," Samuel said, irritated by rain and the closeness of the coming dark. "Damn it, we don't need to hold a committee meeting about it."

He barged his way past Jacob and Shawn to the clearing and stepped into a bullet.

Jacob saw the drift of smoke and thumbed off two fast shots in that direction. Then he ran across the clearing and onto the mesa rim. He looked around and saw nothing but rain-slicked bedrock and scattered pines and juniper.

Below him, Shawn yelled, "Jacob, Sam's all right! He got grazed in the head is all, but he's bleeding pretty bad."

"Get him back to Dromore," Jacob answered, feeding two fresh shells into his Colt.

"He's out like a dead cat, Jake," Shawn said. "It's going to take two of us."

"Then do it, for God's sake," Jacob said. "I'll be all right. I think the bushwhacker made a run for it."

Before Shawn could answer, Jacob sprinted to the cover of a rock pile, a stunted wild oak growing between the boulders like a ragged parasol. Rain drummed on his hat and the shoulders of his slicker, but around him the mesa stretched silently into the distance where there was no clear delineation between sky and land, just a gray curtain that now and then rippled in the wind. Of living creatures, there was no sign.

"Hey, you swine," Jacob yelled, calling into nothingness, "I'm here, so show yourself and we'll have it out."

He heard only quiet, made quieter still by the hushed hiss of the rain.

To Jacob's right the top of the mesa was fairly open, with no obvious places where a man could hide. Behind him lay the rim, and to his left was an area of trees and patches of bunchgrass growing from gravel.

His eyes narrowed in thought, Jacob realized that the bushwhacker, whoever he was, must have run in that direction. The east face of the mesa sloped gently to the flat, and the man had probably escaped in that direction and was now probably long gone.

Jacob straightened from his crouched position. He had little hope of finding the bushwhacker, but he decided to check out the trees and then scout as far as the mesa's east rim.

Stepping carefully, wary of stumbling into an ambush, Jacob made his way to the pines. Around him the unpeopled tableland lay still, eerily watchful, like the windows of an abandoned house. The air smelled of rain and of ozone, lightning flashes flickering on his streaming slicker. But the mesa had been washed clean, and the rancid stench he'd smelled earlier was gone.

Jacob glanced at the sky, dark and growing darker.

He reckoned he had an hour before the day gave way to night and threw a black cloak over the mesa. His time was fast running out.

The Apache war cry split apart the silence like the crack of a bullwhip. Three hard-running, mounted warriors came through the trees at Jacob, surprising him. He'd expected a white man to open the ball, not Indians.

But he'd no time for thought. Now instinct took over as he fought for his life.

An Apache on a rangy steeldust fired at Jacob, and the bullet cracked air close to his skull. He ignored the man and shot at another Indian, who was closer, just a dozen yards away and coming on fast. Jacob hurried his shot and missed. The Apache, his horse dark with rain, didn't slow his pace. He raised a lance and threw it at Jacob, who sidestepped at the last moment. But he'd moved from one danger to another. The third Apache's horse slammed into him, hit Jacob with a shoulder, and sent him sprawling backward to the ground.

Jacob hit the wet caprock hard and his breath gusted out of his chest, but he rolled and his gun came up, searching for a target. An Apache, wearing a blue headband that marked him as a former army scout, sat his horse just five feet away, a Sharps .50 to his shoulder.

"Lay down your gun!" the man yelled.

Jacob snarled his rage. *Savages want to take me alive!*

The two other Apache had dismounted and were now bounding toward him. Jacob fired at the man on the horse. The Indian took the bullet just under his ribs on the left side of his chest and reeled in shock, for the moment at least out of it.

Jacob fell on his back, his gun swinging to engage the Apaches who were already reaching out to grab him.

Blam! Blam!

Two fast shots. Both men went down, as though their legs had been cut from under them with a scythe.

Jacob was startled. He hadn't fired. So who had?

As thunder hammered and lightning scrawled across the sky like the signature of a demented god, Luke Caldwell emerged from the rain and loomed over him.

"Howdy, Jake," he said. "Seems like I showed up just in time, huh?"

The Apache with the blue headband lay on the ground, dead as he was ever going to be, and the other two sprawled at Jacob's feet.

"Caldwell," Jacob said, "are you the one who shot my brother?"

"Did I kill him?" the Texan said, smiling. "A downhill shot is always tricky."

Jacob tensed, ready to bring up his Colt, but the rifle muzzle that rammed into his ear convinced him that now wasn't the time.

"Don't even think about it, O'Brien," Lum said. "Or my bullet will go into your right ear and come out the other." The man kicked Jacob hard in the ribs. "Drop it, by God, or you're a dead man."

Jacob let the revolver drop from his hand. He looked up at Caldwell and said, "This just isn't my day, is it?"

"Nope," Caldwell said, "and it will only go downhill from here."

Chapter Thirty-three

The mesa bulked black against the sky, made barely visible in the growing darkness by rain.

"He should be back by now," Shamus O'Brien said, staring out his study window.

Samuel, wearing a fat bandage around his head, stepped beside his father. "I can't see a thing out there," he said.

"Jacob can take care of himself," Shawn said. "There's nobody around better with a gun than he is."

"That doesn't mean a hill of beans when a rifle is trained on your back," Shamus said. "You said you heard both rifle and revolver shots." He turned his head. "Is that right, Luther?"

"Yeah, Colonel, I reckon that's what we heard. When I went up there to help Jacob he was gone, and three Apaches lay dead on the ground."

Shamus slapped the arm of his wheelchair with

his open hand. "Damn it, where is he? Did other Apaches take him?"

"Colonel, you want I should go look for him again?" Luther said. "I was all over the mesa until it got too dark to see, but I found neither hide nor hair of him."

"No, not in the dark and in a storm," Shamus said. "But you and Shawn will leave at first light." He looked at Samuel. "Why didn't the vaqueros stay with him?"

Samuel and Ironside exchanged glances, then the older man said, "One of them took right poorly, Colonel. And we sent the other one back with him."

Shamus nodded. "Quite right. A sick man is no good in a gunfight."

A servant opened the study door and said, "Dinner is served, Colonel."

Shamus nodded. "We'll be right there, though I don't have much of an appetite thinking that my son could be lying somewhere out there wounded or worse."

"Colonel, I wish you'd let me go now," Ironside said. "I can see like a cat in the dark."

"Luther, you couldn't see a white sheet in a dark closet," Shamus said. "Like me, you're getting as blind as a snubbin' post."

"But Colonel—"

"And like me again, you're getting as stubborn as a government mule."

"Luther, we'll leave before sunup," Shawn smiled.

"That way we'll climb the mesa as soon as it gets light."

"There you go, Luther," Shamus said. "Listen to Shawn."

Lorena came to the door. "I know we're all worried about Jacob," she said, "but we have to eat."

"You're right," Shamus said, "we're coming. Did you ask Sarah to dine with us?"

"I've already sat her at the table," Lorena said.

"So, Sarah, tell me, what did you do before you were unfortunate enough to meet Jacob?" Shawn said.

The girl stopped her soupspoon midway to her mouth and smiled. "I was a whore," she said.

Unfortunately for Samuel, already dizzy from his wound, he was swallowing at that moment and hacked into a fit of coughing. He held a napkin to his mouth and was piqued to see Shawn grinning at him across the table.

"Sarah," Lorena said sweetly, "was a whore, but she wishes to leave that profession. That's why she's now seeking a position at Dromore."

Samuel stopped coughing, glanced around the table, and said, "Sorry."

Shamus angled his son a don't-do-that-again look and said, "Though your previous profession is an ancient one, Sarah—"

"The oldest there is," Luther Ironside said, grinning.

Shamus ignored the interruption and continued, "I don't quite see how it qualifies you for a position at Dromore."

Sarah looked pretty in a russet brown dress given her by Lorena, who had also teased the girl's hair into ringlets in the fashion of the time, set off by a brave display of yellow ribbons.

"I'm a good cook, Colonel," she said. "The culinary arts are something that's always interested me."

"Bravo!" Shawn said. "A woman should be a good cook. I'm a pretty good chef my own self."

"That means, my dear," Ironside said, "that he can fry salt pork and heat up a can of beans." The segundo made a sad little sound in his throat. "I wonder if Jacob is hungry about now," he said.

"Please, Luther, not at the dinner table," Shamus said. "We'll all do our worrying later"—he tapped his stomach—"when we have access to mints." He looked down the table at Lorena. "Did you talk with Mrs. Harrison?"

"Yes, I did, Colonel," Lorena said. "She said she'd love to have Sarah as a kitchen assistant."

"Sarah, does such a situation interest you?" Shamus said.

The girl nodded. "Oh, yes, sir, yes indeed."

"Then it's settled," Shamus said. "I'm sure Mrs. Harrison will discuss wages with you. The only rules of the house are no beaux in your room, though you can entertain gentlemen callers in the kitchen;

no running, dancing, or singing in the hallways; and no profanity." Shamus smiled. "Are you a Catholic, Sarah?"

"No, sir, I'm Protestant."

"Ah well," Shamus said, "who among us is perfect?"

"I also thought that perhaps I could help Mrs. O'Brien with the baby," Sarah said.

"You like babies?" Shamus said.

"Yes indeed, sir."

"Lorena, do you need help with my grandson?" Shamus said.

"A mother always needs help with her baby," Lorena said.

"Then, I'm sure that will be fine," Shamus said. "Just talk to Mrs. Harrison first. She can be very possessive of her kitchen staff."

As the plates were exchanged, Sarah said, "Colonel O'Brien, on my days off could I borrow a horse? I do love to ride."

Samuel laughed. "Then you and my wife will get along splendidly. Lorena loves to ride."

"Yes, I do," Lorena said. She smiled at Sarah. "Perhaps we can ride out together? It would be nice to have a woman as a riding companion for a change. The colonel's vaqueros treat it as a chore."

Sarah clapped her hands. "Oh, I'd love to ride with you, Mrs. O'Brien."

"Then we will," Lorena said. "Tomorrow, just as soon as Jacob gets back."

Chapter Thirty-four

"Well, well, well, look what the cat dragged in," Joshua DeClare said.

"This here is Jacob O'Brien. Says he was up on the mesa hunting me," Luke Caldwell said. "But he got jumped by Apaches an' I had to shoot 'em off his ass."

"I don't think you know me, Mr. O'Brien; allow me to introduce myself," Dora DeClare said. "This is—"

"I know who you are," Jacob said. "Now I know where the stink comes from."

Lum backhanded Jacob across the face so hard blood and saliva flew from his mouth. "Keep a civil tongue in your head," Lum said. "Or I'll tear it out."

"Please, Mr. O'Brien, be seated," Dora said. After she watched Lum and Caldwell force Jacob to the ground she took the pot from the fire and held it up. "May I offer you some coffee?"

"Go to hell," Jacob said, earning another cuff from Lum.

"No coffee then?" Dora said. "Ah well, perhaps later." She smoothed her dress over her knees and said, "Now, what shall we talk about?"

Jacob glanced around him. The DeClares had made camp at the bottom of the mesa in a clearing among the ponderosa. In daylight, anyone up on the rim of the mesa wouldn't see the camp, and even the horses were well hidden. But when Samuel and the others came looking for him, they'd scout this area and find him—if he managed to live that long.

Scarlet firelight danced on Dora's beautiful face and gave her the demonic look of a fallen angel. "Well?" she said.

"You're Nemesis, aren't you?" Jacob said.

"I don't understand the question, Mr. O'Brien."

"You're the avenger."

Dora smiled. "Ah, yes, now I understand." She looked up at Lum and Caldwell. "Did you hear that? Nemesis. Yes, the name suits me very well."

"Then what the hell are you avenging?" Jacob said. He wiped blood from his chin with the back of his hand.

"Why, my father, Mr. O'Brien. Surely you know that?"

"No, I don't know that."

"Well, since you're my guest, I'll explain it to you."

"Dora, you don't have to explain anything to this man," Joshua said. "Just kill him and have done."

"That, dear brother, would be too easy," Dora said. She looked across the fire at Jacob. "Now, where were we? Ah, yes, I remember. Mr. O'Brien, does the name Dace DeClare mean anything to you? Think back ten years."

"Not a damned thing," Jacob said.

"Hmm . . . that's passing strange," Dora said, "because ten years ago on Christmas Eve, your father hanged him. It was of the most singular moment for me, but then the colonel hanged so many, why should I expect you to remember?"

Jacob's head had begun to clear, and he recalled his talk with Sarah. "I recollect someone telling me your pa was hung for a rustler," he said.

Dora clapped her hands. "Quite so! You do remember, bless your heart."

"Rustlers get hung in this territory," Jacob said. "Your pa knew the risk he was taking when he lifted another man's cows."

"One steer, Mr. O'Brien," Dora said. "It was to be a Christmas sacrifice to the dark lord he served. I really do think that in the end that's why Shamus O'Brien hanged him. Papists don't like that sort of thing, do they really?" She smiled. "Are you sure you wouldn't care for coffee?"

Jacob ignored that and said, "Why don't you speak to the colonel, air your grievances? He can be a listening man."

"Oh, no, Mr. O'Brien, I don't wish to speak to the

colonel. You see, I want to destroy him, completely and utterly."

There was a cold, ugly relentlessness in the woman that set Jacob's teeth on edge. But then, in a moment of inspiration, as though a firecracker had gone off in his head, he had a blinding insight into Dora DeClare's plan.

The woman was smart, but even Lum, mentally slower, saw what Jacob was thinking, and he grinned as he read the light that suddenly appeared in the other man's eyes.

"Yes, Mr. O'Brien," Dora said, "a plan ten years in the making began with your brother Patrick."

"You set it up, the rape and murder of Molly Holmes, didn't you?" Jacob said.

"Yes, I did. Oh, dear, Mr. O'Brien, don't kneel on the ground. Please sit. You'll be much more comfy."

"Who murdered Molly Holmes?" Jacob said. He waved a hand in Lum's direction. "This animal?"

"Oh, how silly you are, Mr. O'Brien," Dora said. "Do you think a slut like Molly would welcome Lum between her thighs? I mean, look at his face, what's left of it. I mean, really?"

"Then you recruited Shade Shannon to do the job?"

"Dear Shade. Did you kill him?"

"No, the Apaches did. Slowly."

"Oh, poor thing. Well, yes, Shade raped and strangled the slut. The red-hot-poker finishing touch was all his idea." Dora frowned. "I told him at the time I was not entirely sure that I approved."

"I gave him a piece of my mind, too, Dora," Joshua said.

"As well you should, Josh. As well you should."

"So now you kill me," Jacob said. "Is that the plan?"

"Probably," Dora said. "Shamus O'Brien already grieves for one son, so why not make him grieve for two?"

"Patrick isn't dead," Jacob said. "He's at Dromore."

Dora sat by the fire in thought. Suddenly, she picked up a burning brand and swung it at Jacob's face. He saw it coming and raised his arms to protect himself. The blazing branch exploded against Jacob's hands and showered his face with sparks that stung like scarlet bees.

"Liar!" the woman screamed. "God-cursed liar!"

Jacob rubbed sparks out of his mustache. He smelled burned hair. "I took Patrick out of the Georgetown jail myself," he said. "He's safe now, safe from you."

"I think he's speaking the truth," Joshua said. "He's got no reason to lie."

"So, Shamus O'Brien still lords over Dromore and feels no pain," Dora said.

"Unless you count the Apache lance head in his back," Jacob said. "He got that when he was defending Dromore against those who wanted to take it from him, like your pa."

"Dora, do you want me to shoot this swine?" Lum said.

"No," Dora said. She smiled, her face serene. "Here's a lark! I've just thought of the most precious thing imaginable."

"What is it, my dear?" Joshua said.

"Well, and this is very much *entre nous*, you understand, we'll crucify dear Mr. O'Brien. An appropriate fate for a papist, don't you think?"

"Dora, I'm not catching your drift," Caldwell said.

"If Mr. O'Brien is telling the truth about his brother, then we've suffered a setback," Dora said. "But we can make all right again."

Joshua hugged himself. "This is so exciting."

"I still don't understand," Caldwell said.

"We'll mount a two-pronged attack on Dromore," Dora said.

"And sign your own death warrant, lady," Jacob said.

"Oh, shut up, Mr. O'Brien," Dora said, "and let me talk."

"O'Brien, another word out of you and I'll bust your jaw," Lum said.

"Now, where was I before I was so rudely interrupted?" Dora said. "Ah, yes, I remember. Lum, you and Luke will continue to watch for the O'Brien woman. Now come dawn, a search party will be looking for dear Mr. O'Brien here, so you must stay out of its way." Dora looked at the two men. "Can you do that?"

"Sure," Caldwell said, "we can Injun around the mesa so they'll never find us."

"Good. Now, if after three days you haven't managed to get your hands on the woman, we'll crucify Mr. O'Brien from the rim of the mesa where his sufferings can be seen from Dromore. This will bring his father out."

"And we plug the bastard," Lum said.

"Precisely," Dora said. "You and Luke are both expert riflemen, are you not?"

"Good enough to shoot the gallant colonel off his hoss when he gallops to the rescue," Caldwell said.

"Then your mind will be at rest, Dora, when we travel to Europe," Joshua said.

"I must confess, dear brother, that I'd prefer to see the O'Brien woman captured before we kill the colonel. That would add sauce to the pudding."

"And perhaps you will, my dear," Joshua said. "Is that not so, Lum?"

"I want that O'Brien wench, and I'll get her," the big man said, a gleam in his corpse eyes. "When I'm a-busting her wide open she'll find she's dealing with forces greater than Dromore."

"All praise," Dora said, bowing her head.

Jacob had kept his mouth shut, biding his time. Now, as Lum and Caldwell seemed distracted, he jumped to his feet and made a dive at the Texan's rifle. But Caldwell lived his life constantly on edge, and the man was always a compressed spring ready to uncoil. He easily sidestepped Jacob's bull rush, and at the same time he swung his Winchester. The stock slammed into Jacob's head with a sound like an ax hitting a tree, and he fell headlong to the ground.

Lum stepped closer and, for good measure, slammed the toe of his ankle boot into the prone man's temple.

"Enough, Lum," Dora said. "We don't want to rob poor Mr. O'Brien of his crucifixion, now, do we?"

Chapter Thirty-five

Jacob O'Brien awoke to find himself in a cavern of fire.

He tried to move, but he was paralyzed, bound in place.

There was fire, but no heat, and Jacob thought that strange. Somewhere he heard a trickle of water, a small sound in the stillness, and then, as his consciousness slowly returned, the snap of a log fire.

Now he began to remember . . . the brutal smash of a rifle butt against his head and a descent into darkness.

Caldwell! He'd kill him for that.

Jacob managed to turn his head and look around him. He wasn't in a tunnel but in a cave, and small at that, no more than a shallow depression in the rock. Near the entrance a fire burned, shielded on two sides by a low rock projection, which helped cast flickering scarlet back into the cave. The night had shaded into day, but the light was gray, watery, the color of a mountain pond on a cloudy morning.

He tried to stretch his legs, but they were tied behind him by the same rope that bound his wrists together. He made an attempt to roll toward the fire but grimaced as the rope cut cruelly into him. He gave up and stayed where he was.

But where the hell was he?

Beyond the cave entrance Jacob saw steep, pine-covered hills, but little else revealed a location.

He figured that Dora DeClare and her brother must have left their camp at the base of Glorieta Mesa sometime during the night, knowing that a search party from Dromore would be sure to find them.

The obvious escape route was east across the Pecos and into the hills, maybe even Apache Canyon.

Jacob tried to move again, tugging at his bonds until sweat popped out on his forehead. But it was no use; he'd been trussed like a chicken by somebody who knew his business, probably that sub-human monster Lum.

A smoking man, Jacob had the tobacco hunger, and he was wishful for coffee. He had a feeling that he'd little hope of obtaining either.

Time passed and the fire burned down to an ashy glow. Then a shadow appeared in the cave entrance, and Dora stepped toward Jacob. She had a pan of water in one hand, a white rag in the other. When she kneeled, her split skirt showed more knee and thigh than was necessary.

"Poor Mr. O'Brien," she said, "does your head hurt?"

Jacob said nothing, and the woman continued, "You've got dried blood on your head and down the side of your face. It looks like you've been a very naughty boy."

As the woman wet the rag and dabbed at his head, Jacob said, "Where am I?"

"Well, you're in the hills west of Apache Canyon," Dora said. "Lum and Mr. Caldwell got you up on your horse and helped bring you here."

"Where are they now?"

"My, my, questions, questions, questions. They went back to the mesa, of course."

"My brothers will find them," Jacob said.

"Perhaps, but I think not." Dora leaned back, smiled, and said, "There, you look much better now." The water in the basin was pink.

Jacob nodded toward his shirt pocket. "I've got the makings in there. Untie me so I can have a smoke."

"I'm afraid not, Mr. O'Brien. You must remain bound." Dora lightly laid her fingertips on Jacob's thigh. "It's for your own safety, you know."

"Then roll one for me."

"Sorry, I don't know how." Dora frowned. "Oh, poor dear, you look so disappointed." She smiled. "I know, I'll do something nice for you and make you happy again."

The woman laid down the basin and began to

fumble with the fly buttons of Jacob's pants. "What are you doing?" he said.

"Something nice, as I told you."

"No," Jacob said. "No, don't do that."

"Oh, fiddle-dee-dee, I won't hurt you."

"No!" Jacob yelled, angry as his body betrayed him.

Dora's open, seeking mouth on his silenced him.

"There, wasn't that pleasant?" Dora said, wiping saliva from the mouth with the back of her hand.

"Why the hell did you do that?" Jacob said.

"To prove something."

"Damn it, woman, to prove what?"

"That you're willing to sell your soul as cheaply as the rest of us."

"You forced me."

"Forced you? Was that how it was? It didn't seem that way to me."

"I didn't sell my soul to you, woman. I tried my best to resist you."

"You sold it cheaply, Mr. O'Brien, and to a woman you hate. How weak you are. How weak all men are. You disgust me, every single man jack of you."

Dora stepped to the entrance to the cave, her head bowed because of the low roof. Behind her, Jacob said, "Damn you, I'll see you in hell."

The woman turned. "Why, of course you will, Mr. O'Brien. Where else would you expect to see me?"

* * *

Jacob was in two kinds of pain. The knowledge that his own moral weakness had betrayed him was a special kind of agony, more torturous than the lancing aches that racked his cramped back and especially his hands.

Outside the cave evening had come, but Jacob could see nothing beyond the hatful of fire at the entrance. He heard nothing, no voices, not even the coyote and owl noises of the night.

He wondered with a kind of sickness if they were just going to leave him here and let him starve to death. Or did dying of thirst come earlier? He couldn't remember. He was already very thirsty. Hey, maybe a bear would wander into the cave and end it real quick. If that happened he'd just have to grin and bear it. Jacob giggled. Now that was funny. Even Shawn couldn't make such a good joke.

Where was Shawn? With Samuel and Luther Ironside and them up on the mesa, searching for him. Well, they wouldn't find him, because he wasn't there! *Hah, you're looking for me in all the wrong places, dolts!*

Dora stepped into the cave again. "I'm a little worried about my brother," she said. "He's a bit off his food, and he says he has a headache. He's such a frail creature, Mr. O'Brien, but a fine painter."

"I could use some water," Jacob said.

"Yes, I know you could," Dora said. She smiled at him and left the cave again.

"Damn you!" Jacob yelled. The shout made his parched throat drier, and he began to cough, spasms that shook his body and made the ropes dig into him even tighter, merciless.

He leaned his head against the hard rock, and the sound of trickling water made his thirst unbearable.

"Find me, Pa," he whispered. Depression, deep and dark, covered him like a black cloak. "Please find me."

Chapter Thirty-six

"See any trace of him?" Samuel O'Brien said.

"Nothing," Luther Ironside said. "And we're losing daylight."

"The vaqueros and me have been all over the mesa and the flat to the east," Shawn said. "Seen nothing of him."

"If it was Apaches, they could've carried him away with them," Ironside said.

"God forbid," Samuel said. "More likely he's chasing somebody. Jacob is a mean ranny to tangle with, and he'll go after a man."

"I guess we could make one last sweep of the mesa before dark," Shawn said.

Samuel shook his head. "Waste of time, Shawn. If we haven't found him by now, then he's long gone."

"I bet you're right, boss," Ironside said. "Jacob's chasing after somebody. Hell, he could be halfway to Mexico by now."

"The colonel isn't going to like it, us giving up on him," Shawn said.

Samuel waved a hand, taking in the land to the east and south, miles of craggy peaks, deep shadowed canyons, and dense pine forests. "We'd need a regiment of cavalry to find him out there, and even then it would be next to impossible," he said.

"Then what do we do now?" Ironside said.

"Pray, I guess," Samuel said. He reached down and patted his horse's neck. "Sarah says she'll only trust herself on a tired horse when she rides out with Lorena tomorrow. After the day he's had, this old boy will be good and tired."

Ironside, looking worried, said, "Sam, you know I'm not a praying man."

"Then have a drink on Jacob," Shawn said. "That works just as good."

"Damn it, boy, that's what I'll do," Ironside said. "Not because I care to indulge, you understand, but for Jake's sake, like."

Samuel said, "Luther, you've always been known as a man who only takes strong drink in a good cause."

"Damn right, Sam," Ironside said, pleased.

"I'm concerned, Luther," Shamus O'Brien said. "What do you think happened to my son?"

Ironside shook his head. "The worst is that he was captured by Apaches, Colonel."

"Jacob wouldn't be taken alive by Apaches," Shamus said. "He knows better than that."

Samuel said, "Then he went after somebody he figured was a danger to Dromore."

Shamus nodded. "That sounds more likely." He sighed. "Then all we can do is wait."

Patrick, pale and ten pounds thinner, looked lost in the great leather armchair by the study's fireplace. "I feel responsible for all this," he said. "Suppose that was a Georgetown posse up on the mesa and they arrested Jacob for breaking a condemned prisoner out of jail."

Shamus looked at Ironside. "What do you think about that, Luther?"

"I guess it's possible, Colonel. I never did trust that Wentworth character. He's got sneaky eyes."

"Pa," Patrick said, "I told Lorena I'd go riding with her tomorrow morning. Maybe she could leave me in the hills for a spell and mosey over to Georgetown and talk with Sheriff Moore. He's always been partial to a pretty gal."

"You're not fit to ride anywhere," Shamus said.

"I'm sick and tired of being cooped up in the house," Patrick said. "That new girl Sarah says she isn't much of a horsewoman, so we'll take it easy."

"Then don't ride Rat's Ass, Pat," Ironside said. "That damned mustang of yours will try to buck you off every time."

Patrick's eyes smiled behind his round glasses. "Me and Rat's Ass have an understanding," he said.

"I don't use spurs on him, and he doesn't pull dirty tricks on me."

"What do you think, Samuel?" Shamus said. "Lorena is your wife."

"Lorena is Dromore, and she'll be all right, Pa. She'll wheedle information out of Moore. As Pat says, he has an eye for a well-turned ankle. It'll do Pat good to get out for a while, and Lorena is looking forward to riding. She hasn't been in the saddle since young Shamus was born."

"Well, I'll take your word for it," the colonel said. "Then Lorena will talk to John Moore and see if the damned vigilantes were involved in Jacob's disappearance." He slapped the arms of his wheelchair. "By God, if they were—"

"I'll make sure Lorena knows to say that loud and clear to Moore, Colonel," Samuel said, smiling.

The evening rain had ended, and the morning held promise of a bright day. Patrick, who'd reckoned he'd lain abed too long, delighted in the smell of the horses in the barn and the Havana tobacco tang of leather.

He was still very weak, and a vaquero helped him saddle Rat's Ass, all the time assuring Patrick that the yellow mustang was the meanest, orneriest critter to ever cast a shadow on the earth.

Patrick swung into the saddle, and after the

vaquero passed him his gunbelt he hung it on the horn.

It was a mistake that would cost him dear.

The two women were excited to be riding again, and the weather cooperated fully. The sun climbed higher in the cloudless sky, but the morning was not yet hot. Summer wildflowers added sweetness to the air, and the pines, bathed by rain, smelled fresh and clean, the breeze carrying their scent from high mountain meadows.

"There was a time when we'd see buffalo here," Patrick said, looking around him. "Vast herds of them. But now they're all gone, and Dromore cattle graze where the buffalo once did."

"Progress, I suppose," Lorena said. "But it's a great pity."

"When the buffalo died, so did the Indians," Patrick said. "The Sioux and Cheyenne left their bones on the prairie alongside the buffalo. You can find them if you look long and hard enough."

"You're fond of Lo, Patrick?" Sarah said.

"No, I can't say that I am. But I'm sorry he's gone. Sorry the buffalo are gone, too."

Patrick bent his head and thought, and then came up again, smiling. He said, *"Lo, the poor Indian, whose untutored mind sees God in clouds or hears him in the wind."*

"Did you just make that up, Patrick?" Sarah said. "It's pretty."

"No, it's the opening line of a poem written by an English poet named Alexander Pope. Back in the old days the mountain men loved the poem, but they figured Lo was the poor Indian's name."

"Oh, dear, I won't call the Indians that again," Sarah said.

Patrick grinned. "I wouldn't worry about it. Being called Lo is the least of their problems."

Patrick led the way southeast, then led the women north when he reached Hurtado Mesa. Ahead lay the Pecos, and beyond the river the craggy El Barro peaks stood outlined against the sky.

The Pecos was low at that time of the year, and they rode out of cottonwoods into a foot of water rippled by a sluggish current.

Patrick stopped and let the mustang drink. A moment later, the horse collapsed under him and Patrick heard the flat echo of a rifle as he hit the water.

Chapter Thirty-seven

"Patrick!" Lorena yelled. She kicked her horse forward, and water cascaded from its high-stepping hooves. Behind her Sarah sat her mount, pointing, her mouth open in a soundless scream.

Patrick got to his feet, looking for his gun. The mustang had fallen onto its right side, and the gun-belt lay under the motionless body. He dropped to his knees, and his hands reached under the saddle. The holster was nowhere to be found.

Anyway, it was too late.

A huge man with a horrifically burned face pointed a rifle at Patrick's belly and said, "Get your hands in the air or I'll drop you right where you stand."

Patrick saw Lorena struggle with another man, slashing at him with her riding crop. Suddenly, Lorena relaxed in the sidesaddle, but it was no submission. She kicked her horse into motion and was almost clear of her attacker when the man dived on her back, and the two hit the river, sending up fountains of brown water.

"Go get 'er, Luke," Lum yelled, grinning. "Throw that filly."

Lorena rose to her feet, and again her riding crop slashed at the tall man. He raised an arm to protect his face and waded close to her. When he judged the distance was right, the man backhanded the woman across the face, and she fell at his feet.

"Damn you, Lum!" Caldwell yelled. "The other one's getting away!"

Sarah had regained the bank, bouncing awkwardly on a frightened horse. Lum threw his rifle to his shoulder and fired. The bullet thudded into a cottonwood, and then Sarah was among the trees and out of sight.

"Let her go," Lum yelled. "You've got the one we want."

Patrick had been fishing again around his dead horse. This time he found what he needed: his round spectacles glinting on the river's sandy bottom. He settled the dripping glasses on his nose and yelled at Caldwell, "If you've hurt Lorena, I'll see you hang."

"Told you it was her," Lum yelled.

And Patrick knew with terrible certainty he'd made his second mistake of the morning.

* * *

"Oh, you poor dear, you're soaked, just soaked," Dora said, her hand on Lorena's shoulder. "Lum, bring her to the fire and let's get her dry."

Lum pushed Lorena to the fire, then pushed her onto her knees. He grinned at Dora. "When?"

"Soon," Dora said. "But take her into the woods somewhere. I don't want to see it."

"She's a beauty, though, ain't she?" Lum said.

"Yes," Dora said, "she is very beautiful indeed."

Lum looked at Caldwell. "After I'm finished you can have a taste." He grinned. "If there's anything left of her by then."

Caldwell said nothing, but he reached up, grabbed Patrick by his shirtfront, and dragged him off Lorena's horse. "What do you want done with him, Dora?" he said.

"And which O'Brien are you?" Dora said.

"Patrick. What do you want from us?"

"Much." Dora smiled. "Much will be expected of you." She waved a hand. "Tie him up, Luke, and put him in the cave with his brother. You'll be company for each other, Patrick."

"My brother is being held prisoner here?"

"Not a prisoner. He's my guest, as you are."

After Patrick was dragged kicking into the cave, Dora smiled at Lorena. "Now we can talk woman to woman. Won't that be nice?"

"What do you want?" Lorena said. Her mouth was bruised and her bottom lip split and bleeding. "Ransom money?"

"Oh, dear, no," Dora said. "I have much bigger

plans for you." She raised her slim, elegant hand and ticked off fingers. "And Jacob and Patrick and . . . Samuel and Shaun . . . and Shamus and baby Shamus." Dora let her hand drop. "Oh, I have so many plans."

Lum took a knee beside Lorena. With his forefinger he traced her porcelain skin from cheekbone to chin. When Lorena shrank from him, eyes filled with horror, he scowled and said, "You'll make it easier on yourself if you make nice to me. It won't hurt so much, you understand?"

"Lum, not yet," Dora said. "Lorena and I have so much girlie talk to get through." She kneeled. "Now, I just love your riding habit. English, isn't it? And the silk top hat is just too, too precious. Who is your dressmaker? Pray tell."

"If it's not ransom money you're after, then what do you want?" Lorena said. Her voice was steady, but her eyes were bright with alarm.

"Ah, such a modern woman," Dora sighed. "I do declare, all business, all the time."

"What do you want?" Lorena said, her voice rising.

From inside the cave, Jacob yelled, "Leave her alone, damn you."

Dora looked at Caldwell. "Keep him quiet. Don't kill him, but gag him with something."

To Lorena she said, "You asked me what I want, and the answer, to state the case clearly, is revenge."

"I never did anything to you," Lorena said.

"No, you didn't, but your father-in-law did, and by proxy, your husband and now you."

Lorena's eyes were frantic. "I don't understand," she said.

"What's not to understand, my dear? Shamus O'Brien hanged my father as a rustler, and now it is my plan to destroy the gallant colonel and all he holds dear."

"But . . . but why me?" Lorena said.

"Ah, because you are part of my plan, are you not?"

"Plan . . . ?" Lorena said. She'd been thinking of something else.

"Yes, my plan," Dora said. She stared hard at Lorena again. "Now, how to explain it to a simpleton? Ah, yes, start at the beginning, I suppose. Well, listen, dearie. You're married, so you know what intercourse is? Huh . . . don't you? Or should I use that horribly common word? Do you know what that is?" Dora nodded, smiling. "Why, of course you do. I think I see a little blush on your pretty cheeks."

"You're mad," Lorena said.

"Mad with anger, mad with rage, whatever you want to call it. Yes, I agree. Now here's what's going to happen, and I apologize beforehand because I know it will be most unpleasant for you. You see Lum, standing there, grabbing his crotch? Yes, that's right, dearie, look at him. Why, just seeing the fear in your eyes makes me shiver all over. It really does."

"Let me go," Lorena said. "I'll say nothing of this."

"Oh, that's quite impossible at the moment. But be of good cheer, we do intend to send you back to Dromore. But alas, you won't be the same person who left there this morning. Like me, you'll be quite mad, but in a different way, you understand?"

Now Lorena was genuinely scared. "What are you going to do to me?"

"I'm not going to do anything to you, my dear, but Lum is," Dora said. "He's going to take the little princess into the dark woods and have his way with her until she's quite mad."

"You're right about that, Dora," Lum said. "I never had me a fine lady before, and I'm going to enjoy this one."

"Bring her back here alive, Lum," Dora said. "I don't want you dragging her dead carcass behind your horse."

"Oh, I'll carry her, Dora," Lum said. To Lorena he looked like a living, breathing monster from the worst kind of childhood nightmare.

Suddenly Dora looked bored. "Take her away, someplace far," she said. "I don't want to see or hear your damned rutting." She stood. "Wait, strip that riding habit off her. I wish it for myself, and I don't want it damaged. Oh, and her boots and that absolutely precious hat."

Lorena screamed and struggled as Lum, being careful not to tear the riding habit, removed her clothes. When the woman was stripped to her underwear, Dora picked up the dress and hat.

"Go now, Lum," she said, her voice lashing across the morning like a whip. "And don't bring her back until she's had a foretaste of hell."

Lum grabbed Lorena by the wrist and dragged her away from the cave to his horse. He stepped into the saddle and effortlessly pulled the woman up in front of him.

"You and me is going to a place where we won't be disturbed," Lum said.

"Please," Lorena said, "don't do this. I have a baby at home, and he needs me."

Hope fled from Lorena as Lum rode deeper into the foothills of the Santa Fe Mountains. She knew there would be no rescue, no escape, and she wondered if she could will herself to die—just close her eyes and let her soul flutter free of her body like a rising dove.

When the time came, she was determined to try. Lorena knew it was cowardice on her part, but then she'd never been brave. Even spiders scared her.

"My poor baby," she said.

"Shut your damned trap," Lum said.

And Lorena was surprised that she'd spoken aloud.

As they rode, Lum's hands were all over her body. She shuddered, and Lum whispered, "Ready, girlie? Well, not much longer now."

The man's entire attention was centered on the

woman's body, the smell of her, her perfume as sweet as wildflowers.

When he saw the arroyo, Lum's heart leaped in his chest. He'd found it, the ideal spot for his rustic boudoir. He swung his horse toward the opening, shielded from prying eyes by the branches of a wild oak.

For the first time in her life, Lorena knew true fear.

Chapter Thirty-eight

Sarah Elizabeth Walker, known in the past—when men called her anything—as Letdown Lizzie, rode out of the Pecos and onto the bank among the trees.

She saw the two men ride away with Lorena and Patrick, people who'd been kind to her, and suddenly she was adrift, without direction.

Her obvious choice was to head back to Dromore for help. But she was a poor rider and she'd have to make the trip at a walk, if she could even find the trail. She'd let Patrick do the leading and had paid little attention to landmarks. Besides, by the time she reached Dromore, Lorena and Patrick could be dead.

The man with the burned face had terrified her, and Sarah knew what Lorena's fear must be because she was grappling with her own.

Then the realization came to her in a rush. She was now part of Dromore and all it stood for, and she could not be weak. The colonel would not expect her to turn and run and abandon Lorena and Patrick; none of the O'Briens would.

Fighting down the fear that curled in her stomach like a green snake, Sarah kneed her horse into the Pecos again. She patted the sorrel's neck and said, "Easy now, horse. Don't go too fast."

Keeping to the shallows, Sarah rode in the direction taken by the kidnappers. She wished she'd someone with her, somebody wise like Luther Ironside, who'd say, "You're doing the right thing, Sarah. I'd do the same."

But Luther wasn't there. There was only Sarah, and she was scared almost out of her mind. Then she remembered the Remington derringer that she'd bought a few years earlier. But it was in her room at Dromore, wrapped in an oily cloth in a dresser drawer. It was of no use to her here.

"Nice horse," Sarah said, but only because she needed to hear the reassuring sound of her own voice.

Sarah was not a tracker. Her only relevant experience was to avoid stomping boots as she cut a trail across a crowded dance floor. But a horse with two people on its back leaves deep hoofprints, and the kidnappers had made no attempt to keep their destination a secret.

Sarah followed the trail as best she could, lost it a

couple of times and had to cast around, riding back and forth, before she picked it up again.

She'd never been in this part of the country until now, a raw, untamed wilderness of pine forests, high rocky crags, and shadowed canyons. The sun was high in the sky and the day was hot, and dust settled on Sarah's face and chafed her neck. In the distance the flats between the hills shimmered, waves of heat that crowded closer around her.

She removed her borrowed top hat with its pink chiffon band and wiped her forehead with a scrap of handkerchief. The cloth came away yellow with dust.

"Do you know this country, horse?" she said, patting the sorrel's sweating neck. "No? Well, that makes two of us. Neither do I."

Sarah followed the tracks again, easier now that she rode across grassy ground that was softer from the recent rains. After a few minutes she caught a down-home drift of wood smoke. At first Sarah thought she was imagining things, but then an errant breeze reassured her that she was correct. It was wood smoke, and the odor was strong enough to be close.

Now Sarah faced a dilemma. She realized the need to scout ahead on foot so she wouldn't be seen from the kidnappers' camp, if that were what she had discovered. But if she wanted to get back on the horse in a hurry, would he stand or shy away from her? Mounting and dismounting in a barn was one thing, doing the same thing in the middle of a vast wilderness where a horse might spook was quite another.

She had to take a chance that the sorrel was well trained enough to stand. He was a cow pony, Patrick had told her, and fairly mannered.

Well, she couldn't sit and think about the pony's demeanor all day.

Sarah lifted her leg over the sidesaddle's top pommel, removed her left foot from the stirrup, and slid to the ground. The horse swung his head around to look at her, but apart from that he seemed disinterested.

"Nice horse," Sarah said, relieved. She gathered up the reins, stepped into a stand of trees, and tied the horse to a juniper branch. "Stay," she said, backing out of the trees. "Good horse."

The sorrel tossed his head, the bit chiming, and ignored her.

Crouched low, Sarah took advantage of every scrap of cover as she followed the smoke smell. Her heart hammered in her ears, and fear tied her stomach in knots.

She was unarmed and had no idea what she'd do if this were indeed the outlaw camp. She'd once read a dime novel about a prairie girl who'd rescued her soldier beau from a band of Indians by creeping up on the bloodthirsty savages' camp and untying his bonds.

It was a thought, Sarah decided, something she could try. And right now it was all she had.

But she was about to discover that the reality of what she faced was much more terrifying than anything even Mr. Buntline could imagine.

Sarah's riding habit was a dark green color that helped her blend in with the landscape. The silk top hat with its chiffon band she'd left behind with her horse.

Two paths led ahead of her, winding upward through ponderosa and scattered juniper. Between them rose a massive rock that looked like the prow of a steamship, its north side scabbed all over with yellow lichen. Here the smell of smoke was much stronger, and above the rise Sarah saw a veil of gray lift into the sky, straight as a string.

She took the nearer path and scrambled in the direction of the rock. With every step she smelled a growing stench, the cloying odor of something long dead.

And then, close and loud, the scream of a terrified woman . . . crying out for help, begging to be let go.

Sarah reached the base of the rock and looked over the rise. About fifty yards of meadow sloped gently away from her and ended in a grassy flat that stretched another hundred feet or so to an overhanging cliff face. Doubting her own senses, the woman took in the horrific tableau unfolding beneath her at a glance.

She recognized Dora DeClare, who stood near the entrance of a hollow in the rock, smiling, admiring Lorena's damp riding habit. Her brother sat near the fire, his legs crossed in front of him like bent twigs. A man who had the stamp of Texas gunfighter all over him stepped out of the cave and said something to Dora that Sarah couldn't hear. But what caught and held her attention was the burned man, his face as grotesque as a carnival mask, grinning as he dragged Lorena toward his horse.

In that single, horrific moment as her breath stifled in her throat, Sarah knew that she was in the presence of evil she could not comprehend or fight.

Her instinct was to run back down the path and keep running until she reached her horse. Let Colonel O'Brien deal with it. He was a man of wealth and power with strong sons and a small army of vaqueros . . . and she was . . . just a scared, two-dollar whore . . . a nobody.

Sarah's body tensed as she prepared for head-long flight. Then Lorena screamed again, begged for mercy, her hands beating uselessly against the burned man's chest, and Dora DeClare laughed at the spectacle . . . laughed!

There was little doubt in Sarah's mind about the fate that awaited Lorena. The burned man was hulking and strong, and he'd use her hard, toss her around like a rag doll as his lust dictated.

Then she saw the man ride out, pawing at Lorena who was draped facedown across the pommel of his saddle. He headed north, in the direction of the Santa Fe Mountain foothills, and Sarah turned, hiked up her skirt, and ran down the path as though hounds were on her heels.

To Sarah's relief, the sorrel stood while she mounted. She'd ride south, back along the canyon, then swing north again toward Dromore and tell the colonel what she'd seen.

By then of course, Lorena would be . . .

Sarah drew rein. She sat with her head bowed, her heart racing. No, she couldn't tell the colonel what had happened . . . face the accusation in his eyes, the whispers and sidelong glances of the people who depended on Dromore for their livelihood and loved all that it stood for.

She'd have to take the coward's way out— slink back to Georgetown, like the faithless whore she was.

It was the sorrel that settled things.

He turned smoothly and headed north, his head high, eyes on the trail. Sarah tried to rein him in, but the horse would have none of it. He tossed his head, fighting the bit, and walked on.

Later, looking back on it, Sarah thought she'd

drawn strength from the horse. Or maybe it was a sign . . . from God, providence, whatever.

But if the sorrel was willing to go back, then so was she.

She let the horse have his head. Sarah's experience with horses was limited, but she'd heard cowboys say that they were notional animals that didn't always do what their riders wanted. She was willing to accept that the big red horse was just being ornery and that she wasn't rider enough to correct him.

But he was headed in the right direction, and so was she. And that was all that mattered. The next time she saw Colonel O'Brien she would be able to look him in the eye . . . and suddenly that mattered to her very much.

Chapter Thirty-nine

Sarah followed the rim of Apache Canyon north. The smell of dust was in the air, and the sorrel seemed eager for the trail, eating up one mile, then another with a smooth, distance-eating stride.

The sun was merciless, soaking Sarah's wool riding habit and streaking the sorrel's flanks with sweat.

But the tracks of the burned man's horse were fresher. She was gaining on him. Unbidden, the thought came into her head, *Gee, I bet he's real scared!*

That mental image made her giggle uncontrollably—and she knew the sun and hammering heat were having an effect on her.

There was no breeze to help alleviate Sarah's misery. The sun was a flaming ball in a molten sky, and around her the land spread still, as though too hot to make the effort to move. She saw a Gila monster lying inert on a rock, its sides pulsing, and without warning a covey of quail scattered from a mesquite bush, apparently startled by the nearness of the horse.

A canteen hung from the English sidesaddle's leaping pommel by a canvas strap. Sarah drank, and then drank again. The water was warm but it slaked her thirst, and, for a few minutes at least, it helped against the worst effects of the heat.

Then, a ways ahead, she saw dust—just a wisp that hung in the air for a moment—but it soon vanished. Now Lorena and the burned man were not far ahead.

Sarah knew much was at stake and she must be careful. She eased back on the reins, and the sorrel responded, slowing his walk, the heat finally tiring him.

Crushed grass and the occasional track told Sarah where the burned man was headed. She followed his tracks over a low hill and then crossed a dry wash, her horse stepping around the white skeleton of a dead cottonwood. Ahead lay another grassy humpback, scarred by a narrow game trail. Dust still hung over the trail and was only now beginning to settle.

Cautiously, Sarah rode to the bottom of the rise and then slid from the saddle. Immediately, her knees buckled and forced her into a little dance to keep upright. Whether from tiredness or fear, Sarah pretended not to know. But the butterflies fluttering in her stomach assured her the latter was the case.

Stepping carefully, the girl took the game trail until she could just look over the rim. She was barely in time to see the rump of the burned man's horse disappear into the narrow slot of an arroyo.

A hundred yards of grass, studded with juniper, piñon, and tangled stands of prickly pear cactus, separated Sarah from the arroyo. She didn't dare take the horse, because a whinny or even a bit-jangling toss of the head could betray her. Turning, she glanced back at the sorrel. He was grazing peacefully in tree shade and showed no indication to wander away.

Now that she was close to the burned man again, Sarah felt the presence of evil, overwhelming, threatening to devour her. It tore out her heart and took her courage with it, leaving her to feel naked, weak, vulnerable, and, worst of all, alone. She swallowed hard, fighting down the urge to cut and run, and walked down the trail to the flat.

She felt an unfriendly breeze pushing at her, teasing her hair and slapping her skirt against her trembling legs. Telling her to get away from here.

Sarah kept walking. She stopped at the brush-choked entrance of the arroyo and looked around for a weapon, a rock, a tree branch . . . anything. She found nothing. From somewhere inside the arroyo Lorena screamed and kept on screaming. Sarah heard the burned man laugh, breathless from exertion, as though he was struggling with his victim.

Sarah had her riding crop, attached to her wrist by a leather strap. It was little enough, but it would have to do. She stepped into the arroyo and was hit by a mailed fist of sound . . .

Lorena's desperate screams.

After ten yards the arroyo narrowed to a few feet, and cactus tore viciously at Sarah's skirt and arms. The dank air smelled damp, of rotten vegetation and squeaking things, and there was no light from the sun. After a while the walls opened, and the arroyo ended at a gray wall of rock. From high up water fell, splashing into a stone tank, and near there, the burned man, naked, lay on top of Lorena.

The man's horse grazed on scant grass off to one side, and his clothes were scattered, obviously removed with much urgency. He'd carelessly thrown his gunbelt on top of a flat rock, and the Colt was halfway out of the holster.

Lorena struggled under the burned man, fighting back with all her woman's strength. Finally he forced her legs apart and pushed the back of her thighs with his forearms, forcing her hips upward, her knees bent all the way to her naked breasts.

Sarah ran for the Colt and grabbed it out of the holster. The burned man's horrendous face turned toward her, and his lipless mouth twisted in a snarl. "Get away from here," he said. "This female is mine."

"Get off her!" Sarah yelled. She held the revolver straight out in front of her, the muzzle shaking.

Lum rolled off Lorena. "Give me that gun," he said, rising to his feet. "Give me the gun or I'll tear you apart," he said.

Sarah backed off a couple of steps. Her eyes were terrified, and the big Colt shook uncontrollably in her hands.

"Give me the gun," Lum said again. "And I'll let you go. I don't want you, girlie; my business is with the O'Brien woman."

Sarah fired, and the bullet fountained dirt near Lum's feet. He kept coming, his unwavering stare black with death.

"Oh, please, go away," Sarah said. "I don't want to shoot you."

Lorena sprang to her feet and charged at Sarah. She shouldered into the girl hard and grabbed the revolver before Sarah went sprawling.

Lum covered the distance between himself and Lorena very fast. But the woman had been taught to shoot by Shawn O'Brien, and well she knew the way of the Colt.

She slammed a shot into Lum's chest. The big man slowed, stopped, and looked down at the sudden, blossoming blood. He roared at Lorena, his outstretched hands reaching for her throat like claws. The woman took a split second to steady her aim, and then she fired again.

This time the bullet crashed into Lum's skull, right in the middle of his forehead. The man stood there, his eyes wide open, staring into distance. Then he shrieked, a terrible, keening screech, so piercing it echoed its stark terror among the surrounding hills.

In the ringing silence that followed, Lum stood where he was, dead, but standing upright, his eyes fixed on something only he could see.

Sarah approached the dead man hesitantly, taking tiny, fearful steps.

"Lorena, why did he do that?" she said. The girl's face was drained of color. "Why did he scream like that?"

Lorena seemed almost calm. "I think he caught his first glimpse of hell," she said.

Sarah ran around frantically picking up scraps of Lorena's clothing. "Put these on," she said. "No, don't put them on. Not yet." She took the smoking Colt from Lorena's hand. "Did . . . did he . . . ?"

"No," Lorena said. "He didn't."

"Wash," Sarah said. She pointed to the water cascading from the rock wall. "Over there. Wash yourself clean. His stink is on you, and me."

Sarah rapidly stripped off her clothes, and the two women stood naked in the clearing. The girl grabbed Lorena's hand, and they ran to the falling water.

Sarah let out a little squeal. "Ow, it's cold!" she said.

"Freezing," Lorena said. She turned her face to

the tumbling stream. "But it feels good," she said, her soaked hair falling over her shoulders.

"Wash," Sarah said, "down there. Get every bit of him off you."

The women stayed under the torrent for ten minutes, laughing, splashing each other like children, the terrors of the morning washing away with every drop of water.

Finally, numb from cold, they stepped into the warming sun.

"Look," Sarah said.

"I know," Lorena said. "It's almost as though he was standing there watching us."

Sarah's voice quavered. "Lorena is . . . is he really dead?"

"He's dead all right. And he knows it."

"It's creepy, the way he just stands there and doesn't fall down," Sarah said. "He scared me when he was alive, and he's scaring me now."

Stepping carefully, looking out for cactus, Lorena walked to Lum and spat in his face. She looked at Sarah. "He still didn't fall." She raised her bare foot and pushed on the man's belly. This time Lum fell on his back and lay still.

"Wash your foot, Lorena," Sarah said.

Between them, the women salvaged enough clothing to cover their nakedness. Lorena carefully wiped off Lum's saddle before she led his horse out of the arroyo.

As they walked to the rise, Lorena said, "Dora DeClare has Patrick and Jacob. We have to rescue them."

"She has a man with her, Lorena," Sarah said. "I've seen his kind before. He's a gunfighter up from Texas."

"There's a rifle in the boot," Lorena said.

"Can you hit anything with a rifle?" Sarah said.

"I don't know. Maybe."

"What if you miss? They'd shoot Patrick and Jacob for sure."

Lorena said nothing, and Sarah continued, "I think we should ride straight to Dromore for help. I don't think either of us is in a fit state to take on a Texas gunfighter. And I'm such a coward."

"Sarah, you're not a coward; you proved that today," Lorena said.

"I couldn't shoot that . . . monster."

"Not everyone can kill a man, Sarah." Lorena let a silence stretch, then she said, "But you're right. We need Samuel and Shawn and Luther Ironside, as well as the vaqueros."

"Yes, we do," Sarah said. "I don't think we should try to do it alone. And you've got your baby to consider."

Lorena said, "I have been thinking about him. Nanny's probably worried by this time, and little Shamus will want to be fed."

Sarah glanced at the other woman's swollen breasts. "Are you full?"

"Uh-huh. I'm leaking."

"I really don't think we want to go up against a gunfighter, do you?"

Lorena smiled. "No, I guess not. But I'm so worried about Patrick and Jacob."

"The colonel will take care of things," Sarah said.

"Yes, he will," Lorena said. "He always does."

Chapter Forty

Jacob O'Brien was in a world of pain, and extreme thirst ravaged him. The cave was hot and the air smoky and hard to breathe.

"How are you holding up, brother?" Patrick asked.

Jacob managed a smile. "Tip-top, Pat."

Patrick saw that his brother's water-deprived lips were dry and cracked, and his hands were swollen to twice their size as the ropes cut savagely into his wrists.

Bound hand and foot himself, Patrick could offer little help, but he tried. "Caldwell, you bastard!" he yelled. "We need water in here."

The Texan stepped into the cave, bowing his head under the low rock roof. He looked at Jacob and smiled. "Getting thirsty, O'Brien?"

"Yeah, he's thirsty," Patrick said, "and what have you done with my brother's wife?"

"Right at the moment, I'd say she's layin' with

Lum. You know, the big feller with the burned face." Caldwell grinned. "I bet she's enjoying it."

Patrick tried to kick out at his tormentor. "You sorry piece of trash," he said, "I'll kill you."

The Texan sidestepped the clumsy attempt and drove his boot hard into Patrick's side. "You lie still, or I'll bust all of your ribs," he said.

"Caldwell," Jacob croaked, as he saw his brother double over in pain, "I swear, I'll gun you for this."

"You don't say?" the Texan said. "Well, I'll give you your chance. Call it professional courtesy."

He grabbed Jacob by his shirtfront and dragged him into the middle of the cave. Quickly he untied the rope around his wrists. Then he pulled his Colt and dropped it in front of him.

"Pick it up, O'Brien," he said. "Let's see how good you are."

Jacob reached for the revolver, but he couldn't open his grotesquely swollen hand. His fingers were purple and dead, and no matter how much he willed them to move, he couldn't. The gun was just inches away, but it might have well been on the moon.

"I always took you for a yellowbelly, O'Brien," he said. "And now you've proved it. Look, I'm unarmed; let's see if you have the guts to pick up the gun and get to your work."

Jacob tried again, desperate now. Even the slightest movement of his fingers caused him intense pain. He couldn't open his hand. It was impossible. He bowed his head. Beaten.

Caldwell's boot came up fast, crashed into Jacob's face, and sent him reeling backward as blood sprayed around his head. "I called you for a damned yellowbelly," the Texan said, grinning.

He bound up Jacob's wrists again and ignored Patrick, who was cursing at him wildly as he tried to pull free of his own bonds.

Caldwell rose to his feet. "I wonder how your brother's wife is doing, O'Brien?" he said. "Must be on her tenth or eleventh go-round by now, huh?"

"If that filthy animal has harmed Lorena, I'll—"

"Do nothing," Caldwell said. "You'll be dead soon, O'Brien, so don't worry about a thing. Your sister-in-law is Lum's woman now, and after what she's tasted today, she'll never leave him."

"Luke, I'm so worried about Lum," Dora DeClare said. "He should be back by now, don't you think?"

Caldwell grinned. "Hell, he could be with the O'Brien gal all night."

"I suppose so, but I do worry about him," Dora said. "He's so naïve and vulnerable in a way, like an overgrown schoolboy sometimes."

Caldwell lifted the pot from the fire and poured coffee into his cup. "I wouldn't worry about him. He can take care of himself."

"Oh, in my heart of hearts I know Lum will be fine." She shook her head. "I'm acting like a silly, overanxious mother, I guess."

After rolling a cigarette, Caldwell lit it with a

brand from the fire. Through a cloud of smoke, he said, "We've got two of the O'Briens. So where do we go from here?"

"Well, when Lum gets back, we send Lorena O'Brien back to Dromore." She smiled. "I wish I could see her husband's face when he sees the state she's in. Of course I'm hoping against hope that Lum did enough to drive her completely insane."

"And then?"

"And then we bargain with Dromore, with the O'Brien brothers as pawns." Dora looked quizzically at Caldwell. "Do you play chess?"

"I know what pawns are."

"Good. Then you know where my plan is taking me."

"Not quite. After Lum and me crucify them two on top of the mesa, where does the bargaining come in?"

"When the time comes I'll let you know," Dora said. She pushed a tendril of hair from her forehead. "I'm so hot."

Caldwell looked to the north where the hills were gathering shadows around them. "Be dark soon," he said. "You'll cool down."

"No, Luke, I won't," Dora said. "I'm in heat. The thought of that O'Brien slut getting something I'm not is troubling me."

Joshua, who'd been dozing by the fire, said, "There you go, Caldwell. An invitation if ever I heard one."

The Texan threw away the dregs of his coffee.

"She doesn't have to write it out," he said. "Not for me."

Dora lay on her back, smiling.

Joshua, idly watching Caldwell on top of his sister, decided that the master was so correct about humans—they were such a worthless bunch of garbage.

Joshua DeClare fed the fire with twigs and studied the play of light and shade among the hills as the great red ball of the sun sank slowly in the west over the Santa Fe Mountains. He memorized the colors, the shades of crimson, jade, and lilac that he would one day commit to canvas.

He was alone. Dora had gone to bathe in a stream deeper in the hills, and Caldwell, like a cur dog following a bitch in heat, had gone with her.

Judging by the shadows of the pine trees, they'd been gone an hour, maybe a little longer. Good riddance to them both. His sister's single-minded quest for revenge and all the hardship it entailed had tired him. He hadn't eaten in a couple of days, and before that his only sustenance had been a slice of blackened salt pork, hardly food for an invalid. He felt ill, very weak, and his hands trembled, a bad thing for a painter.

Joshua fed a twig into the fire, and from inside the cave he heard a man moan, probably that Jacob O'Brien person who was slowly dying of thirst. And his brother with him.

He stared into the flames, thinking. Unlike Dora, Joshua's need for revenge on the O'Briens didn't burn with a white-hot heat. He wished to avenge his father, of course, but he and Dace had never been close, though the old man adored Dora. After Joshua's accident, Dace had lost what little interest he had in his son. Who could take pride in a cripple?

But Dace had taken time to teach him about the old religion, much more ancient than Christianity, its simple tenants easy to grasp and understand:

To do good is evil. To do evil is good.

"A thing to always remember, Joshua."

Love is hate. Hate is love.

"The most meaningless of all emotions is love, remember that, Joshua."

To the best of his ability, Joshua had tried to live by the code, but somewhere along the way he'd failed. His landscapes brought pleasure, maybe even hope and faith, to thousands of people, and that was not the way of the master.

Beauty is ugliness. Ugliness is beauty.

Joshua knew that his sense of failure had twisted his mind like the falling horse had twisted his body; yet in truth he lived for his art, and if he ever had to stop painting he'd die a little death each day until life mercifully left him completely.

Lies are truth. Truth is a lie.

Well, he was living a lie. A great artist cannot be a true disciple of the ancient religion, and that thought, as darkness crowded around him, tore Joshua DeClare apart.

Later, Luke Caldwell told Dora that her brother welcomed the bullet that killed him.

"He just sat there, smiling at me, and took it," Caldwell said. "I mean, smack! Right between the eyes, and he smiled at me."

"I don't want to hear about it, Luke," Dora said. "Did you get rid of the body?"

"Yeah, I took it far."

Dora sat by the fire, and her beautiful eyes lifted to the Texan. "We had to kill him, didn't we?"

"Of course we did," Caldwell said. "He was slowing us down, Dora. Once we make our play against Dromore, we'll need to ride far and fast. We couldn't do that with a cripple hanging on to our coattails."

"He was all right," Dora said. "A fine oil painter."

"He was a crippled piece of dung," Caldwell said. "We're better off without him."

Dora nodded. "As you say, Luke."

She listened, frowning, as Caldwell said, "We better give water to those two in the cave. I don't want them dying on us. At least just yet, I don't."

"Couldn't we make them suffer just a little longer?" Dora said.

"No, we'd kill them, and you'd be tossing away your bargaining chips."

"Oh, water them, then," Dora said. "Then tie their ropes all the tighter."

After Caldwell stepped into the cave with a canteen, Dora drew her knees up to her chin and stared at the haloed moon. Coyotes called in the foothills, and night birds rustled in the pines. Beyond the circle of firelight the darkness hung close, like sable drapes closing off a brighter world beyond. The fire cracked sparks, and the lid of the coffeepot bounced as its contents bubbled.

Dora felt no sense of loss at Josh's death because she understood the necessity, but he'd been a fine artist and his talents would be missed. Well, at least by those who were interested in that kind of thing.

More urgently, her brother's death would leave her without an income for a while until his paintings sold more regularly. The works of dead artists were always in demand, and Joshua's agent in London had dozens, but it took time.

When Caldwell sat by the fire again, Dora poured him coffee and said, "Dromore will burn to the ground. We're agreed on that, are we not?"

Caldwell nodded. "Yeah, I guess it will."

"But we need money, Luke."

"I can always sell my gun."

"That's a shrinking market, don't you think?"

"Out here in the West, maybe. But there's always a demand for guns in the cities. I hear New Orleans is hiring."

Dora shook her head. "You're talking pie in the

sky, Luke. We need to make a grandstand play to score and score big."

"I could rob a bank," Caldwell said.

"For once use your brain instead of your gun," Dora said. "Dromore is the answer."

"I don't catch your drift."

"How much would Colonel O'Brien pay to get his sons back alive?"

Caldwell grinned. "Hell, a lot."

"Then all we have to do is set our price," Dora said. "I don't think fifty thousand would be too high."

"We could live high on the hog with that," Caldwell said, his eyes shining. "Buy us a big house and a carriage and four and—"

"Well, we could live on it for a while anyway," Dora said. She didn't add, *"But you won't be sharing it, idiot."* She said that only to herself.

"So we get the money, then gun the O'Briens and light a shuck, huh?" Caldwell said.

"Not quite. We use the O'Briens to burn Dromore to the ground and then we kill them."

"How the hell are we going to do that?" Caldwell said.

And Dora told him.

Chapter Forty-one

"How is she?" Shamus O'Brien said.

"She'll be fine, Colonel," Sarah said. "She has the baby with her, and she's resting. But she wants to talk with you."

"Girl, you look all used up yourself," Shamus said.

"I'm all right," Sarah said. "Lorena had it worse than me."

Anguish showed on the colonel's face. "She told me she wasn't—"

"She wasn't," Sarah said, her face calm.

"Thank God and all the saints in heaven for their tender mercies," Shamus said.

"Lorena?" Sarah said.

"Ah, yes, I'll go talk to her. And Sarah, lie down and rest."

The girl smiled. "I will, Colonel."

Shamus rolled his chair to the back of the house, tapped on Lorena's door, and made his way inside.

The woman sat up in her pillows, baby Shamus asleep beside her.

"You wanted to see me, Lorena?" Shamus asked.

"Yes, I have to tell you something."

The colonel rolled closer to the bed. "Are Nanny and the others taking good care of you?" he said.

Lorena smiled. "Spoiling me. I'm a bit tired is all, not sick."

"You've had a terrifying experience, and you need to rest quietly," Shamus said. "And I'm sure you're worried about Patrick and Jacob. We all are."

"Are you going after them, Colonel?"

"Yes, at first light. I'll ride with Samuel, Shawn, and the vaqueros, and I plan to bring those fiends all to justice, including the woman."

"Her name is Dora DeClare, and she says you hanged her father," Lorena said.

"I don't recollect the name," Shamus said. He whispered DeClare a few times, turning it over in his mind, then said, "No, I don't remember."

"She told me you hanged him for a rustler," Lorena said.

"I hanged a lot of rustlers," Shamus said.

"She means harm to you and Dromore, Colonel. I think she's a woman to be feared."

"Not after tomorrow. If the law doesn't hang her, she'll go to prison for a long time, her and that Texas gunfighter."

Lorena sat forward in the bed. "Colonel, they might shoot Patrick and Jacob, just out of spite."

"I'll hit them so hard and so fast they won't have

time," Shamus said. "One of my vaqueros is the best tracker in the territory. I'll run them to ground, never fear. They won't get a chance to shoot."

"It's thin, Colonel."

Suddenly, Shamus looked old and very tired. He nodded. "Yes, I know it is."

"You're worried," Lorena said.

"I'd be telling a lie if I said otherwise."

"Colonel, what are the chances of Patrick and Jacob surviving?"

Shamus tried to make his whole face a confident smile. He failed miserably because he knew Lorena was an intelligent woman and wanted it straight.

"Fifty-fifty," he said.

"Maybe less?"

"It depends on the gunfighter. A man who fights for wages might cut and run, or he might not."

"If he doesn't run?"

"Then there might be one chance in ten that he won't shoot my sons," Shamus said.

Lorena swallowed hard. "Shamus, I'm scared."

"So am I," the colonel said. "So am I."

"He says he's coming with us," Samuel O'Brien said. "Wants to be tied to his horse."

"I'm not going to try and talk him out of it," Shawn said. "Are you?"

"Hell, no," Samuel said. "He says maybe the gunfighter will cut and run."

"Maybe. But he could kill Pat and Jake just for the fun of it."

"We're going about this the wrong way," Luther Ironside said, helping himself to whiskey. "The way the colonel is setting it up, it's too dangerous."

"For whom?" Shawn said.

"Jake and Pat, that's for whom," Ironside said.

He pulled his chair and sat. "It's a job for one man. In, shoot the gunfighter and the gal, then out with Pat and Jacob." Ironside looked at Samuel, then Shawn. "We ride in there with an army like Grant taking Richmond, and we could end up with a lot of men dead on the ground."

"There's sense in what you say, Luther," Samuel said. "But the colonel wants to lead the charge. He's got his heart set on it."

Ironside nodded. "That's his style, charge regardless. Sure, we killed a whole heap of Yankees during the war doing just that, but we also lost a lot of lively lads who wore the gray. The colonel's about to repeat his mistake."

"Mistake?" Samuel said.

"Yeah," Ironside said. "It's a mistake to think we can charge into the camp of that woman—whatever her name is—and rescue Pat and Jake without them taking lead and maybe getting themselves killed."

Shawn looked at his brother. "Sam, I think Luther is right. I'll do it by myself."

"I was thinking I'd do it," Ironside said.

"Maybe the three of us," Samuel said. "Ride out without telling the colonel."

"How's Lorena, Sam?" Shawn said.

"She's doing just fine," Samuel said. "Why do you ask?"

"Because your place is here with her," Shawn said. "Right now she needs her husband by her side. Luther, since you're so all-fired set on going, we'll do it together."

"Two ain't one," Ironside said.

"We do it together or you stay home, old man," Shawn said.

Ironside opened his mouth to speak, but thought the better of it. When Shawn made up his mind about a thing, he meant it.

"All right," he said, "let's saddle up."

"Where's Pa?" Shawn said.

"He's in the chapel, talking to Ma," Samuel said.

"He's worried," Shawn said.

"Damn right he's worried," Ironside said. "He knows he could lose two sons, and that would kill him faster than any bullet."

"Stall him, Sam," Shawn said. "Stall him for as long as you can."

"I'll do my best. But the colonel's a mighty stubborn man, and he doesn't take to being stalled."

Shawn and Ironside rose to their feet but stayed where they were as the butler tapped on the door and stepped inside.

"A gentleman wishes to see Shawn," the man said. "He says his name is Ernest Thistledown."

"Thistledown!" Shawn said. "What the hell is he doing here?"

"There's one way to find out," Samuel remarked. And to the butler he said, "Show him in, please."

Thistledown, meek and insignificant, sidled into the study; his body was postured into a walking apology. "I'm so sorry to intrude," he said.

"I thought you'd be back east by this time," Shawn said. He gestured to the decanters. "Can I get you a drink?"

"A brandy would be excellent," Thistledown said. He rubbed his hands together. "Against the inclement chill of the evening."

Shawn introduced Samuel and Ironside, handed Thistledown his brandy, and then said, "What brings you to Dromore?" He hesitated a moment and added, "I was just about to leave."

The little man sat in a chair proffered by Ironside, who towered over him like a grizzled giant, and said, "I'm here to confirm a story, Mr. O'Brien, hence my unwarranted intrusion into, as it were, the bosom of your family."

Samuel cast Shawn an amused, quizzical look. He'd heard his brother speak of Ernest Thistledown, the feared bounty hunter, but this little man seemed about as dangerous as a mouse's shadow.

"You heard about Lum?" Shawn said.

"Admirably put, Mr. O'Brien, succinct and to the point. Yes, indeed, I'm enquiring about the man named Lum. I was accepting the hospitality of a rancher south of here when one of his drovers rode in and said that a Dromore servant girl had killed a man who was trying to . . . well, shall we just say subject her to a fate worse than death."

"Word gets around," Ironside said, suddenly irritable.

"Well, drovers talk to drovers, I suppose," Thistledown said. "The gentleman in question said he'd been told the attacker's name was Lowe or Lawson, but he wasn't sure. But it sounded close enough to Lum to cause me considerable agitation."

"It was Lum, and it was my wife who shot him, not a servant girl," Samuel said.

"Is he dead for certain, Mr. O'Brien?"

"As dead as a bullet in the brain can make a man," Samuel said.

Thistledown considered that, then said, "And the body of the deceased? Is it, as they say, still in situ?"

"Yes. We're sure as hell not going to bury the lout."

"Of course, and quite right, too," Thistledown said. He sipped his drink, then said, "This is a matter of some delicacy, Mr. O'Brien, but did your lady wife say where the . . . ah, assault took place?"

"In an arroyo in the Santa Fe foothills," Samuel said. "Head north along the west wall of Apache Canyon, and you'll be in the general area."

"My employers will expect me to confirm that Lum is in fact the deceased person," Thistledown said. "Even though, in all good conscience, I can't claim the kill."

Samuel looked into the little man's eyes, saw a glint of steel, and realized he'd been wrong about him. It was the fact that he looked so harmless that made Ernest Thistledown so dangerous.

"You can ride along with Luther and me," Shawn said. "We'll point you in the right direction."

Ironside looked Thistledown over, not liking what he saw. "You heeled?" he said.

"Yes, but I left my weapon at the door. I didn't think it would be mannerly to step into your parlor with a sawn-off shotgun hanging from my shoulder."

"Unhealthy," Ironside said.

"Quite," Thistledown said. He turned to Shawn. "May I inquire why you are night riding?"

"My brothers Jacob and Patrick have been kidnapped," Shawn said, "by friends of yours, Dora DeClare and her brother. They've got a Texas gunfighter with them." He picked up his hat from the table beside him. "We're going to save my brothers."

"The gunfighter's name is Luke Caldwell," Thistledown said.

Shawn was taken aback. "Are you sure?"

"When a man shoots at me, I tend to remember his name."

Ironside's eyes asked a question of Shawn. "He's one of the best there is," Shawn said. "Lightning fast on the draw and a born killer whose conscience doesn't trouble him none."

"Then we're doing right," Ironside said.

Shawn nodded. "Yes, Luther, we're doing right."

"I have a score to settle with Dora DeClare and Luke Caldwell," Thistledown said. "They scared me, and I don't like being scared."

Shawn headed for the door. "You'll have to keep up. Where we're headed isn't country for a buggy."

"I'm riding my horse," Thistledown said. "Reluctantly, but there it is."

"You finally trade for a real horse?" Shawn said.

"No. It's the same animal."

"Then it's a mule," Shawn said.

"Well, whatever it is, to my considerable discomfort, that's what I'm sitting on," Thistledown said.

Chapter Forty-two

"Something has happened," Dora DeClare said. "Lum should be back by now with the woman."

"Maybe he's taking her to Old Mexico," Luke Caldwell said, grinning, "on account of how he's fallen madly in love with her."

"Don't be ridiculous," Dora said. "Something's happened to him."

"You think the little lady loved him to death?" Caldwell said.

Dora rose to her feet. In the reflected firelight she looked like a pillar of flame. "We'll get those two up onto the mesa," she said.

"Now? In the dark?"

"Yes, now, Luke. And then you head for Dromore."

"Shouldn't we wait and see if Lum gets back first?" Caldwell said. "The O'Brien woman could carry our demands."

"Poor Lum is not coming back," Dora said. "I

think the O'Brien brothers were out looking for these two and stumbled on him. The damned barbarians must have shot him out of hand or strung him up, like they have so many others."

Caldwell got to his feet. "All right, we'll play it your way, Dora. I just hope you're right."

"Luke, don't think," Dora said. "You're not equipped for it. Just get the O'Briens out here, and we'll head onto the mesa."

Caldwell stepped into the cave, a knife in his hand.

Jacob was in bad shape and seemed to be unconscious, but Patrick glared at the Texan with hate in his eyes.

Caldwell was amused, and he grinned as he reached down and cut the rope that bound Patrick's ankles. "We're getting out of here," he said.

"Where is Lorena?" Patrick said.

"Who knows?" Caldwell said, studying Jacob's body, a trussed-up comma of bruises and blood on the cave floor. "Maybe they killed each other."

He dragged Patrick to his feet. "Get out," he said.

"What about my brother?"

"I'll take care of him. Now get out of here, and don't try any fancy moves. Dora is waiting for you outside with a rifle."

Patrick could barely move, his cramped legs stiff and sore. He took a couple of stumbling steps, then stopped as Caldwell cut Jacob's ankles free. "Be careful with him," he said. "He's been tied up for a long time. He won't be able to walk."

"Then he'll crawl," Caldwell said. "Now get out of here or I'll put a bullet into you."

A couple of vicious kicks to his ribs drew only a groan from Jacob, but no movement. Caldwell grabbed him by the shirtfront and dragged him out of the cave.

"This one's in bad shape," he said to Dora, who held a rifle on Patrick.

"You kept him tied up and denied him water," Patrick said. "What did you damned animals expect?"

"Give him water," Dora said. She motioned to Patrick with the rifle. "Another word out of you and I'll shoot you in the belly," she said. "I assure you, it will take you many painful hours to die."

"What do you want from us?" Patrick said.

"Money," Dora smiled. "And Dromore in ashes."

The woman's madness was obvious, and Patrick said nothing. He knew if he said a word she would shoot him—and display no emotion as she pulled the trigger.

Jacob groaned as the water moistened his bloody mouth and reached his parched throat. He opened his eyes and looked around him. But Patrick couldn't tell if he knew where he was, or who he was.

"Can he stand?" Dora said.

Caldwell dragged Jacob to his feet, but he immediately fell in a heap, like a marionette whose strings had just been cut.

"You'll have to put a loop on him and drag him up to the mesa behind your horse," Dora said. "Hurry, we don't have any time to lose."

The moon had dropped lower, and the sky was radiant with stars. A north breeze, bringing with it a tang of pine, stirred the air around Patrick's cheeks and made him realize how good it was to be alive. He wondered if Lorena felt that same breeze, or was her face, the color of marble, turned to a sky she could no longer see.

The thought disturbed Patrick so badly he was barely aware of the noose Caldwell dropped around his neck. The gunman passed the end to Dora, and then he looped a second rope across Jacob's chest under his armpits.

Caldwell left and returned leading two horses. He waited until Dora mounted, then said, "Tie the rope around your saddle horn, and if he gives you any trouble just drag him. Once he figures he's strangling, he'll walk willingly enough."

Caldwell mounted and took the gradual slope that led to the top of the mesa, dragging Jacob's inert body behind him. Dora followed, and Patrick felt the cruel jerk and tightening of the noose around his neck. He stumbled after the woman, his boots seeking traction on the grass and gravel rise.

The hopelessness and futility of his situation

filled Patrick with despair. He saw no way out, no path to freedom for him and Jacob. In the books he'd read as a child, the hero tied to a burning stake as the cannibals danced around him always escaped. "With a single bound he was free," the authors wrote, as though it was the easiest thing in the world.

Trussed up as he was, he could make no bound, and no dash to freedom. He and Jacob were at the mercy of a killer and a madwoman, and Patrick felt only fear and the death of hope.

The night air on top of the mesa was cool and clear, and the stars were above and around them.

"Take them to the rim," Dora said, "and tie their feet again."

Caldwell did as he was told, then backed away from the edge. He smiled at the woman. "If they as much as twitch, they'll both go over," he said.

"Good. Now you know what you have to do," Dora said. She stood at the rim, held on to the branch of a wind-twisted juniper, and peered over. "There are lights at Dromore," she said. "What does that portend?"

"Beats me," Caldwell said. "Maybe the colonel is so worried about his sons and daughter-in-law he can't sleep."

"I hope so," Dora said. "Soon his days of restful slumber will be over forever."

* * *

Luke Caldwell stared through starlight at the ravine ahead of him, a V of rock filled with brush and trees that slanted steeply to the flat. It would be a dangerous descent, but it would save time. He had to be back on top of the mesa by first light for Dora's plan to work.

A shard of Apache pottery, its color faded by time and weather to dark amber, lay at Caldwell's feet. He kicked the triangular-shaped piece of bowl into the ravine, and it seemed like forever before he heard it shatter on the rocks below.

Caldwell swallowed hard. One slip and . . .

He started his downward climb.

Chapter Forty-three

"What was that?" Shawn O'Brien said.

"Sounded like a rock," Luther Ironside said. He turned his gaze to the dark bulk of the mesa outlined against the star-scattered sky. "Must be an animal up there. Cougar maybe."

"Damn it," Shawn said, "I'm as jumpy as hell."

"Night riding was never one of my favorite pastimes," Ironside said. "Did it a few times in the war, but I never took to it. It can spook a man."

"I'll smell him," Ernest Thistledown said.

"Huh?" Ironside said.

"I've been thinking about how I will find Lum's body, if it is indeed he who has passed on," the little man said. "But if the sun's worked on him, he'll stink."

"Thistledown," Shawn said, "anybody ever tell you that you're a real pleasure to be around?"

"No. They have not."

"I wonder why?" Ironside said. "I mean, you being such a cheerful cuss an' all."

"In my line of work, the needs of the client always come first," Thistledown said. "They will ask, nay, demand, proof that Lum is dead and all danger from him has passed. Until I impart that information many people won't sleep soundly o' nights."

"He's dead," Shawn said. "Lorena shot him."

"The proof of the pudding, Mr. O'Brien. The proof of the pudding."

Shawn nodded. "All right, Thistledown, just follow your nose."

The little bounty hunter smiled. "Hah, a good joke, Mr. O'Brien."

A few sentinel stars still clung to the sky, and there was a growing light in the east when the three riders crossed the Pecos and swung north along Apache Canyon.

Thistledown, who claimed to have learned the rudiments of tracking from army scout Al Sieber and his protégé, a bright youngster by the name of Tom Horn, rode on ahead.

"Al helped me track down a breed over to the Mogollon Rim country a few years back," he'd said. "Him and young Tom. I shared a two thousand bounty with the pair of them and never regretted it."

But Luther Ironside doubted the story and had little confidence in Thistledown's abilities.

"If the little runt can follow a cold trail, then I'm the queen of England's uncle," he said.

But Thistledown did discover something—the body of Joshua DeClare.

Shawn and Ironside followed him into a clearing a few hundred yards to the west of the canyon. The area was a small meadow, bounded by pine and a few juniper, aspen growing on the slopes above.

DeClare's body was wedged into a rock overhang, his twisted legs dangling in space.

"Somebody arranged the little bastard like that," Ironside said. "As a joke, maybe."

"He's shot between the eyes," Shawn said. "Nothing funny about that."

Ironside looked at him. "Jake?"

Shawn shook his head. "Jacob's mean, but he wouldn't do something like that to a man."

"Boot tracks all over the place, so it wasn't Apaches," Ironside said.

"Then it had to be Luke Caldwell," Thistledown said.

"Why would Caldwell gun a cripple?" Ironside said.

"He was slowing them maybe, him and Dora," Thistledown said.

"I guess we should take him down from there, huh?" Ironside said.

"Why?" Shawn said. "He's nothing to us but an enemy." He swung his horse away. "Let's go find Patrick and Jake."

* * *

Thistledown again proved that he wasn't on the brag when he mentioned his ability as a scout. He read sign like an Apache and found the cave and the ashy circle of a campfire.

"They were here all right," Ironside said. He swung out of the saddle and laid a hand over the fire. "Cold," he said, "and they've been gone for a spell. Maybe they saw us coming and skedaddled."

Shawn dismounted, glanced at a noisy whiskey-jack jay attracted by the presence of humans, and stepped into the cave.

At first he could see little, but as his eyes accustomed to the gloom, he caught a metallic glint at the back of the cave. Shane kneeled, thumbed a match into flame, and studied the ground. He saw bloodstains and something else—Jacob's ivory-handled Buck knife lying on a flat section of rock.

It didn't look like the knife had fallen from Jake's pocket; rather, it seemed as though it had been carefully placed. The top bolster pointed west, in the direction of Glorieta Mesa.

Jacob was wounded, as the splashes of dried blood indicated, but somehow he'd managed to reach his knife and use it as a signpost.

Shawn stepped out of the cave and said to Ironside, "They're on top of the mesa."

Answering the question on the older man's face, he told how he'd found Jacob's knife and added,

"There's bloodstains all over the floor of the cave. Both Jacob and Patrick could be wounded."

"Then let's get up there," Ironside said.

"I'll tag along if you don't mind," Thistledown said. "Allow Lum to ripen, as it were, before I go looking for him."

"You're welcome," Shawn said. "But be careful with the scattergun. If it comes to shooting, which it will, we don't want to harm our own."

Chapter Forty-four

The remains of the night still clung to the mesa when Luke Caldwell climbed the ravine and reached the top. Dora DeClare, her rifle trained on the two prostrate O'Brien brothers, was waiting for him.

"Well?" she said.

"It went perfectly," Caldwell grinned. He saw Dora looking at him expectantly and said, "I pinned it to the door with my knife, then hightailed it. Even if somebody had come out right away, they wouldn't have been able to spot me in the dark."

"Are you sure they'll see it?" Dora said. The sky to the east was aflame, and her golden hair was touched with red.

"They'll see it," Caldwell said. He stepped to the mesa rim and looked over. "Still too dark to see, but Colonel O'Brien will be there soon. Count on it." Caldwell hesitated, then said, "Dora, I've never been able to read and write and do my ciphers. What did the note say?"

Dora stared at him in disbelief. She told herself again that she'd need to get rid of this illiterate, ignorant lout at the first opportunity.

"Why, Luke, I'll teach you how to do those things," she said, smiling. "We'll have lots and lots of time when we go back east." Dora glanced at the O'Briens to make sure they were still in no fit state to fight. "As for the note, it said just what we discussed. If he wants his sons back alive, the colonel must pay us fifty thousand dollars and burn down Dromore."

"Do you think he'll do it?" Caldwell said.

"Of course he'll do it. But we won't live up to our part of the bargain. What I didn't tell you earlier is that you'll drag those two back from the rim and quietly cut their throats. Then, before Colonel O'Brien even knows what's happening, we'll be halfway to Santa Fe."

A grin split Caldwell's face. "Damn it, Dora, you're brilliant."

"Yes, I know I am," Dora said. She looked at the sky. "Will the morning never come?"

"It'll be here soon enough, Caldwell said. "I'll take the horses to the north edge of the mesa so we can make a fast getaway, like you said."

"Yes, do it, and hurry. I want the O'Briens right on the rim when their dear papa sees them."

After Caldwell led the horses away, Dora shivered, but not from cold. She felt as though she was being watched . . . watched by someone with hostile eyes.

She glanced behind her, then, startled, turned and looked again.

A sudden spike of fear hit her in the belly, like a steel arrowhead. It was a trick of the early morning light, nothing else. She closed her eyes, then opened them again.

He was still there.

"Damn you, what do you want?" she called.

He made no answer. He stood silent and still as a statue, his brown robe flapping in the morning breeze.

Staring at her.

"What do you want?" Dora yelled, her voice almost a scream. "Go back to your God."

The monk stood, said nothing, staring.

Dora heard the pound of feet behind her. She swung around, the Winchester coming up fast.

"Don't shoot! It's Luke!" Caldwell came at a run, then stopped beside her. "I heard you shout. Is O'Brien here?"

"It was the monk. Remember in El Cerrito, the damned monk?"

Caldwell's gun flashed into his hand. "Where?"

Dora turned and pointed. "Over there."

"I see nothing," Caldwell said. "A tree. There's a twisted old tree."

The woman's eyes speared into the dawning light. She saw only the stunted juniper.

"He was there," she said. "I saw him."

Caldwell holstered his gun. "A trick of the light, Dora, was all. And you're as nervous as a horse on a high wire. You'll be all right when we reach Santa Fe."

"Yes," Dora said, managing a smile, "of course I'll be just fine in Santa Fe."

"You scared me there," Caldwell said. "I thought the O'Briens had got you fer sure."

The shout came faint but clear in the morning air.

"You on up there on the mesa!"

Dora stepped to the edge, then turned to Caldwell. "Get them on their feet at the rim."

Caldwell hoisted Patrick to a standing position, but Jacob was a dead weight and couldn't be lifted.

"Just prop him up against the other one," Dora said. She waited until Jacob's unconscious body leaned against Patrick's legs, then she called out, "What do you want?"

She saw Shamus O'Brien at the bottom of the slope, roped to a horse. But a dozen of his vaqueros were higher, making their way through tree and brush cover toward the top.

"Luke," Dora said, "climb lower. You have to get close enough to tell O'Brien to leave the money and pull his men away."

Suddenly, Caldwell didn't like this. He didn't like it one bit. Things were not going as planned. For one thing, they'd not considered how difficult conversation would be. And second, the Dromore hands were still climbing the slope.

He ran to the gorge and clambered part of the way down. When he figured he was within hailing distance, he shouted, "O'Brien, call off your hounds or your sons are dead men."

Shamus heard that, because he yelled, "You damned scoundrel, if you harm my boys I'll hang you."

"Where's the money?" Caldwell yelled.

"What?" Shamus answered, throwing his voice as he'd done on a dozen cannon-blasted battlefields.

"Leave the money!" Caldwell yelled.

"Not one red cent and be damned to ye," Shamus yelled.

A bullet *spaaang*ed off a rock near Caldwell's head and drove splinters into his cheek. His fingers came away bloody, and a surge of panic stabbed at him.

Damn him, O'Brien was making a fight of it!

Caldwell turned and scrambled back up the ravine, round after round smashing close, throwing dirt and gravel into his face. He reached the top of the mesa where Dora worked her rifle, shooting at targets on the flat.

She saw Caldwell and screamed, "Kill the O'Briens! Cut their throats!"

The Texan, frantically moving through a haze of fright and alarm, drew his knife. But he stayed where he was, rooted to the spot. Below him he heard voices, vaqueros yelling back and forth in Spanish he didn't understand.

"Kill them!" Dora screamed. "I want their throats cut!"

She stood at the rim and fired, racked the Winchester and fired again.

Anger is temporary madness, and Caldwell used it to overcome his fear. He worked himself into a killing rage, wanting only to smash, destroy, wipe the damned O'Briens from the face of their earth. Yes, cut their throats and watch the blood spurt, their smug faces dissolve into the terrifying knowledge of their own deaths.

Knife in hand, Caldwell advanced on Patrick and Jacob, his face savage.

Then Jacob moved.

He swung his bound legs and hit Patrick hard behind the knees. Patrick yelled, collapsed in a heap, and took a header over the rim. Jacob rolled and followed him, he and his brother hollering as they tumbled through empty air.

Caldwell, cheated of his prey and mad clean through, ran to the edge of the mesa, his gun in hand. A bullet split daylight an inch from his right ear, and he yelped in fright and surprise.

That shot had come from behind him!

Caldwell turned and saw three mounted men walk their horses toward him, two of them firing rifles from the shoulder. He was aware of Dora shooting at the riders, and for the moment she had them pinned in place.

The Texan saw his chance and took it.

He ran for his saddled horse, bullets kicking

around him. Behind him he heard Dora scream, "Caldwell, you bastard!"

He kept on running.

A small man riding a red mule split from the other two and charged at Caldwell, his mount's hooves clanging on the hard caprock. He held a scattergun in his right hand, wide of his body.

A scared gunfighter running like a maiden aunt from an unbuttoned fly is still dangerous and a man to contend with.

Caldwell stopped, turned, set his feet, and thumbed off two fast shots. Ernest Thistledown threw up his hands and tumbled off his mule, his shotgun spinning away from him.

Caldwell ran to his horse, mounted, and galloped toward the north rim of the mesa. A few shots followed the Texan before he disappeared from sight.

Dora DeClare had run her Winchester dry. But she pulled Jacob's short-barreled Colt from the pocket of her dress and cut loose at Shawn and Ironside.

Shawn hesitated, reluctant to shoot at a woman, but Ironside, hardened by war, had no such compunction. Firing his rifle from the hip, he hit Dora twice and calmly watched her fall.

Ironside's hard blue eyes looked beyond the woman to the north of the mesa. "Caldwell got away, damn him," he said.

"We'll get him," Shawn said. "I'll go take a look at Thistledown."

But before he could move, Dora, the front of her

dress covered with a scarlet bib of blood, rose to her feet. She ignored the Dromore riders and staggered to the mesa rim. There she did something strange that perplexed Ironside and troubled Shawn.

Dora DeClare turned in the direction of Dromore. She lifted her hands, nails extended like talons, and made clawing motions, as though trying to tear down the house. A noise came from her throat that sounded like an animal growl, low, threatening, filled with hate.

"Damn you, that's enough," Ironside yelled. He triggered another shot, and the woman toppled over the rim.

But what had been strange before became stranger still.

Later, when they talked about it, only Shamus, Samuel, and Shawn saw the phenomenon. None of the vaqueros saw it, nor did Luther Ironside, much to his chagrin.

When Shamus described what he'd seen, he said, "A holy monk, a man of God, stood over the woman's body, as though he was waiting for something. Then, after a few minutes he swung away, his arms extended, as though he was dragging away a person that I couldn't see. And then I heard a terrible scream, and then nothing." He crossed himself. "Jesus, Mary, and Joseph, and all the saints in heaven, it was an awful sight for a Christian man to see."

Shawn and Patrick said they'd witnessed the same thing and heard the scream.

But Ironside said, "I saw an eagle flying around, and he could've made the scream you heard. As for the holy monk"—here he'd looked hard at the colonel—"it could be that three superstitious Irishmen saw a thing that wasn't there, like see the banshee."

"Is that what you think, Luther?" Shamus said.

"It's what I know, Colonel."

"Then you could be right. But you're not."

Dora DeClare and her brother were buried in unmarked graves on the open range. No one said words over them. A search was made by the Dromore vaqueros, but Lum's body was never found.

Chapter Forty-five

The first snow flurries of fall tossed in a cold late September wind when Sheriff John Moore paid a visit to Dromore.

The three invalids who sat with Shamus, Samuel, and Luther Ironside in the study were all on the mend.

Patrick had suffered a broken leg in the fall from the mesa, Jacob three broken ribs and a fractured left wrist, and doctors had dug two bullets out of Ernest Thistledown's chest. For a while the little man's survival had been touch and go, but to everybody's surprise he'd pulled through and was now talking about heading back east. Even Luther Ironside allowed that Thistledown was as tough as a trail drive steak and a credit to the bounty hunter profession.

"The reason I'm here, Colonel, is about the recent misunderstanding involving your son Patrick," Moore said. "In a word, I am the bearer of a written apology from Mr. James Wentworth on behalf of himself and the Georgetown Vigilance Committee." He beamed as though about to say something important. "And it's in duplicate."

With a flourish, he produced two sealed envelopes. "One for you, Colonel O'Brien." He handed Shamus the letter. "And, last but not least, one for you, Patrick."

Shamus sat in his wheelchair, the unopened envelope in his hand. "I would hardly call condemning a man to death by mistake a misunderstanding," he said.

"For which Mr. Wentworth is most sorry," Moore said. He looked anxiously at the envelope. "As you will read, Colonel."

"Later," Shamus said. "Samuel, get the sheriff a drink."

"Not a single drop, if you please," Moore said. "My recent brush with death has convinced me that the future of John Moore lies not in debauchery but in sobriety and a strict avoidance of fancy women."

Moore saw with some alarm that Samuel was about to sit down again and said, "Well now, Sam, as I think about it, I could have just a modicum to wet me pipe, like."

The sheriff watched anxiously as Samuel poured a dash of whiskey into a glass. "Ah, Sam, perhaps a slightly larger modicum."

After he saw Moore settled with a volume of

whiskey that satisfied him, Jacob said, "Any word of Luke Caldwell?"

"Jake, a man called Cassidy or Clifton was involved in a cutting in Santa Fe a month ago," Moore said. "It could've been him."

"Anything else?"

"Not that I've heard."

"If you learn anything, let me know right away."

"Oh, I will. How are your hands, Jake?"

"They're just fine, good enough to draw down on a snake like Caldwell."

Moore shook his head. "The whole affair with Dora DeClare and her brother was a bad business. Some of what happened I don't understand myself, and some of it I played badly."

"No, you played a man's part, Moore," Thistledown said. "You have no call to beat up on yourself."

"Thank'ee for the kind words," the sheriff said. He looked over at Shamus. "Colonel, did you ever recollect the woman's pa that she said you hung?"

"No, I didn't," Shamus said. "Luther, do you remember stringing up a rustler called DeClare?"

"Sure don't recollect, Colonel. When I hang a man, the last thing I want is to know his name."

"A bad business," Moore said again. "So many dead people." He held his empty glass out to Samuel. "Sam, I'm just so upset, another if you please."

"A modicum?" Samuel said, smiling.

"Well, maybe a tad larger modicum than the last one."

"Hell, Moore, why don't you just take the bottle?" Ironside said, his face sour.

"Oh, no," the sheriff said. "Remember what I told you, Luther? I'm done with strong drink. Well, in large quantities, that is."

As Moore rose to leave, a little unsteadily, he said to the entire room, "I heard this just yesterday. The morning Dora DeClare died, the Mexicans say the church bell in El Cerrito rang. Only thing was, there was nobody pulling on the rope." He looked around him. "Strange, that."

"The wind," Ironside said. "A prairie wind that blew in the right direction."

"Big bell," Moore said. Nothing more.

Sheriff Moore rode to Dromore again a week later and asked to talk with Jacob "on a matter of extreme urgency."

"Caldwell?" Jacob said.

"Seems like."

"Where?"

"A town called McGowan, north of the Malpais. Whiskey drummer just got into town, and he says his stage changed horses in McGowan and he met the new town marshal, a big feller by the name of Caldwell."

"Is it the same man, John?"

"Could be. Seems that Caldwell was given a star

just before he gunned a drifter an' would-be badman by the name of Henry Sims. The drummer says Sims claimed to be the cock o' the walk in McGowan—until Caldwell taught him otherwise."

"Straight-up fight?" Jacob said.

"Uh-huh. The drummer says he was in the Stage Stop saloon when it came down. Sims was drinking at the bar when Caldwell walked in and said that Sims had been making some mighty loud noises around town and that he was sick and tired of hearing them. He told Sims to mount his horse, put a heap of git between him and McGowan, and never come back."

Moore put a hand to his throat. "All this talking is making me dry, Jake."

Jacob poured a whiskey for Moore, then the lawman continued, "The drummer says Sims said he was goin' nowhere and that Caldwell could go stick his head up his ass. Well, Caldwell wasn't gonna take that kind of sass, and he drew down on Sims. After the smoke cleared, the drummer put his business card on Sims's chest and he says it covered all three bullet holes."

Moore sipped his bourbon and smacked his lips in appreciation. "That was good shootin', Jake," he said.

"Depends on how fast Sims was," Jacob said. "If a man has time, he can place three shots pretty close."

"Well," Moore said, "I thought you might like to know." He pointed the index finger of the hand that held his glass at the deep scar that ran from Jacob's throat to the corner of his left eye. "On account of that."

"Yeah, he put the spur to me pretty good," Jacob said. "He owes me."

"Big-time," Moore said, turning away. He didn't like to look at the scar.

"Jacob, you're still not completely well," Lorena said. "And so skinny you're nothing but breath and breeches."

"Better than anybody, Lorena, you know what we faced," Jacob said. "It was an evil thing, and Luke Caldwell was a big part of it."

"Jake, your hands still haven't healed," Shawn said. "Maybe another six months and you could take Caldwell, but not now."

Jacob's fingers strayed to the scar on his throat and face. "Forget this?"

Shamus said, "Sit down, Jacob, and play me a little Chopin, perhaps the Nocturne in G Minor. It's not a demanding piece, is it?"

"No, Colonel, it's not. It makes few technical demands of the pianist."

"Well, let me hear the intermezzo. I always think it sounds almost like a choral work."

Jacob sat and looked at his hands. They were still stiff in the knuckles and pale, as though the blood would never come back into them.

"I can't," he said.

Shamus nodded. "I know you can't. Then, if you can't play the piano, how in God's name are you ever going to throw down on a practiced gunfighter who just killed a man?"

"Luke Caldwell needs killing, and on the day I'll be faster than he is," Jacob said.

"Hell, Jake, I'll go after him," Luther Ironside said.

"You're not fast enough," Jacob said.

"Then I'll outlast the demon."

"Luther, listen to what Jacob told you—you're too slow and too old," Shamus said.

As Ironside muttered objections, Jacob rose to his feet. "I want no more discussion about this. It's my job. I've got it to do."

He stepped to Shamus's side, and for the first time in years touched him, placing his hand on his father's shoulder. "Pa, you didn't give ransom money to Dora DeClare because Dromore pays tribute to no one. Instead you fought, but the battle isn't over yet. As long as Caldwell's shadow falls on the earth, it still rages."

Shamus put his hand on Jacob's. "And we don't surrender to anyone or forgive a wrong, do we?"

"No, Colonel, we don't."

"Then do what you have to do, son. But come back to us when the final bugle sounds."

Jacob nodded. "I feel a calling. I don't know what it is, but when I've answered it, I'll return to Dromore."

"May Jesus, Mary, and Joseph, and all the saints

protect you, Jacob. And when you've answered your calling, return to this house."

Sarah waited by Jacob's horse as he swung into the saddle.

"You take care of yourself," she said.

Jacob said, "We haven't spoken for a spell. How's Dromore treating you?"

"Very well. Samuel gave me the sorrel horse I rode when . . ."

"Yes, he told me. The sorrel will make you a fine mount," Jacob said.

"Yes. Yes, he will."

After a moment, Jacob touched his hat brim. "Well, so long, Sarah."

"Jacob, I'll worry, so please take care."

"I surely will."

Sarah watched Jacob ride away until he disappeared into distance and a shimmering heat haze. She felt a sense of loss, as though a part of her had gone with him.

Chapter Forty-six

McGowan, huddled close to the foothills of the San Mateo Mountains, was a cow town like any other, maybe a little less dusty, a little less shabby, and a lot more crowded. But it still boasted only a single street flanked by saloons, stores, and business premises, a stage and telegraph office, and, with a new town's optimism, a half-constructed train station. But no railroad.

It was full dark when Jacob rode into town. The saloons were ablaze with light, and reflector lamps lined the boardwalks, casting an alternating pattern of orange and black on the street.

When he'd ridden only twenty-five yards he saw a livery stable, its doors wide open to catch the night breeze. An old-timer wearing somebody's cast-off suit was tipped back in a chair near the door as he watched the world and his life go by.

Jacob drew rein. "Howdy," he said.

"Right back at ya, I'm sure, sonny," the oldster said.

"Got room for my horse?" Jacob said.

"Got room fer fifty hosses. Cost you two bits a night, another two bits fer oats."

"Your prices come high," Jacob said.

"You're the one that needs a stable, sonny."

"I also need a place to wash up," Jacob said.

"There's a pump around back, cost you two bits. Soap and towel is two bits extry."

Jacob swung out of the saddle. "You'll be a rich man one day," he said.

"And who's to say I ain't already," the oldster said.

He looked over Jacob and his gaunt mount. "You come from the Malpais way?"

"Hell, no."

"Just wondered. If you don't mind me sayin' so, you look all used up."

"Feel that way, too."

Jacob followed the old man into the stable, unsaddled his horse, and forked him some hay. He poured a scoop of oats into the bucket hanging in the stall, then said, "I'll use the pump now."

"Soap and a towel?" the oldster said.

"Sure, why not? I don't mind making you richer."

After he washed his face and hands and combed his wet hair, Jacob paid the old man. As casually as he could, he said, "Marshal in town?"

Now the oldster looked at him more closely, his eyes lingering on Jacob's Colt and the scar on his face. "He's out of town," he said, "over to Haystack

Mountain way chasing a thief who robbed . . . well, you don't care who he robbed, but he got away with two dollars and a silver-backed comb."

"Know when the marshal will be back?"

"Maybe tomorrow, maybe tonight. Our new lawman don't like being away from his whiskey an' whores too long."

Jacob absorbed that and then said, "I need a room for the night."

"Only one hotel in town, sonny, an' that's run by the widder Milroy, but she tole me earlier today that she's all full up, every nook an' cranny."

The old man jerked a thumb over his shoulder. "You can bed down here. Got me a stall back there with an iron cot, an' it'll sleep you just fine. Cost you—"

"I know, two bits."

"You learn fast, sonny."

Jacob O'Brien stepped along the boardwalk to a Chinaman's restaurant recommended by the old-timer. He hadn't been in a town of this size in a long time and noticed how both men and women gave him the road, their wary eyes angling to his gun and the terrible scar on his face.

Jacob smiled, thinking that he must look like a real desperate character. When they looked past the scar, people saw a tall, lanky man with iron-colored eyes who wore a Colt like it was part of him. Apart from his gunbelt, boots, and spurs, all of them top quality, the raggedy rest of what he wore wouldn't have sold for fifty cents in a used clothing store, and that included his battered hat and scuffed shotgun chaps.

The restaurant was called Charlie O'Donnell's Bar and Grill, because the Chinese family who bought it had never gotten around to changing the name. Without waiting for his order, the proprietor, a smiling, bowing man with a long pigtail, served Jacob a clear chicken soup with dumplings, some kind of pork stew with rice on the side, and a glass of beer.

The food was good, and Jacob ate heartily. A pot of hot tea and delicate pink rice cakes completed the meal, and Jacob vowed that in future he'd be more favorably inclined toward the entire Celestial race.

Now he'd eaten, Jacob felt better, but he was on edge, a niggling sick feeling deep in his gut. He smoked a cigarette and tried to relax, but when he stretched the fingers of his gun hand they were stiff and sore. He knew he was in no shape to go toe-to-toe with a gunfighter like Caldwell and beat him on the draw-and-shoot.

Jacob had to face reality. Tonight or tomorrow he'd get into a gunfight he couldn't win. There was no way around that stark fact. All he could hope to do was put enough lead into Caldwell to drop him before . . .

He worked the fingers of his hand, opened and closed them, but after a few minutes, the pain and stiffness were as bad as ever. No, they were worse. Much worse.

Suddenly, the Chinese man glided to his side, smiling. He turned toward the kitchen, waved, and jabbered words that Jacob couldn't understand.

A young girl, no more than sixteen, stepped to the table. The Chinaman talked to the girl, who listened intently. After the man finished speaking, the girl bowed to both him and Jacob and hurried away.

Before Jacob could wonder at this strange behavior, the girl came back, carrying a small jade jar. A tiny carved dragon with ruby eyes adorned the lid, and when the girl removed it, Jacob smelled incense.

The Chinese girl sat in a chair opposite Jacob. She took the cigarette from his fingers, ground it out in an ashtray, and then placed his right hand palm down on the table. The girl smiled at him and smeared a little of the jar's contents on the back of his hand. The white ointment was strangely cool and slick without being greasy.

"Make feel good, you see," the proprietor said, beaming.

The girl worked the ointment into the tendons of Jacob's hand and then his wrist where the tight hemp had left scars. The pain was intense, and Jacob breathed through clenched teeth as the girl's strong fingers dug deep.

After ten minutes she moved to his knuckles

and then the finger joints, and the pain grew, blossoming like fire. Jacob, fearful of being crippled, was tempted to pull his hand away, but the Chinese girl's serene expression and focused concentration helped reassure him.

It took thirty minutes, then the girl sat back in her chair and said, "Drink tea now and do not move hand. I come back soon."

The girl left, and Jacob used his other hand to pour tea into a tiny porcelain cup. He was trembling, the pain he'd felt an all too vivid memory.

Two cups of tea and twenty minutes later, the girl returned. She smiled at Jacob and lifted his hand from the table. "Move now," she said.

Jacob did as he was told. Expecting pain, he was surprised when his clenching fist felt supple, the stiffness gone. He tried wiggling his fingers, and the result was the same.

"My hand feels better than it ever did before," he said.

The girl smiled and showed her own hands, the knuckles red and swollen. "I have taken your pain," she said. "But in a while it will leave me."

The Chinese refused any payment for the massage, saying only that relieving the pain of another human being was its own reward.

His conscience flaying him, Jacob didn't tell them his motives were considerably less pure—he wanted his hand to move smoothly because he needed it to kill a man.

Chapter Forty-seven

When the morning light woke Jacob O'Brien, he sat up with a start, the mission bells ringing in his ears.

Even as the remnants of the dream faded, his heart still pounded and his mouth was dry. He glanced around him wildly, reestablished where he was in reality, and then he remembered . . . the dream returning piece by piece, as though he looked into a kaleidoscope and saw the fragments come together to form pictures in his mind . . .

The mission's walls were the color of sand, and behind it stood a green apple tree. The monk with blue eyes who stood at the open oak doors, said, "Jacob, it is harvest time. Help us pick the apples."

The monk handed him a basket. "When all the green apples are gathered, you may leave."

Jacob took the basket and picked the apples. But the

more fruit he took from the tree, the more green apples grew to take their place.

"My basket is full," Jacob told the monk, "but there are more apples on the tree."

"You have many baskets to fill," the monk said, "many green apples to pick. You must stay here at the mission until your work is done."

"But how long will that be?" Jacob said.

"After the winter, after the spring, after the summer until autumn and the next harvest comes," the monk said.

"I'm a prisoner here!" Jacob said.

"No, my son," the monk said, "you are a tormented soul that needs rest and light in your darkness."

Jacob remembered no more because he woke up at that point, as the mission bells rang. He smiled and flexed his supple gun hand. It was not bells ringing he'd heard in his sleep, but the sound of a hammer on an anvil.

He arose from the creaking iron cot, stretched the kinks out of his back, and stepped outside the rear of the barn to where the old-timer had a blacksmith shop. The man had been shaping a horseshoe on the anvil horn, but now he stopped and looked at Jacob.

"You like green apples, sonny?" he said.

"Talking in my sleep, huh?" Jacob said.

"Yeah, about monks an' missions an' green apple trees."

"Sorry."

The oldster shrugged. "Ain't nothing to me, but most gents that sleep here talk about whiskey and whores, though I've had a couple that had conversations with their mothers." He nodded toward the front of the barn. "Coffee in the office."

"Two bits?"

"No, I provide hot coffee as a courtesy to my guests."

"You're all heart," Jacob said, smiling, taking the sting out of the remark.

"I know. That's why I ain't gettin' any richer."

The old man tonged the cooling horseshoe and plunged it into the cherry-red glow of the forge. Jacob left him to it and went after coffee.

For the first time in months, he was able to build and light a cigarette without his useless fingers spilling tobacco down his front. His hand felt good. Now would it be fast enough to match Caldwell's speed on the draw?

Time will tell, Jacob thought.

He buckled on his gunbelt and stood with his shoulder against the frame of the open barn door, drinking coffee with one hand and smoking with the other.

The sun was only now lifting above the San Mateo Mountains, but McGowan had already come to life. Businessmen in broadcloth and housewives wearing bonnets, wicker baskets on their arms, trod the boardwalks while a few slugabed merchants hurried to open awnings and unlock doors. The sporting crowd, late sleepers, was nowhere to be seen, and the saloons were as yet not open for business.

Jacob was drinking his third cup of weak coffee when Luke Caldwell rode into town.

Stepping out from the angled shadow of the barn, Jacob saw people on the boardwalks stop to watch their new lawman ride down the middle of the street. Caldwell sat upright in the saddle, his face grim as befitted the town marshal who expected a hero's welcome. He led a mustang pony, a man draped across its back, his wrists and ankles tied together under the animal's belly.

From what Jacob could see the dead man was a small towhead, thin and dressed only in pants and a faded red shirt, his feet bare.

"What happened, Marshal?" a man on the boardwalk said.

"He drew down on me," Caldwell said.

Jacob figured that a man desperate enough to steal two dollars and a silver-backed comb was unlikely to own a belt gun. If any of the onlookers thought the same, they didn't let it show.

Caldwell reined up, and the mustang stopped behind him, its ugly head hanging. "He tried to drygulch me," Caldwell said. "Then, when I attempted to arrest him, he pulled a gun on me."

"You were quite right, Marshal," a storekeeper

with a florid face and white apron said. "Mathias Knowles was a damned nuisance."

"You kill a man in this town for being a nuisance?"

Jacob had stepped onto the boardwalk, and he stood watching Caldwell, his hand close to his holstered Colt.

The Texan's face registered alarm, then anger, and finally mild amusement. "Howdy, Jacob," he said.

Jacob nodded. "Luke."

"What are you doing here?" Caldwell said, as though talking to an old friend.

"Passing through. I've got a job to do, and then I'm riding."

Caldwell's eyes hardened, then he looked over to the growing crowd. "One of you men get Abe Clay," he said. "He's got a burying to do."

"Where's his gun, Luke?" Jacob said.

"What the hell are you talking about?" Caldwell said.

"You claim he drew down on you. Where's his gun?"

A few people muttered to one another, and a couple of men nodded, as though they expected an answer.

"Hell, I don't know," Caldwell said. "I forgot to pick it up."

"What kind of gun was it?" Jacob said, pushing it.

"I don't know. A man draws down on you, you

don't take time to see what kind of revolver he's got in his hand." He looked to the crowd again. "Ain't that right, folks?"

"That's right, Marshal," the florid man said.

"After you shot him, did he drop his gun?" Jacob asked, enjoying himself.

But Caldwell, his face furious, knew he was being railroaded and didn't answer. He was saved from further questions by the appearance of the under-taker, who glanced at the ragged corpse and said glumly, "City rates?"

"Speak to the mayor," Caldwell said.

Abe Clay nodded. "City rates."

As Clay took the mustang in tow, Caldwell threw a single, vicious glance at Jacob, then rode down the street and dismounted outside the marshal's office.

After Caldwell vanished inside the adobe build-ing, the florid storekeeper said to Jacob, "What are you, mister? A troublemaker?"

"I sure am," Jacob said. "You want me to make some?"

The man looked into Jacob's eyes and didn't like what he read there. Muttering to himself, he walked into his store and slammed the door behind him.

Jacob stood for a while, watching the marshal's office. He'd opened the ball. How would Caldwell respond?

* * *

Whitey Morehead answered that question.

He found Jacob in the Oxtail, a saloon and dancehall that had a tuned piano and a tolerant bartender.

"Been looking fer you all over, Jake," Morehead said. He was a short, wiry man with hair so blond it looked white. He wore a deputy's star on his vest, but no belt gun.

Jacob had taken the precaution of turning the piano to face the door. He watched Morehead's hands but continued to play.

"What do you need, Whitey?" he said.

"Me? Nothing. But Luke wants to buy you a drink at the Lone Star tonight. He says around seven if that's convenient."

"Why would Caldwell want to buy me a drink?" Jacob said.

Morehead shrugged. "Hell, I don't know. Maybe he likes you."

"I heard you were in Yuma doing twenty to life, Whitey," Jacob said.

"You heard wrong, Jake." He took a couple of steps closer to the piano. "What the hell is that tune?"

"Chopin."

"Never heard of him."

"No, Whitey, you wouldn't," Jacob said. "And a word of advice—if you take a step closer you'll have to skin the hogleg you got shoved into the back of your pants."

"I came peaceful," Morehead said.

"You're a snake, Whitey, and just as low-down."

"That's a hell of a thing to say to a man, Jake. I've got friends in this town."

"I know. Caldwell's one of them, and with friends like him, who needs enemies, huh?"

Jacob continued to play as Morehead said, "Bob Lambert's in town. He's a deputy like me."

"And he's an even meaner and lower-down snake than you, Whitey." Jacob shook his head. "You're in some mighty bad company."

"Damn you, Jake, do you accept Luke's invitation or no?" Morehead said.

"Tell him I'll be there."

The gunman smiled. "I'm looking forward to it, Jake."

"Crawl out of here, Whitey," Jacob said.

After Morehead left, the bartender stepped to the piano, a towel over his shoulder and a worried expression on his heroically mustached face.

"Mister," he said to Jacob, "you don't know me and I don't know you, so here's a word of advice I'd give to my own son—get on your horse and ride, and don't come back to McGowan again."

Jacob looked up from the piano keyboard. "Who is it?"

"All three of them. Caldwell's fast, so is Whitey, but Bob Lambert is pure pizen. When you get an invite like that, they mean to kill you. It's happened before."

"I know about Lambert," Jacob said. "Uses a crossdraw pretty well. He killed Steve Lupton up in the Nations six month ago, and nobody, including me, considered Lupton a bargain. Whitey's a snake. When bullets start flying there's no saying which way he'll wriggle."

"Well, anyway, now you know."

"I guess I do."

The bartender stood listening for a while, then said, "I've always liked Chopin's Nocturne in G Minor. It departs from his usual ternary form, and I find that refreshing."

Jacob shook his head and smiled. "Is there anything western men haven't done or don't know?"

"If you mean collectively, the answer is, damned little," the bartender said.

The railroad clock on the wall chimed six, and suddenly Jacob was on a high lonesome, and the black dog that was his depression crouched in a corner, waiting.

Chapter Forty-eight

A gunfight is a sudden thing, but Jacob O'Brien had time to think about it. In an hour he'd face three fast guns, two of them with whom he had no quarrel.

Bob Lambert worked both sides of the law. He'd been a shotgun guard for Wells Fargo and had done a couple of hellfire stints as a boomtown lawman. Some said he'd ridden with Jesse and Frank and them, but for sure, and until recently, he'd hired out his gun as a range detective up Montana way. Whitey Morehead would kill anybody if the pay was enough, and he'd always been on the wrong side. He'd spent time in Yuma Territorial Prison, and Jacob reckoned he'd only been enjoying the outdoors for a few months.

Both men were professional gunfighters, and their services didn't come cheap. Luke Caldwell must have big plans for McGowan if he'd hired those two.

Jacob finished playing and closed the lid on the piano. His gun hand felt good, and it would have to be.

"You're not taking my advice, huh?" the bartender said.

"Seems like," Jacob said.

"Then have a drink on me; take the edge off."

The bartender passed a glass to Jacob and poured a shot. "You hungry?" he said. "I got some cheese and green apples."

"Green apples?" Jacob repeated, surprised.

"They're tart, but folks like them with a piece of Stilton."

"No, I guess I'll pass," Jacob said.

"Maybe that's best," the bartender said. "Green apples can give a man a bellyache."

"There's a mission where green apples grow," Jacob said.

"Is that a fact?"

"Uh-huh. There's a tree full of them behind the mission. And there's a blue-eyed monk in a brown robe, and he looks after the tree."

"Now where would that be?"

"I don't know."

The bartender was silent, staring into Jacob's eyes. Then he said, "Drink your whiskey, piano player. It's almost time."

Jacob O'Brien's spurs rang on the boardwalk as he walked in the direction of the Oxtail saloon.

Night shadowed the town, and a warm breeze from the south carried the cinder and timber smell of the Malpais lava beds. Ahead of Jacob a sudden gust lifted a scrap of newspaper from the street. It hung in the air for what seemed an eternity, then fluttered back to earth like a stricken dove.

Jacob stepped into the Oxtail.

The night was young, but the sporting crowd was out in force, gamblers, whores, loungers, and a few miners and cowboys rubbing shoulders with big-bellied men in broadcloth.

Jacob smiled to himself. It seemed that the word had gotten around that a man would die in the saloon that night, and folks wanted to see the action.

A piano man had been tickling the ivories, but the music strayed to a stop when Jacob stepped to the bar. The crowd that had been laughing and noisy when he'd entered now fell silent and cleared a space to give him room. Jacob glanced at the faces of the people around him. A few showed sympathy, even concern, but most revealed a feral anticipation of what was to come. This promised to be a big night in McGowan, and the excited crowd didn't want to miss a single moment of it.

"What can I get you, mister?" the bartender said. He used a dirty towel to describe a beer-streaked circle in the mahogany in front of Jacob.

"Luke Caldwell," Jacob said. "But I guess he already knows I'm here."

The mirror behind the bar provided Jacob with a view of the crowd. He watched it part, like a wave breaking over a rock, as Caldwell pushed his way through. Whitey Morehead and Bob Lambert followed in his wake, grinning their arrogance.

"Right on time, Jake," Caldwell said. "Must be that good Irish breeding of your'n."

Jake turned and smiled. "What would a mongrel like you know about breeding, Caldwell?"

Morehead and Lambert flanked the Texan and saw the sudden fury in his face. They moved aside a couple of feet and cleared room for their gun hands. Behind them, the crowd shuffled away from the line of fire, and a saloon girl giggled in nervous anticipation.

Caldwell was on the prod, but he refused to be baited; he was prepared to let the pre-gunfight ritual run its course.

Jacob tried for an edge, anything to get the Texan rattled.

"Still worshipping the dark forces, Luke, or have you given up on that after what happened to Dora DeClare?" he said.

"Nah, I never held with that hell, Jake," Caldwell said. "And Dora, well she was a hack for rent, any man's ride. Besides that, she was crazy."

Jacob made no answer, and Caldwell let the silence

stretch taut before he said, "You said some hard words to me out in the street, Jake."

"I reckon I did," Jacob said. "You killed an unarmed man, like the lowdown, dirty yellow dog you are."

Fighting talk. But Caldwell again let it slide.

"I'm going to buy you a drink and then I'm arresting you," he said.

"On what charge?"

"I'll come up with something."

"You think I'll let you and those two coyotes with you take me into your jail?" Jacob said. "What are the chances I'd come out alive?"

"About the same chance as you've got right here and now if you don't come along quiet."

"Morehead, Lambert, I've got no quarrel with you," Jacob said. "You can step away from this."

"Go to hell," Lambert said. And Whitey Morehead grinned.

Jacob nodded. "You two were notified." He met Caldwell's eyes. "The sand has run through the glass, Luke. My talking is done."

And he drew.

Jacob fired at Lambert first, figuring he was the fastest of the three. He saw Whitey hesitate, not liking this, and switched to Caldwell. Jacob and the Texan fired at the same time. Caldwell took the hit, staggered, and fired again; his bullet tore into Jacob's waist an inch above his empty holster. Lambert was sprawled on the sawdust, out of it, but Whitey decided to make his play. Jacob's bullet hit Whitey in the chest and clipped a half moon from the little man's tobacco tag. Sudden blood erupted from Whitey's mouth. His eyes wide with shock and disbelief, he raised onto his toes, then fell, dead when he hit the floor. A bullet burned across Jacob's right bicep. He saw Caldwell, his gun up, back to the far wall of the saloon, blood on his shoulder, and he fired at the Texan. The bullet hit the trigger guard of Caldwell's Colt, ranged downward, and clipped off his pinkie finger before it slammed into the revolver butt. The big .45 round, now jagged and misshapen, caromed into Caldwell's right kneecap and splintered bone. Caldwell screamed, hit the floor, and the Colt dropped from his hand.

"Two and a half seconds, folks," a man in broadcloth yelled, holding up a gold watch for all to see. He grinned, and a front tooth made from the same metal as his watch gleamed. "Three men down in two and a half seconds."

This announcement drew a few cheers from the sporting crowd, but most of the onlookers stood in stunned silence, gun smoke drifting thick, pungent, and gray around them in the roaring silence.

Jacob ignored the crowd. He stepped around Lambert's body and walked to Caldwell, his chiming spurs knelling an elegy.

"Pick up the Colt, Caldwell," he said. "Get back to your work."

"Damn you, O'Brien, my gun hand's all shot to pieces," the Texan wailed, his eyes scared.

"Pick it up," Jacob said again, holstering his own revolver.

"I have no chance with you," Caldwell said.

"I'm giving you the same chance you gave me in the cave, remember?"

"And you didn't pick it up," Caldwell said.

"I tried, and so will you."

Caldwell looked around him and spread his arms wide. Blood dripped from the stump of his finger. "I have friends here. Step forward and help me."

No one moved. The saloon girl giggled again, and a man told her, "Shut up."

Caldwell glanced up at Jacob. "Damn you to hell," he said.

He dived for his gun, and Jacob shot him in the head.

Caldwell died with his face in the sawdust.

After he took time to reload from his cartridge belt, Jacob glanced around the silent saloon and then stepped to the door. To the man with the gold tooth and watch, he said, "Add another half-second."

Then he opened the door and walked into the bone-white glow of the moonlit street.

Chapter Forty-nine

Jacob O'Brien rode in the shadow of the Zuni Mountains, a high-country caravan of rawboned peaks, hanging valleys, deep canyons, and piñon and pine forests marching parallel to the Continental Divide.

He rode at a walk on a tired horse, heading nowhere through a vast and aloof wilderness of trees and rock that wore its majestic quiet like a cloak.

Blood, long crusted and black, fanned up above Jacob's belt on the right side and caused him pain. Caldwell's bullet had ripped away two inches of flesh and skin and left a wound that was raw and hard to heal.

Following a faint trail, Jacob came up on the ruin of an ancient pueblo, three of its adobe walls still standing. He drew rein in the shade of a wall and built a cigarette, a man without purpose or direction, a deep, dark depression weighing on him like an anvil.

He could have returned to Dromore, but the thought of burdening the colonel and the others with a wounded man didn't enter into Jacob's thinking. They'd been through enough recently without him adding to their troubles.

Only the mountains offered a refuge where he would be a burden to no one. Maybe come winter he'd find a cave, snuggle next to a big mama cougar, and sleep until spring. Or he could crawl into a hollow log. Now that would be right cozy when the snows came.

Jacob ground out the cigarette butt on his boot heel.

A complex, often troubled man, Jacob felt the need to be alone, to think, to plan his future, if such even existed. He was tired, sick of killing and death, and he was uneasily aware that Dora DeClare had opened a gateway to the darker recesses of his mind that should have remained forever closed.

He felt the need, for the first time in his life, to get closer to his God.

Again, where better to find him than the mountains?

Jacob rode away from the pueblo, a terrible weariness on him.

Damn, he was exhausted, body and soul.

Jacob took to the ribbon of trail again and then swung his horse toward the mountains. He followed a switchback game trail back and forth up a piñon-covered slope, then into ponderosa where there was dappled shade. He kept to the dim trail until suddenly it led into a hanging valley of high grassland. The surrounding slopes were covered in pine, and here and there outcroppings of sandstone rock, formed into grotesque shapes by erosion, perched like gargoyles on the façade of a Gothic cathedral.

Jacob kneed his horse forward, and it walked slowly, neck arched and ears pricked, wondering, as its rider did, at the building a hundred yards away, sitting on a shelf of rock among the trees.

The valley was an isolated, lonely place where shadows came early and lingered late. A stream, fed by an underground spring, bubbled over a pebbled bottom near the house, and on its banks a few willows struggled for life, raising their thin arms in supplication to an uncaring sky.

Despite the heat of the day, the breeze blowing off the surrounding crags was cool and smelled of pine and of the bitter loneliness of a place lost between earth and sky, an odor like ancient rock.

When he was fifty yards from the house, Jacob drew rein and took stock.

The building was a mission in the Old Spanish style, but constructed of gray stone, not adobe, and it glowed with the patina of centuries.

Jacob was tempted to slide the Winchester from under his knee, but he dismissed the idea. He sensed no threat. There was a strange peace about the place, quiet, like a hush of a confessional.

He rode forward again. A stable backed against the west wall of the mission, and behind that a smokehouse, forge, and other outbuildings. A pyramid of firewood was stacked high near one of the structures, against the coming winter.

But what caught and held Jacob's attention was a tree—a green apple tree with swelling fruit on its leafy limbs.

The mission's iron-studded oak door opened, and a monk wearing a brown robe stepped outside. He looked at Jacob and smiled. "Welcome," he said.

"You knew I was coming?" Jacob said.

"Yes, I did."

"I'd like to help you pick the green apples," Jacob said.

"I think the crop will be even heavier next year," the monk said. His eyes were very blue. "Can you stay until then?"

"Yes," Jacob said. "I'd like to stay. I'm wounded and very tired."

"I know you are."

Jacob dismounted, and the monk put his arm around his shoulder and led him into the mission that smelled of candle smoke and yellow parchment.

"I'll see to your wound," the monk said, "and then you must sleep . . . sleep for a long, long time."

"And then I'll pick the green apples?" Jacob said.

"Yes. You can gather them one by one until the tree is bare," the monk said.

Turn the page for an exciting preview . . .

From the bestselling masters of the American West comes a heart-racing story of frontier justice, pioneer spirit, and one town's last-chance miracle . . .

Three weeks before Christmas, the little town of Chug Water in Wyoming Territory is stunned by a brutal crime. The mayor's family has been slaughtered in cold blood on their ranch outside of Rawhide Buttes. As the townsfolk gather to pay their last respects, Duff MacCallister saddles up to go after the killers. He returns with two outlaws— a cold-blooded, nasty pair of snakes, Jesse and T. Bob Cave. But the day before they're sentenced to hang, the Cave brothers escape their fate . . .

Into this holiday hell storm ride three friendly travelers, Smoke, Sally, and Matt Jensen, come to spend Christmas with Duff. But a deadly diphtheria outbreak leaves the town beholden to the mercy of the Cave brothers. It's a desperate bind to be stuck in, but Duff and his friends will use every bullet they can find to shoot their way into a merry but bloody Christmas.

A FRONTIER CHRISTMAS
by William W. Johnstone
with J. A. Johnstone

On sale now, wherever Pinnacle Books are sold.

Chapter One

Greeley, Colorado

Ralph Walters stood on the depot platform, waiting for the train. He had a long trip in front of him—to Cheyenne by rail, then by stagecoach up to Rawhide Buttes, Wyoming. He was a traveling troubadour, someone who could play the guitar, banjo, fiddle, harmonica, and drum. In one of his acts, he would pass himself off as a one-man band, and play the banjo, harmonica, and drum all at the same time. He was also a skilled magician.

Because entertainment was rare and much appreciated, especially in the small towns, he did a good business.

He was going to Rawhide Buttes to perform for a firemen's benefit show, and for the students in the Rawhide School. Schools didn't pay as much as some of the more adult venues, but he could almost always schedule a school in conjunction with his adult show, and that's what he had done in Rawhide Buttes.

He'd skipped breakfast and lunch because he wasn't hungry. It was probably a pretty good thing that he still wasn't very hungry. He had awakened with a sore throat and wasn't sure he would be able to swallow, anyway. Reaching up, he wrapped his hand around his throat and thought he felt some swelling there.

"Here she comes!" somebody shouted, and several people moved closer to the track.

Walters remained in place as the big engine came roaring into the station with steam gushing from the drive cylinders and glowing coals dripping from the firebox. The engineer was leaning on the windowsill of the cab, his jutting chin and hooked nose looking as if they were about to join. Brakes were applied, and the train came to a halt. It sat there with wisps of steam wreathing the drive wheels, the journals and gearboxes popping and snapping as they cooled.

"Board!" the conductor shouted.

Those who were about to make the trip rushed to climb onto the train.

This was old hat to Walters, who had made hundreds of trips on trains as he went from town to town.

The conductor recognized him, and smiled. "Hello, Mr. Walters, riding with us again, I see."

"Yes, but only as far as Cheyenne. There I must take a coach."

"Welcome aboard. I see that your regular seat hasn't been taken."

"Good, thank you." Walters moved down the aisle to the last seat on the left.

With a series of starts and jerks, the train resumed its journey a moment later.

Walters leaned his head back against the seat. He believed he might also be getting a fever.

Sugarloaf Ranch, Colorado

When Smoke Jensen came back from town he had a letter from his friend Duff MacCallister. "Sally, I heard from Duff." Smoke reached for a hot bear claw.

"Don't eat more than one. I'm doing this for the boys in the bunkhouse. What does Duff have to say?"

"I don't know I haven't opened it yet. I thought we would read it together."

Sally smiled. "That was nice of you." She put another tray of dough puffs into the oven.

"How many of those things are you making?"

"We have eight hands spending the entire winter with us, and you know very well that Cal and Pearlie could eat this entire tray by themselves."

Smoke chuckled. "I guess you're right." He opened the envelope and began to read, silently.

"Well, what does he say?"

"He has invited us to come to Chugwater to spend Christmas with him."

"Christmas in Chugwater? That's very nice of him. I wonder why he invited us, though. You would think he would have invited someone like Falcon, or one of the other MacCallisters."

Smoke nodded in agreement. "But he not only invited us, he invited Matt, too, since he's here to spend the holidays with us."

"Well, be gentle when you turn Duff down. The poor man is so far away from his ancestral home, I'm sure that Christmas is a difficult time for him."

Smoke's eyebrows rose. "Why would I turn him down? I'm the one who hinted that we would be receptive to an invitation in the first place."

"What? Smoke, I thought we were going to New York for Christmas."

"Whatever gave you that idea?"

Sally frowned. "Didn't we make that decision this past summer?"

"You said it had been a long time since you were in New York, and you'd like to go back for a visit sometime. That's not making a decision, that's talking about it. Besides, Matt and I have to be at Fort Russell, Wyoming, in December to sell our horses, so it just seems natural that, since we are going to be up there, anyway, that we drop in on Duff."

"But, Smoke—"

"And didn't you just say that you thought Christmas might be a difficult time for him? Where is your compassion?"

Sally laughed. "I hate it when we are arguing and you use my own words on me."

"Were we just arguing?"

"Of a sort, I suppose."

Smoke smiled then reached for her. "Good. The best part of arguing is making up," he said, pulling her to him.

Big Rock, Colorado

At the moment, Matt Jensen was in Longmont's Saloon, watching a three-card game that Louis Longmont was playing with a traveling gambler named Sherman who had not given a first name.

He had been having an inordinate run of luck since he came to town, so much luck that Longmont was convinced Sherman was helping his odds with a little card manipulation.

Sherman didn't know that Longmont wasn't just a saloon owner. He was also an exceptionally skilled gambler. Practically a magician with cards.

The game they were playing was a simple game, not too unlike the game of finding the pea under the shell. In this case, Sherman had to find the ace after watching Longmont shift the cards around in front of him. Sherman had tried his luck three times, and every time he had lost.

Another patron engaged the saloon owner in conversation. It wasn't idle conversation. It was a setup. The patron was a secret partner, sometimes letting Sherman know by coded signals what cards the mark was holding. In this case, his only purpose was to divert Longmont's attention.

With his opponent's attention shifted, Sherman reached across the table and put a small, barely noticeable, crease on one corner of the ace. Longmont could switch the cards around any way he wanted. Sherman wouldn't even attempt to follow him. He would simply select the card with the creased corner.

"You going to play cards, or are you going to talk all day?" Sherman asked.

Longmont turned back to the table. "Why, I'm going to play cards, Mr. Sherman," Longmont said, smiling easily.

"Only, this time, let's bet some real money," Sherman suggested. He put ten twenty-dollar gold pieces on the table.

"That's a pretty steep bet for a little friendly game like this, isn't it?"

"You own the saloon. Surely you can afford it."

Longmont smiled. "Oh, I can afford it."

As he put his own money on the table matching the bet, Sherman took one last look at the creased card. So far, Longmont hadn't noticed it. How could he? It was so subtle a crease that it was barely discernible, even to Sherman, and he was the one who put it there.

Longmont picked up the three cards and began shuffling them around. Sherman looked over at his partner and nodded. Longmont put the cards down on the table, then began moving them around, in and out, over and under with such lightning speed that the cards were nearly a blur. When he stopped, the three cards lay in front of him, waiting for Sherman to pick the ace.

Smiling confidently, Sherman reached across the table to make his selection . . . then suddenly froze in mid-motion. The smile left his face. His hand hung suspended over the table as he stared at the three cards with a sickly expression on his face.

"Hard to pick out the ace when they all look alike, isn't it, *mon ami*?" Longmont asked.

"Yeah," Sherman said with a weak response. He had been had. Somehow Longmont had not only picked up on the card with the tiny crease, he had duplicated that crease on the other two cards, doing it so perfectly that Sherman had no idea which was the one he had marked.

"Are you going to pick a card or not?"

Sherman turned up a card. It was a queen. "Damn!"

"Maybe this isn't your game," Longmont suggested as he pulled back the money from the center of the table.

"I don't believe the ace is even on the table."

"Oh, it's on the table, all right." Longmont reached for one of the cards.

"Wait a minute. I'll turn it over," Sherman said. "For all I know you have an ace palmed. You can make it appear anywhere you want."

"All right. You turn it over."

Sherman reached for the card Longmont had started for and flipped it over. It was the ace. "Damn," he said again.

"Actually, I can make an ace appear anywhere I want." Longmont picked up a new deck of cards, shuffled them, then spread them all out, facedown, on the table. "Here's the ace of diamonds," he said, turning it up. "The ace of clubs, the ace of hearts, and the ace of spades."

"What? How the hell did you do that?"

"Here are the four kings," Longmont added, pulling them from the spread-out deck. "Here are the queens, and here are the jacks."

"I . . ."

"You have run into someone who was not only able to catch you, but is a hell of a lot better at it than you," Matt said.

The others gathered around the table to watch laughed.

"I tell you what, Mr. Sherman," Longmont said, sliding ten of the twenty-dollar gold pieces back across the table. "Take your money, but leave my saloon and don't come back. When my customers play cards in here, they have a right to expect an honest game."

Sherman stared at the money for a moment, then he reached for it. "A man has to make a living."

"Yes, and most of my customers do that by the sweat of their brow, not by sitting at a table, cheating others."

Sherman nodded.

"And take your partner with you," Longmont added, looking at the man who had attempted to divert his attention earlier. "You can have one last drink, then both of you go."

"Thanks anyway, but we aren't thirsty." With a glance toward his partner, Sherman started toward the door.

"Oh, and *Joyeux Noël*," Longmont called as the two men left.

Chapter Two

Chugwater, Wyoming

When Duff MacCallister rode into town, he was curious at the number of people gathered in the street in front of Fiddlers' Green Saloon. Dismounting, he tied off his horse Sky, then called out to Fred Matthews.

"What's going on, Fred? Why all the people?"

"There's a man standing in front of the apothecary, holding a gun to Damon White's head. He's demanding that a thousand dollars be brought to him within an hour, or he's goin' to kill our druggist."

"At the apothecary, you say?"

"Yes."

"Where is Marshal Craig?"

"He has gone to Cheyenne. He left Johnny Baldwin in charge."

Duff pulled his pistol and stepped out into the street.

"Duff, where are you going?"

"Well, we cannae be losing our druggist now, can we? And I'm afraid that Mr. Baldwin is too old to have to deal with something like this. I'll be going to talk to the gentlemen who's holding Mr. White. I'll be asking him, nicely, to abandon this project."

"With a gun in your hand?"

"Aye. 'Tis no secret, Fred, that I'm not one of those men who has the talent to quickly extract my firearm. If any shooting is to be done, I'd best have the gun in my hand before it starts."

"I would try and talk you out of it, but I can see that you have already made up your mind."

"Aye, 'tis something I feel I must do."

Holding his pistol down by his side, Duff started toward the apothecary at the far end of the street. As he got closer, he could hear the gunman shouting.

"Bring me the money! One thousand dollars! Bring me the money or this man dies! One thousand dollars!"

All the stores immediately around the apothecary had emptied. No one was on the street close to the gunman and Damon White.

"Bring me the money!" The gunman continued to shout from the wooden porch that extended from the front of the drugstore. He was about to shout something again, when he saw Duff walking toward him. "Who are you? What are you doing here?"

"The name is MacCallister, lad. Duff MacCallister. I'm here because 'tis needin' a bit of cough syrup I am, so I'd be grateful if you'd let the druggist go."

The gunman kept the gun pointed at White's head. "That'll cost you a thousand dollars."

"A thousand dollars, you say." Duff shook his head. "*Och*, isn't that a mite dear, for a wee bit of cough syrup?"

"No. I mean, I'm not going to let this man go until I get a thousand dollars."

"From who?"

"What?"

"Who is it that you expect to give you a thousand dollars?"

"I don't care. Are you dumb? Can't you see I'm holding a gun to this man's head?"

"Aye, that I can see." Duff continued walking until he was at the bottom step.

"You've come far enough. Stop, right there, right now!" the gunman called down to Duff.

"I'll nae be doing that. I told you, 'tis a bit of cough syrup I'm needing."

"If you don't stop right where you are, I'm going to shoot this man."

Duff raised his pistol and pointed it straight at the gunman's head. He was so close that they were separated by less than ten feet. "If you shoot him, I'll shoot you."

"Don't you understand? I'm going to shoot him, if you don't drop that gun!"

"Oh, I'm nae goin' to drop the gun, lad. I'll be

needing it, you see, so I can shoot you after you shoot Mr. White." Duff pulled the hammer back and the pistol made a deadly, double clicking sound as the sear was engaged.

For a long moment the two men stood there, a macabre tableau, Duff holding his pistol pointed directly at the gunman, while the gunman held his pistol to Damon White's head.

The gunman began to sweat, even though the weather was cold. The pupils of his eyes grew large.

"Tell me, lad, don't you think 'tis a bit cold out here?" Duff asked.

The gunman didn't reply.

"If you drop the gun, I can take you down to the jailhouse. I know that they keep the jail warm. Deputy Baldwin is an old man, and old men get cold awfully easily. You could be lying on a bunk in the cell, warm and waiting for your supper.

"Or, we can just carry this out, and you'll wind up in a place a lot warmer than the jail. I'm sure you know what I mean."

The gunman began to shake, then he took the gun away from the druggist's head and pointed it toward the porch. Damon White moved away quickly.

Duff didn't move. "Drop the gun, lad. Drop it, and this whole business will be over."

"You're crazy," the gunman said. "Walking up on me like that. You're crazy."

"Aye, so I've been told."

The man was still holding the pistol in his hand, though the barrel was pointing straight down.

"I'll nae be telling you again to drop the gun."

The gunman opened his hand, and the gun fell to the porch with a loud thump.

"Mr. White, you have a telephone in your establishment, I believe?" Duff asked.

"Y-yes," White said, relief from fear visible on his face.

"Would ye be so kind as to call the marshal's office 'n ask Deputy Baldwin if he would come collect his prisoner?"

"I'd be glad to. And the cough medicine is on the house."

Duff smiled. "'Tis a funny thing. I no longer feel the need for the elixir."

When Duff returned to where he had left his horse, several people applauded him.

"Come into the saloon, Duff, and I'll buy you a drink," someone said.

"I thank you for the offer, Mr. Miller, but I must step into this shop for a few moments," Duff replied, nodding toward the building next door to the saloon. A sign on the front of the building read MEAGAN'S DRESS EMPORIUM.

A bell on the door jingled as Duff stepped inside.

"I'll be with you in a moment," a woman's voice called from the back of the room.

Stepping toward the sound of the voice, Duff saw Meagan Parker on her knees, pinning up the skirt on a dress being worn by Martha Guthrie, wife of the mayor of Chugwater.

"Mrs. Guthrie, 'tis a beautiful picture you make in that dress. You'll be warming R.W.'s heart, and that's for sure.

Martha, who was a short and rather rotund woman, blushed and giggled at the compliment. "Oh, do you think so?"

"That's exactly what I've been telling her," Meagan said, standing up.

"I'm buying the dress for a Christmas party we'll be giving John, his wife, and our grandchildren," Martha said. "They're coming to town for Christmas."

"Oh, and what a joyous event that will be. I'll have to stop by to say hello," Duff replied.

"Please do."

"All right, Mrs. Guthrie, if you'll go back there and take off the dress, I'll have it finished for you in plenty of time," Meagan said.

"Thank you, dear." Martha took one more look at herself in the mirror. "You do such beautiful work."

Meagan waited until Martha disappeared into the back room, then she kissed Duff. "What brings you here, today?"

"Smoke, Sally, and Matt will be coming to Sky Meadow. I want you to come out for dinner Wednesday night while they are here."

"I'd be glad to." Meagan frowned. "Didn't I see several people gathered in front of the Fiddlers' a few minutes ago? What was that all about, do you know?"

"Aye, 'twas a small disturbance down at the apothecary is all. 'Tis over now."

She examined Duff with a quizzical smile. "Why is it that I think it might have been more than that, and that you had something to do with it?"

"Because you are a woman with a very suspicious heart," Duff said.

"You are aware, are you not, Duff, that there is to be a dance on Christmas Eve?"

"And are you asking me to the dance?" Duff replied with a teasing smile.

"No, you are supposed to ask me."

"Oh. Well then, lass, would you be so kind as to attend the dance with me?"

"Let me think about it," Meagan replied. Then, with a wide smile she continued. "All right, I suppose I can." She was about to kiss Duff again, but at that moment, Martha Guthrie reappeared.

"I left the dress on the table," she said. "How soon will it be ready? I also want to wear it for R.W.'s Christmas dinner for the businessmen of the town."

"Oh, you can pick it up tomorrow," Meagan said.

"Wonderful. Thank you. Mr. MacCallister, please do drop by when John and his family are in town. I know they would love to see you."

"I'll do that," Duff promised.

As soon as Martha left, Duff turned back to Meagan. "I believe you were about to kiss me?"

"I will, but then you must go. I have work to do and, for some reason, I find you distracting."

They kissed again, then Duff turned to leave. "I'll see you at dinner when Smoke and the others arrive."

Elmer Gleason, Duff's foreman, had a most interesting background. He had been a guerilla with Quantrill during the war; had ridden some with Jesse and Frank James after the war; had lived with the Indians for a while, taking an Indian wife; and had gone to sea as an able-bodied seaman, sailing all over the Pacific.

In a way, one could say that Duff had inherited him with the ranch, because when Duff came to develop the land he had filed upon, Elmer was already there.

"They say the place is hainted," R.W. Guthrie had told Duff when he'd first arrived in the territory. He was talking about Little Horse Mine, a worked-out and abandoned gold mine that was on the land Duff had just taken title to.

"Course, I ain't sayin' that I believe in haints, mind you. But that is what they say. Some say it wasn't the Spanish, but injuns, that first found the gold, and they was all kilt off by white men who wanted the gold for themselves. What happened was, after the injuns was all kilt, they became ghosts, and now they haint the mine and kill any white man who comes around tryin' to find the gold.

Now, mind, I don't believe none of that. I'm just tellin' you what folks say about it."

As it turned out, the haint Guthrie was speaking of was Elmer Gleason.

Elmer had located a new vein of gold in the mine, and unable to capitalize on it, was living a hand-to-mouth existence in the mine, unshaved and dressed only in skins.

Duff discovered him in the mine, which was on the property Duff had just filed upon. Everything Elmer had taken from it actually belonged to Duff, giving him every right to drive Elmer off, but he didn't. He offered Elmer a one-half partnership in the mine. That partnership had paid off handsomely for both of them.

Elmer had been with Duff from the beginning and was now Duff's foreman and closest friend.

Duff's half of the proceeds from the mine had built Sky Meadow into one of the most productive ranches in Wyoming. His operation was large enough to employ fourteen men.

When Duff returned to the ranch, Elmer was talking to the three other cowboys who had been with him for a very long time. Al Woodward, Case Goodrich, and Brax Walker not only worked for him, but were extremely loyal and top hands, occupying positions of responsibility.

"Get the men out to bust up the ice so's the cows can get to water," Elmer was telling them. "And you'd better send a couple men out to check if any of the beeves have wandered off."

The three men nodded in acquiescence, spoke to Duff a minute, then left to attend to their duties.

"Anything interesting happen in town?" Elmer asked.

"I invited Meagan to come to dinner when Smoke and the others are here."

"Uh-huh. And you talked some feller outta shootin' Damon White, too, is what I heered."

"Where did you hear that?"

"I sent Dooley into town to get some things, and he told me about it when he got back."

"There wasn't much to it," Duff said. "Are you goin' to ask your friend Vi to come to dinner?"

"You mean you don't mind?"

"Why should I mind?"

Elmer smiled. "Well, then, if you don't mind, I'll ride on into town and take care of that."

Duff nodded, then rode on to the barn to get his horse out of the cold.